HEDGING YOUR BETS

ALSO BY JAYNE DENKER

The Rom-Com Agenda

ST. MARTIN'S GRIFFIN
NEW YORK

This is a work of fiction. All of the characters, organizations, and events portrayed in this novel are either products of the author's imagination or are used fictitiously.

First published in the United States by St. Martin's Griffin, an imprint of St. Martin's Publishing Group

www.stmartins.com

Designed by Jen Edwards

Library of Congress Cataloging-in-Publication Data

Names: Denker, Jayne, 1966– author.
Title: Hedging your bets : a novel / Jayne Denker.
Description: First edition. | New York : St. Martin's Griffin, 2024.
Identifiers: LCCN 2023033021 | ISBN 9781250821508 (trade paperback) | ISBN 9781250821515 (ebook)
Subjects: LCGFT: Romance fiction. | Novels.
Classification: LCC PS3604.E58553 H44 2024 | DDC 813/.6—dc23/eng/20230721
LC record available at https://lccn.loc.gov/2023033021

First Edition: 2024

10 9 8 7 6 5 4 3 2 1

For goddesses of all shapes and sizes

HEDGING YOUR BETS

CHAPTER 1

Nearly getting headbutted by a stranger in a tiny pharmacy foyer was the last thing anybody needed after a long day at work, but Gillian Pritchard took it in stride. Besides, it was partially her own fault. She'd been distracted by a text alert and wasn't looking where she was going.

A tall man, sneezing repeatedly into a large bandanna covering most of his face, hurtling into her and nearly breaking her nose, put Gillian back in pharmacist mode even though she was off the clock and on her way out the door. She didn't mind. Gillian had been a pharmacist for years, and she was good at it. Nothing made her happier than being able to serve the citizens of the small town of Willow Cove.

"Allergies?" she murmured sympathetically, and the man nodded as he pushed past her into the building.

Gillian didn't take offense at his brusqueness; he was obviously suffering. She would have followed him back inside to help him out if it weren't for her text. A quick glance at her phone to see that it was from her elderly neighbor, Carol, and it only said *Come quick,* was enough to send a zing of alarm through her.

Cursing the fact that the gorgeous spring weather had enticed her to walk to work that day, Gillian hurried through town and into her residential neighborhood as fast as she could, but it still took far too long to get home. She tried calling Carol back on the way, but there was no answer. Practically at a jog when she rounded the corner onto her own block, she nearly barreled into her three neighbors, Carol, Arnette, and Judy, clustered on the sidewalk. When they all turned to her en masse, their eyes wide, Gillian's heart seized.

"What's wrong?" she gasped. "Are you all right? Carol, why didn't you answer my—"

"It's Retha," Arnette stage-whispered, clutching the sides of her cardigan and pulling them tighter around her.

Gillian's heart skipped a beat at the mention of the ladies' fourth senior friend, her next-door neighbor. "Retha?"

"She's *gone*!" Carol burst out, breathless.

"Wait . . . *gone* gone?"

All the women nodded.

Gillian felt sudden tears prick her eyes, shock and grief constricting her throat. "But . . . but I saw her yesterday. She was fine!"

Her third neighbor, Judy, shrugged and said with venom, "And now she's in *Tampa*."

"My God," Gillian whispered, staring unseeing at the pavement. "I can't believe she's . . . wait." Her head snapped up and she narrowed her eyes. *"Tampa?"*

Carol nodded vigorously. "Took up with that Norman character she met the last time she was visiting her nephew's family in February. Just up and moved in with him!"

"For God's sake!" Gillian burst out, trying to calm her rabbiting heart. "Don't *do* that! I thought—"

"That she'd kicked it?" Judy muttered. "Might as well have. I mean . . . *Tampa*?"

"Some people like Tampa," Arnette sniffed.

"Some people take up with random widowers without thinking it through too," Judy countered.

"Just because you can't be bothered to find true love in your twilight years doesn't mean the rest of us have given up, you know," Carol cut in, gently patting her white-blond, gravity-defying, blown-out bob that was equal parts hair, hair spray, and air.

"I never said I was against it," Judy said, pulling up an errant bra strap. "But I sure wouldn't count on it being found with *Norman* in *Tampa*."

"Judy," Arnette hissed, flicking a glance at Gillian. "Remember what we talked about. Positivity!"

Gillian fought back a weary sigh. Subtlety was not their strong suit. "Cut it out, ladies."

Carol wheedled, "We just want to see you happy. Is that so wrong?"

"Second chances happen all the time," Arnette said.

Gillian's neighbors knew she was perfectly content with her home and her job and her friends, and that "finding a new man," as they always urged her to do, would simply be a pleasant addition to her already happy life. Gillian actually had started dabbling in online dating, signing up with a couple of dating apps recently. She wasn't averse to finding someone to care about, someone who cared about her, but five years of blessed solitude since her divorce had made her pretty darn comfortable with her life as it was. She'd gone on a few dates, but apparently she wasn't working fast enough for the ladies' liking.

"If you'd only let me give my stepson your number—" Carol started, for the thousandth time.

"Not right now, okay?" She gazed across the street and felt a pang of loss. She'd really liked Retha. "What's going to happen to the house?"

"We don't know," Carol said. "Retha didn't say boo about anything, not even that she was leaving, until today. She said she was moving to Tampa, hopped in an Uber with nothing but two suitcases and the urn with her husband's ashes, waved to us out the window, and off she went to the airport. Poof, she was gone."

"It must be true love if she paid for an Uber to drive her all the way to Syracuse to catch a flight. Must have cost a fortune," Judy said. "Hey, if Norm's loaded, that could explain a lot."

"Judy!" Carol and Arnette snapped.

There was a lot of Judy's name being snapped when the ladies were together. Judy had no filter. Gillian kind of liked that about her.

"I guess the house will go on the market soon enough, to catch the summer crowd," Gillian said.

Sometimes visitors fell so deeply in love with the little town of Willow Cove, and the Thousand Islands region in general, that they couldn't resist buying a summer home there. Gillian understood. The town, on the banks of the powerful St. Lawrence River in the North Country of New York State, with Canada to the north and the Adirondack Mountains to the southeast, was a charmer. Gillian had lived there more than half her life, and she absolutely loved it, even in the cold, blustery winter season. Which was finally over. The restaurants, wine bars, art galleries, and shops would throw open their doors soon, and the tourists and summer residents would arrive to enjoy life on the river.

"It should sell pretty quick . . . ly . . ."

Gillian's words died in her throat just as Carol let out a little squeak. A large, dark pickup truck had barreled around the corner and pulled up to the house as they were talking. Now a tall, lean man jumped down from the cab and, hands on his hips, stared up at Retha's former home. His well-worn jeans sagged a little at his waist; his bluish-green heathered T-shirt strained against his ample chest and then slouched above his belt. As he squinted upward, he casually scratched the back of his neck, where his light-brown hair faded to a close crop. He was surprisingly tan for early May.

"Real estate agent?" Arnette speculated.

"Not slick enough," Judy countered. "Contractor, I'd bet. Retha mentioned she might need a new roof."

"Gillian," Carol whispered eagerly, "go find out."

"Carol, stop."

"Gillian Pritchard," Arnette said in her scoldy voice, which was no less effective at reduced volume, "I want you to take a good look at those shoulders. And if you don't go over and introduce yourself right now, there's no hope for you."

Gillian scanned her friends, who were all eagerly watching her. Arnette, her sharp eyes bright against her warm brown skin. Carol, sprightly and girlish, smiling hopefully. Judy, short and broad, cynicism oozing out of every pore. Gillian knew what they wanted of her. Even Judy, though she didn't show it. So with a heavy, resigned sigh, she nodded wearily and started across the street.

She heard a definite Carol-is-excited squeal behind her and only felt a little bad for deceiving them, swerving to the right at the last minute and marching into her own house without a second glance at the man in Retha's front yard. A chorus of boos assaulted her from across the street. Gillian laughed to herself as she shut her front door.

Noah West tentatively entered his new house and looked around. Yep, it was a house. Not the kind he was used to—not the least of which because it was filled with someone else's belongings—and not for the first time, he wondered what the hell he'd just done, buying a house sight unseen from thousands of miles away.

But he didn't have the energy to examine the motivations behind his life choices. Not right now. Later. When he was strong enough to face all that had happened. Now he preferred to take comfort in facts. He liked those. Those were easy to grab on to, analyze, fix. Assessing this house, for instance, and making a list of necessary repairs. That was safe. That was logical. Unlike other events in his life recently, which had ceased to make sense about five or six decisions ago.

All he knew was one minute he was in the desert outside Palm Springs, and the next he was standing in the suffocating greenery of the far northern reaches of New York State in a picturesque town on the shore of a vast, heaving river. Not quite what he was used to.

But maybe exactly what he needed.

That also remained to be seen.

He wandered through the rooms on the second floor, ending up in the master bedroom. The sight of his reflection in the scrollwork-framed mirror over a French provincial dresser was anomalous, to say the very least. It was as if he were a ghost passing through. Either he didn't belong or the furniture didn't. Well, here he was, so it was the furnishings that would have to be rethought. He was pretty sure he'd seen a thrift store on Main Street. It was about to get a huge donation.

Noah sat on the edge of the mattress, bounced once or twice. Bed could stay. He crossed to one of the bedroom's windows. The house next door was surprisingly close—he wasn't sure he liked exactly how close—separated only by his driveway and the neighbor's driveway, with a narrow strip of grass between the two stretches of blacktop. He opened the window to get rid of the cloying odor of floral-scented facial powder and started to drop the blinds but paused when there was a sudden flash of movement behind the glass across the way. That window was flung upward, and Billy Idol's "To Be a Lover" hit him full in the face. He blinked. He hadn't heard the song in years, maybe decades. He was impressed all over again with its throbbing energy . . . and the energy of his neighbor, who was dancing to the powerful beat.

At that point Noah's brain stuttered into glitch mode, only capable of registering random impressions. Pale skin. Blond hair. White tank top. Cleavage. And . . . good grief. Thighs. And the briefest flash of underwear.

"Have mercy," Noah chorused with Billy under his breath, even though he was alone. It was as if that was all his voice could muster, under the circumstances . . . the circumstances being that his neighbor had divested herself of any semblance of pants.

Noah clapped his eyes shut. He hadn't meant to see any of that.

But he had.

He didn't dare move for . . . what was it . . . thirty seconds, a minute? Half an hour? He wasn't sure. But the song couldn't have been any longer than four minutes at most, and Billy was still snarling. So time stood still. That made as much sense as anything else in his life lately. Why not?

He would have continued to let time stretch out indefinitely as Billy roared for all he was worth. But all good things must come to an end, sometimes rudely and abruptly.

He sneezed.

Stupid North Country.

Noah had forgotten he had allergies. Living in the desert for years made it easy to forget. But here they were, and worse than he remembered. His sinuses tickled by the grass and tree pollen so foreign to his system, he let loose a second powerful explosion, and he cursed the local pharmacist who'd assured him the antihistamine she'd recommended would control his symptoms for hours. These pills didn't seem to mute them one bit. Window open for two minutes, and his nose felt like it was full of feathers.

A third window-rattling sneeze, and he cracked one eye to locate the sash to shut out the pollen. That was when he saw his neighbor at her own window, looking around for the source of the explosion.

Her eyes met his. Again, time stood still. Noah was pinned by those eyes. Cat's-eye–shaped, glittering. He found himself wondering what color they were instead of mustering up enough effort to retreat. She was going to scream, wasn't she? Or at least run off and call the cops. That'd be about right. He'd deserve it.

The woman's eyes narrowed, just a bit. Then she smiled. And Noah's stomach leapt. She spun around—giving him a generous view of her lush backside, clad in dark purple satin—and started dancing once more. No scream. No frantic rush to hide. Or to put on pants. Defiant, his neighbor dared him to keep watching.

"Whoa," he whispered.

Noah was grateful the woman moved away from the window, farther into her room, because that finally broke the spell he was under. He was able to move as well, out of the bedroom, down the stairs, and out the front door, which he latched securely behind him.

This was not what he had signed up for. Granted, it was just a random occurrence, but for some reason a heavy weight settled in his gut as his skittering brain attached some sort of ominous portent to the dancing woman. But that was all it was, Noah reminded himself—just a woman. Dancing in her house. Minding her own business. It did not, in fact, mean anything. It had no bearing on his life.

As he made his way to his truck parked at the curb, he was relieved to see the street was empty. When he'd pulled up, he'd spotted a small cluster of women watching him, although he'd pointedly not made eye contact. Small towns, man. Every one had busybodies. Well, he was going to hightail it out of there and—

Noah nearly clocked himself in the head with the corner of his truck's door when the tiniest of the blue-hairs suddenly popped up from behind her wheeled garbage tote. Just great—stealth grannies. Completely unaware she'd practically given him a heart attack, she waved cheerfully, her small hand engulfed in an overlarge, rough gardening glove clutching a fistful of what appeared to be errant weeds. Where she found them in the golf-course-quality lawn of hers was a mystery, but not one he wanted to expend brainpower ruminating on. Instead, he waved back reluctantly and retreated to his truck cab, slamming the door. Because . . . there. Now she'd gotten that . . . that *look* in her eye. He knew that look. It meant she took his wave as an invitation to cross the street and chat, and . . .

Before the woman—who looked harmless enough, he had to admit—could take the first step off the curb, he started his truck, threw it in gear, and sped off down the street. Not today, overly friendly future neighbor. Not today.

∽

Noah sat in his truck outside the marina, immobile. For the past five minutes, he'd been unable to get out of the cab. "I can't do it," he muttered to himself. He scrubbed his face with his hands. The statement was simple enough, wasn't it? He wouldn't need to explain any further when he repeated just that to the attorney. Who wouldn't care anyway. He was just an intermediary, the person who'd drawn up the papers, held out a pen, and waited patiently while Noah scribbled his name and initials a dozen times, officially making him the new owner of Spencer's Marina. The attorney could do the same thing, in reverse, when Noah resold the place. Yes, he'd just bought it, but all these changes all at once . . . it was just too much.

Not to say his current situation wasn't of his own making. Well. It hadn't been, at first. The first thunderbolt had been Corinne stating, quite matter-of-factly, that she believed she and Noah had come to the end of their "journey" together and now it was time to "respectfully continue onward apart." Or something. A buzzing had started in the back of his brain right around the time his suddenly ex-girlfriend uttered the words "You need to move out," and it hadn't completely abated yet.

What had happened after, however, had been all him. He'd indeed packed up and moved out, sleeping in his office at his small art gallery in Palm Springs until it sold. Then he found himself staring at a pile of money without quite knowing what to do with it. Until his uncle Manny, in one of his rare phone calls to his nephew, had mentioned in passing that Jerry Spencer, owner of the town marina and Noah's former boss, had died. Noah wasn't really a firm believer in serendipity or fate or any of that stuff, but he couldn't deny the universe was taking a hand in his future this time. As in, he was looking for a new life that had nothing whatsoever to do with the one he was leaving behind. And here it was on a silver platter.

It could have been hazy nostalgia for the marina, where he'd worked as a teenager, and for the charming town of Willow Cove in general, where he'd spent so many of his summers with his family, staying at Manny's place—or maybe he was romanticizing the ruggedly independent single life Manny had cultivated over the years, and he wanted that for himself now—but suddenly Noah found himself turning over a giant chunk of cash in exchange for the keys to the marina.

Now here he was: new town, new house, new business, and a rebellious immune system.

As if to confirm that, he let loose a sneeze powerful enough to nearly knock his head against the steering wheel.

Dammit.

Noah blew his nose into his bandanna and stared at the familiar storefront. It looked like nothing about the marina had changed. If he could bring himself to go inside, he knew he'd be surrounded by the familiar sights and smells of all things boating: engine parts, life vests, cleaning supplies, the whiff of rubber components, oils, resins . . . all of it would bring back sense memories of his younger days. Of course, why he thought he could jump right back into selling boating gear and fixing watercraft after not having so much as lived or worked near water in more than fifteen years was a mystery. But he had loved it years ago. He could love it again. Right?

Noah blew his nose once more, girded his loins, and forced

himself out of his truck. He pushed on the building's door and strode into the showroom. He was right—going inside was like stepping back in time. Absolutely everything was the same. But he didn't feel a warm, fuzzy nostalgia. He felt a grip of anxiety so tight he wanted nothing more than to run right back out again.

"Good work, West," he muttered. "Dragged every single thing you own three thousand miles across the country in a U-Haul trailer that is currently taking up three spaces, crosswise, at a 'motor court,' whatever that is. Ended up in a place you haven't seen in years, smothered by pollen, humidity, and talcum powder. Stalked by old ladies and flashed by your hot neighbor. But hey, everything's cool."

A tall, dark-haired man who had been perusing some canoe oars propped up in racks along the wall was now side-eyeing him warily. Of course he was. Noah stood up straighter, tried to look confident, and nodded at the man once. The man nodded back. All right, then.

He approached the customer and asked, "Can I help you with anything?"

The guy glanced around, perplexed. "You work here?"

Right. This person had just seen him lurch through the front door like a marionette whose operator had lost control of his strings and then start talking to himself. It hardly communicated that he was the newest member of Willow Cove's business community.

"I'm the marina's new owner." He stuck out his hand. "Noah West."

The man nodded slowly and shook Noah's hand. "Eli Masterson. Sorry to hear about Jerry. He was a good guy."

"He was."

"No offense, but I thought Jerry's family was going to keep running the place."

Noah shook his head. "They weren't interested and put it up

for sale. I couldn't resist. I used to work here years ago, when I came up for the summers."

Eli squinted at him. "West, you said? Are you related to Manny?"

"He's my uncle."

Now that he could place Noah on the Willow Cove social map, Eli looked a bit more willing to talk. "I haven't seen you around."

"I haven't lived here for a while. But I do now. So what can I help you with?"

At that moment an actual employee, as evidenced by the polo shirt with the Spencer's Marina logo on it, approached them. More side-eyeing ensued. Noah figured he probably deserved it, since he hadn't formally introduced himself to . . . well, anyone. Including the actual staff.

"You know, I've got some urgent . . . owner stuff . . . to take care of. I'm sure . . ." He squinted at the kid's name tag. ". . . Parker can help you out. Excuse me."

Noah could feel Eli's and Parker's eyes on him as he walked the length of the store, back toward the front door. He had intended to visit the repair shop and check out the boat rentals and slips, but he'd do that another time. When he was better prepared. Right now it was all he could do to make his way outside and wait for his flipping stomach to settle.

He needed someone to talk to. He needed to make sense of all of this. Trouble was, he had no idea who would understand everything he was going through, except . . .

"Corinne." It came out embarrassingly breathless as soon as she answered the phone, but he was too desperate to care much.

"Noah? What—"

"How . . ." Noah swallowed heavily. "How are you doing? How's everything?"

"Everything's good." She sounded wary, and Noah didn't

blame her. They hadn't spoken since he left town nearly a week ago. "How did the move go?"

Noah wandered restlessly into the pedestrian passage between buildings. At the other end of the brick walkway, sunlight glinted off the lapping waves of the river, making him squint. "Not bad. The house is nice. I'm still staying at a motel, but I'll be moving in pretty soon."

Ugh, platitudes. He wanted to stuff these social niceties into a rocket and fire them into the sun.

"Is Willow Cove everything you remember?"

Of course he'd told Corinne about Willow Cove. He'd told Corinne everything—his entire life story, every tiny detail—about growing up downstate but spending summers up here, his family, his business degree at odds with his interest in art, his subsequent move to California, his life there before he met her. That's what you did when you thought you'd met the love of your life and felt like there was nothing more important than burrowing deep into each other's histories, into each other's selves, until you couldn't tell where you ended and the other began. That was their life together, for two and a half years. Until Corinne got other ideas. And now here he was, thousands of miles away, and they were chatting like friendly acquaintances.

Noah couldn't wait any longer. "How's Aidan?"

"He's fine. His new tooth is coming in weird. It's giving me nightmares about braces."

"If you need any help—"

Corinne's voice had a sharp edge when she said, "Noah. I'm not trolling for money."

"I know, I know." It was just . . . this was the only way he could help with Aidan. Now. "Sorry."

"We're fine, okay?"

"Okay." He knew why they were fine. He couldn't bring himself to ask about Corinne's new boyfriend. Noah and Corinne were supposed to be congenial exes, and he was trying to be, but the thought of this new guy taking up space in Corinne's house, hanging his toothbrush where Noah's had been, taking Aidan to the petting zoo that had been their favorite place to go . . . nope. He wasn't as enlightened and laid-back as he wanted to think he was.

"Is Aidan around? Can I talk to him?"

"He's in school," she said, and Noah picked up on an accusatory tinge to her voice, implying he was less of a person because he'd forgotten what time it was in California and Aidan's schedule. He could just picture her impatiently pushing her long black hair out of her angular face, the silver and mother-of-pearl bangles she liked to wear jangling on her wrist.

"Right, right. Well, can you tell him I said hi, and I'm thinking about him? Can I call another time, when he's home, maybe a video call—?"

"Noah."

There was that clipped command again. *Noah.*

Sit. Stay. Heel.

"Yeah." If his voice got any tighter, his throat would snap like a PEZ dispenser.

"We need . . . we need some space. Okay?"

"Wh . . . *space*? Seems to me I just gave you three thousand miles' worth of space."

"I know, but—"

"Are you trying to keep Aidan from me?"

There was an uncomfortable pause—more uncomfortable than the conversation, if that was at all possible—before Corinne spoke again.

"Yes," she said simply, plainly, brooking no argument.

Noah choked, shocked. Eventually he fought out, "Are you *serious*?"

"We've been over this. I have to think about what's best for

Aidan, and I don't want him upset. You've confused him enough by moving out—"

"You threw me out!"

"I did what you didn't have the courage to do. We should have ended things a long time ago."

"But Aidan—"

"He's not your son, Noah."

Noah had only been in two physical fights in his entire life, but he certainly remembered what a well-timed punch to the gut felt like. It felt exactly like this.

He fought to get his breath back, and then every one of his nerve endings was on fire. The fact that Corinne could be so calm as she blithely destroyed what had been his whole world for more than two years made him want to rage, to throw his phone against the brick wall of the alley in a satisfyingly palpable explosion—anything to expend this restless energy that had plagued him for weeks.

For the moment, though, the only thing he could find to do to save his sanity was hang up on his ex, spout a few choice expletives, and walk away before he really did destroy his phone or punch the brick wall. All these months, and his frustration hadn't lessened one bit. He wondered if it ever would.

CHAPTER 3

"My movie night, my house, my movie."

"Seems to me you'd let your guests choose," Jenna groused at Gillian, pouring wine until it was precariously close to the rim of the glass. Delia reached for it, but Jenna slapped her hand away. "Get your own."

When Jenna wasn't looking, Gillian stole the glass out from under her. "My movie night, my house, my wine."

"Tch. Attitude."

"And that's why you love me."

"When you don't steal my wine, sure. What's got you so riled up, anyway?"

"Nothing! I'm fine! Busy, that's all."

Jenna narrowed her eyes. "Pharmacy work following you home? Should we check your purse for jugs of pills?"

"It isn't the dating, is it?" Delia asked sympathetically.

Gillian sighed and dropped into her favorite silk linen chair as two of her best friends, Jenna Masterson-Page and Delia Dupree, settled on the striped sofa nearby. "I don't want to talk about it."

"Yes, you do." Leah entered the room last, sitting on the floor with her back against the couch, between Jenna's and Delia's legs. "You'll feel better if you let it out, and then you'll have the strength to get right back in the game."

"See here, Keegan," Gillian scolded the newest addition to their friend group, "I don't want to hear platitudes out of anyone as disgustingly in love as you and Eli are. It's disturbing."

Leah couldn't hide her small smile or the blush suffusing her cheeks. It was true Leah and Eli had fallen hard for each other last winter.

"Besides," Gillian went on, "if you think about it, this is all your fault."

"Aw, because you saw how happy Leah and Eli are and you wanted the same thing for yourself?" Delia exclaimed. "How sweet!"

What had started out as a project for the group of friends to "class up" Eli so he could win back Victoria, his ex-girlfriend, had turned into something else entirely when he and Leah started spending more and more time together. Now they were inseparable and deliriously happy, and the rest of their friends couldn't have been happier for them.

"No," Gillian countered forcefully, "because as soon as Eli was settled with Leah, the rest of you got bored. 'You need someone, Gillian. Let's find you someone, Gillian.' And like a dope I listened. Now look at me."

"We just want you to find love," Delia said.

"And that's another thing." Gillian pointed at Delia so sharply that some wine sloshed out of her glass. "It wasn't supposed to be me next. It was supposed to be you and Gray."

Delia snorted. "Yeah, like that'll happen in this lifetime."

"Eli and Leah, you and Gray, you all just sort of ended up in one another's orbits like magic. But the rest of us have to . . ."—Gillian shuddered—"sign up on dating apps."

"Oh, it hasn't been so bad, has it? At least tell us you've found *someone* with some potential," Delia begged.

Gillian winced and picked up her TV remote. "How about that movie?"

"Come on."

Gillian didn't know where to start, so she just didn't. She wasn't about to tell her closest friends about the first date she'd gone on with someone she'd met through one of the apps, when she was bright-eyed, pure, and hopeful, envisioning meeting someone kind and charming and handsome who would sweep her off her feet. And how she'd felt her pulse flutter in her wrist when the stylish, good-looking man had appeared in the café doorway. He'd locked eyes with her, looked her up and down . . . and then walked out immediately.

She hadn't felt that demoralized since she was twelve years old and had a crush on Nick Rehnquist . . . and confessed her crush to her friends. When it got back to Nick, he laughed out loud—right in the middle of the cafeteria, right in front of her and her friends, his friends, and everyone else—and snorted that he'd never like a girl like her. Ever. And he'd called her fat.

The guy from the dating app had the same energy, just the grown-up version. And for a split second, Gillian had felt the same kind of twist in her gut that she'd felt when she was twelve. Even though, at this point in her life, she knew her size meant nothing. Gillian was a larger woman, it was true. She'd never been, and never would be, a svelte model—her ample breasts alone negated that quite handily—but she also was heavier than even her above-average height of five foot eight allowed. By society's standards, anyway. And the damn BMI chart that had been dogging her her whole life.

Left to her own devices, she didn't give her size a second thought. Gillian was perfectly content with her appearance and, more important, was in perfect health, which her doctor confirmed at every physical. No heart problems, no cholesterol problems, no blood pressure problems, no blood sugar problems. As Gillian's beloved physician said, human beings come in all shapes and sizes. As for *her* shape, it was true she had curves in all the right places . . . as well as a few some people would consider all the wrong places.

And she knew, when it came to those people, there was no point in trying to convince them she was not, in fact, a perpetual couch potato shoveling mass quantities of Ding Dongs into her insatiable maw. Every time anyone was superficial enough to make assumptions about her based on her clothing size, she wrote them off. With a smile, though. Because she was nothing if not 96.3 percent sweetness and light.

So she had shrugged off the guy who'd walked out without even meeting her and moved on to other men she'd matched with. She'd have been a liar, though, if she hadn't admitted to herself that her first experience had made her more cautious, and she'd set up fewer dates because of it.

All she said now was, "The dates aren't always bad, okay? There have been one or two nice guys, but nothing . . . *special*, you know? Is it too much to want to hold out for someone remarkable?" She shook herself. "Never mind. Rome wasn't built in a day and all that nonsense. But tonight I want to watch a movie with my besties. And I'm warning you, Dupree," she said to Delia, "if you make even the slightest complaint about this being in black and white, you're banned from movie nights for the foreseeable future."

"Oh no. What did you pick?"

"No, no, this is good," Jenna said, turning to the screen as Gillian cued up the film. "*All About Eve.* Deception, betrayal, scandal—"

"But a really good group of friends," Gillian said. "And for the romance junkies in the house, Bette Davis's character has a loyal boyfriend. Best of all, nobody does cynical and biting like Bette."

"Her Margo Channing is a classic," Leah agreed. "And her clothes are to die for. Roll it. Delia, you'll love it—promise."

They all loved it, even Delia, and well into the movie, possibly bolstered by the bottles of wine they emptied, the friends were loudly cheering the embattled heroine Margo and enthusiastically booing the scheming villain Eve.

"I think we missed half of the dialogue," Leah said when it was over. "Still worth it."

"I now officially aspire to be as glib as Bette Davis. Life goal," Gillian declared, switching off the TV and scrutinizing the last bottle of wine only to find it didn't have so much as a drop left. "Oh. We're out."

"I think that's our cue," Jenna said, standing and stretching as Delia gathered up the glasses and took them into the kitchen. "I have to terrorize a bunch of teenagers tomorrow—almost prom night, gotta scare 'em straight with grisly car-crash videos. But right now I need to check on the home situation. Taking bets on whether Ben managed to get the girls to sleep on time or if they're still bouncing around while he's snoring in the lower bunk bed. Anyone? Anyone?"

"Snoring," everyone else chorused. Jenna and Ben's daughters were adorable, but their batteries never ran down.

"Hey," Delia called from the kitchen, "did I hear something about Retha leaving town?"

"Yeah," Gillian said, hoisting the empties in the crook of her arm, "she's following her heart, which is now in the possession of some widower in Tampa. Why?"

"Because somebody's in her house. The lights are on."

Gillian hurried into the kitchen and joined Delia at the side door. Across the houses' conjoined driveways, Retha's place was absolutely ablaze, light pouring out of every window.

"Should we call the police?" Delia asked.

Jenna came up behind them. "I don't think burglars advertise what they're doing by turning on all the lights in the place, Delia."

"Then what . . ." She trailed off, then breathed, "Holy hootenanny."

"Now what?" Gillian, who had turned away to put the empties in the recycling bin, returned to see what was dazzling Delia besides the bright lights.

Half silhouetted in the rectangle of a downstairs window, a tall man moved around in Retha's dining room. With his back to the window, Gillian could only make out broad shoulders, muscled arms. A slight turn of his head, and she spied a strong jaw.

"Oh," she whispered, impressed.

Then he turned a little more, threw back his head, and let go a massive sneeze. A familiar one.

"Oh. Oh . . . no. Nope."

"You *know* him?" Delia squeaked.

Gillian shrugged, avoiding her friend's eyes.

"Are you holding out on us?" she demanded. "Who *is* that?"

"I don't know. He was checking out the house earlier. Contractor or something. Maybe a flipper."

"He's *amazingly* hot."

Oh, she knew that.

"Please tell me you have more details."

"Did you talk to him?" Leah asked, also intrigued.

Gillian shook her head. She wasn't about to tell her friends about her little window flirtation from this afternoon. God, that look of his. It had practically burned her clothes off—well, what clothes she was still wearing, as she'd been in the middle of stripping off her work outfit—even across two driveways and through several panes of glass. Not that she had let it show, of course. If Mr. Hotness thought he was going to shock her by drooling on Retha's window like that, he was sorely mistaken. It was easy to keep dancing, and she was pretty proud of the parting booty-shake she'd gifted him. He didn't need to know she'd been forced to take a minute in her upstairs hallway, out of view, to put herself back together, calm those susceptible ladybits of hers, and get her knees to stop knocking before she could continue with her evening.

"I think you should go talk to him," Delia said, still staring at him rapturously. "He's just perfect."

Gillian laughed, patted Delia's purple hair affectionately, and turned away once and for all. "Even if he were single—which we don't know—it'd be a terrible idea."

"What? Why?"

"Because," Leah said, "if he's a flipper he'll be working on Retha's house for who knows how long, and if things didn't work out between him and Gillian, it could get awkward, trying to avoid somebody crawling all over the house next door for months."

"Exactly. See? New girl gets it," Gillian said.

"I think you should go for it," Jenna mused.

"Oh, not you too."

"Well, he can't be any worse than the guys you've found online," Leah said. "If he's a flipper, he's gainfully employed, which is a plus. Worst-case scenario, if it doesn't work out, I've got a spare house you can stay in."

"Um, you don't own that house free and clear yet," Jenna reminded Leah.

Leah was the reluctant owner of a dilapidated house in town. When Cathy, her foster mother, had died, Leah had been surprised to find out she had left the place to Leah instead of her biological son, Patrick. As expected, Patrick was contesting the will, and Delia was handling the case. Even though she'd given up her career as an attorney, she still had her license.

Delia snorted, flipping her hand dismissively. "It's nearly in the bag."

"Well, I think I'll take the path of least resistance," Gillian said. "If I don't get involved with the flipper, or whoever he is, then I won't have to leave my home to avoid him. See how simple that is?"

"Simple and *boring*," Jenna snorted.

"Besides, I can't leave. I've got gardening to do."

"The competition isn't for months."

"So little time, I know. But I *am* going to win this thing. I mean it."

"You came so close last year," Delia said. "Isn't third place enough?"

"*Too* close. It only makes me want it more. So shoo, all of you. I've got planning to do."

Once her friends left, Gillian pulled on a cardigan and wandered out into the cool, quiet night. She took a breath, thinking about everything she had to do to get her garden ready for the competition. She walked the length of her driveway to enter her backyard the way the judges would, to see it through their eyes. The view was unencumbered by a garage. While most homeowners would balk at being denied one, Gillian didn't mind at all. Retha's house didn't have one either. Her driveway and Retha's both ended abruptly just past the back corners of their houses, giving way to lawns separated only by a tall hedge stretching from the ends of their driveways to the back property line.

Gillian stood by the boxwood hedge and looked out over the lush expanse of her garden, trying to be as objective as the judges would be—correction: as harsh as they would be; no sense in sugarcoating it—as they assessed the composition of her flower beds, trees, and lawn. She liked the promise her yard held already.

She'd been working her fifth-of-an-acre patch long enough

that she could have coasted on what she'd already cultivated, but if she wanted to win this competition once and for all, she was going to have to step up her game. Especially because she had to clear an extra hurdle on the way to claiming the trophy: Louise March, chair of the gardening club, lead judge of the competition, and a thorn in Gillian's side for more than fifteen years. Every year that Gillian entered the garden competition, Louise took the opportunity to judge her work ruthlessly. It was a miracle she had managed to take third place in the last competition; before that, she'd never even been granted an honorable mention.

As Gillian had stood there last year, clutching her sad little third-place certificate and a gift card to the garden center, she'd sworn to herself she'd go all out for the next competition. She was now well on her way to a full English garden. Color. Scents. Multilayered beds bursting with hollyhocks and peonies and snapdragons and clematis. Her roses were more than respectable, her perennials ready to bounce back this season. She had seedlings burgeoning under grow lights in her basement, she had a fountain she'd bought from the garden center with her third-place gift card. She had been planning and sketching all winter, and fertilizing with her homemade compost since the ground thawed in the spring. She was ready, and so was her garden.

Gillian made her way to the back corner by the shed and turned the handle on the rotating composter a few times. She examined the yard from that angle, picturing the cascades of flowers, the brilliant pink creeping phlox and deeply glowing purple lobelia, that would bloom in heaping mounds soon. Would she stick to strictly English flowers? No. It would be an American take on a British classic. Not straying too far, however. Just enough to put her own stamp on it. But what it would be, she knew, was beautiful and romantic.

Well, that was ironic. A romantic garden created by someone

with absolutely no romance in her life. She told herself she was making an effort to rectify that, but was she really? Or was her love life hobbled by the specter of her previous terrible relationship? Gillian had been elated to get rid of her domineering husband, Tucker. She'd rejoiced when she'd won her freedom and no longer had to justify her every move, explain her every action, or check with him before making any decision. There was no reason for his shadow to loom over her life now. He was long gone, after all. Blew out of town as easily as he'd blown into it six years ago, when he'd swept Gillian off her feet. Bad judgment call on her part, falling for him. She had been young and naive and had taken leave of her senses for a while. But it wouldn't happen again. It couldn't. Since her divorce, whenever she looked in any man's eyes, chatted with him, even flirted a bit when she was so inclined, there was now a cold, hard cynic lurking inside her, sitting back with a cocktail, drawling, *And just what is this one hiding, hm?* Her cold, hard inner cynic looked and sounded an awful lot like Bette Davis in her prime, she realized. No wonder she'd been adamant about watching *All About Eve* tonight—Bette Davis was her love language. Or lack thereof.

Gillian's eyes drifted up over the tall hedge separating her yard from Retha's and to the windows of the house next door. The lights were going out one by one, and without their glow streaming out of the windows, her yard fell into almost total darkness. She listened hard but didn't hear a door close, didn't hear a vehicle engine start. Was the mystery man staying in the house? Would she be running into him on a regular basis? And if so, would she introduce herself, like Delia had suggested? Flirt? Give him her number? Ask him to take a look at the loose floorboard in the upstairs hall that constantly plagued her, and then jump him?

Ridiculous.

Just like those muscles. And that jawline. Who looked like

that? Nobody, that's who. She'd have convinced herself he'd been a figment of her imagination if her friends hadn't seen him as well.

Gillian's Inner Bette took a long drag on her cigarette and let loose a dry, affected laugh as she tossed her permed hair. *Married, probably,* Inner Bette drawled. *Or gay. Or an oaf. And we don't want oafs, do we, darling?*

"No, we do not, Bette," Gillian whispered, tearing her eyes away from Retha's house. "We certainly do not."

~

It was 3:34 A.M. when Gillian let out a strangled gasp and found herself staring at the ceiling, her heart pounding, as she tried to find her way out of an impromptu straitjacket made from her twisted sheets.

Well, this was just perfect.

She groaned and kicked at her bindings. The absolute last thing she needed or wanted was some stranger making an appearance in her dreams, and yet there he was. Was that all it took these days? One sight of a marginally attractive man—okay, a scorching hot guy with to-die-for muscles and a strong jawline—and her subconscious was suddenly obsessed with him to the point of dragging him into her dreams and having her way with him?

Gillian kicked at her sheets again and splayed herself out like a starfish. Certain parts of her body still had some residual throbbing going on, which was downright embarrassing. Sure, she had needs, but the last thing she wanted was for some random guy she didn't even know to address those needs, even in her subconscious.

Ick.

Well, okay, not ick. He clearly wasn't repulsive. He was sex on a stick, if she was going to be honest with herself. And the way he'd looked at her when he saw her through the window . . .

She shivered. No wonder he'd entered her dreams when she had her guard down. And had done very, very wicked things to her in said dream. It was almost as though she could still feel his lips on hers, on her neck, on her . . .

"Bette!" Gillian whimpered, renewing her fight with her sheets so she could focus on something other than the throbbing, which had intensified. "Help."

Inner Bette appeared in her doorway, wrapped in a bathrobe, her face covered in cold cream except for her eyes, which made her look remarkably like a raccoon. *Leave me alone. Even figments of your imagination need their beauty sleep.* And she vanished.

"Thanks for nothing, Bette," Gillian grumbled.

∾

"Mick, you stinker, don't you dare sell those bricks," Gillian threatened down her phone line as she hunted in a bathroom cabinet for her sunscreen. "I still need them."

"Yeah, but they been here a long time," the owner of the salvage yard protested. "I gotta move 'em."

"They weren't bothering you all winter."

"And now it's spring, and people are doing clearouts I want a piece of. I hear some rich idiots bought the Cabot place and want to tear down the barn. If I get their business I'm gonna need every square inch of the yard to store the stuff. You want these bricks buried under a hundred vintage milk cans, that's your business—"

"All right, all right, I get the picture." She crossed from her bathroom back into her bedroom to collect her best gardening hat. "You could deliver them, you know."

"Nope, no can do. It's the busy season—"

"Yeah, yeah, I heard you the first time."

"Get here soon, is all I'm saying."

Gillian grunted, irritated, and ended the call. Good thing she was about to take out her frustrations by digging some dirt—her favorite pastime, and a very soothing one. She wasn't about to admit to Mick she probably should have picked up those bricks already. She could have started putting in her garden path today if her planting went well and she had some extra time.

Her plans for the day were to plant the seedlings she'd been nurturing in her basement after she prepped the beds along Retha's property line and trimmed the hedge. Gillian always lovingly and precisely shaped her side of the dividing greenery, one wayward sprig at a time, with small pruners. It was the perfect neutral backdrop for the cacophony of color produced by her flower beds, with the tall, narrow, purple salvia and pink foxgloves and lupins butted up against it, then shorter flowering plants in front of those. She made a mental note to add even more color to that bed, maybe move the pink yarrow there. It wasn't doing well in its current location on the other side of the yard . . .

Then she was startled out of her reverie by the roar of a car engine making the panes of her bedroom window buzz with the vibration. It was so close to the house it had to be coming from her driveway or Retha's. She moved the curtains aside and looked down, but it was hard to see over the lower eaves. Someone was definitely in one of their driveways, though.

Although she couldn't see exactly what was going on, she could hear the engine rev. Then she saw a familiar black pickup truck charge down Retha's driveway toward the street at top speed . . . with a huge chunk of the boxwood hedge flailing helplessly behind the bumper as it was dragged along the blacktop, spindly roots bobbing, mounds of dirt shaken off in its wake. She could practically hear it screaming . . . Oh, wait. That was her.

Gillian hurtled down the stairs and outside. "Stop! *Stop!*"

The pickup did stop, but not because she was shouting. The driver reached the end of the driveway, hopped out, unwound a heavy chain from the base of the plant, and unceremoniously flung the carcass onto the apron.

It was him. She recognized that profile. The magnificent posture, the strong arms, the wide shoulders, the trim waist. The perfect set of the jeans smudged with dirt from murdering plants (was that considered floricide?) and the strain of the T-shirt across that broad chest. It was the flipper again. Or whatever he was.

"Hey!"

Oblivious, the guy climbed into the truck and charged back up the driveway, going as fast in reverse as he had gone forward. Gillian jumped out of the way before he ran over her toes, but the minute the vehicle stopped she was at the driver's side door before he had a chance to open it.

"What the *hell* do you think you're doing?" she demanded, glaring at him through his open window.

The man blinked, a surprised double take. Was it because she was ambushing him, or did he recognize her from her little, er, underwear-flashing dance? Gillian was too furious to give it more than a half second's thought, or to give him more than a half second to answer, which he didn't.

"How *dare* you?"

There was a moment's silence as the man studied her. Even through the haze of her rage, she couldn't help noticing how ridiculously good-looking he was. At a distance, his physique was striking, but she could shrug off the siren song of a few muscles. Up close like this, she couldn't tear her eyes away from his. They were light brownish green, with lashes that should have been against the law. The guy was too pretty for his own good. He looked her up and down, and when those lashes fanned out across the tops of his cheeks, Gillian felt a little tug in her gut.

His quirked lips, defined by a bit of hadn't-shaved-in-a-few-days scruff, scowled. "Feeling a little attached to the greenery, are we?" he grunted. "Well, these aren't worth it. Best to just get rid of 'em."

The flora destroyer flung open the truck door, and Gillian had no choice but to retreat. She wasn't about to back down, though.

"That's Retha's hedge," she stated, hands on her hips.

"Eh, gonna stop you there. Actually . . . it's mine."

"You can't just . . ." It took a second for Gillian to tweak to what he was saying. *"Yours?"*

"Funny story—buy a house, yard is included in the price. Noah West," he introduced himself. "Your new neighbor."

He extended a dirt-encrusted hand. Gillian stared at it like it was a three-day-old dead fish and didn't say a word.

"What, no welcome to the neighborhood?"

"Are you going to keep destroying it? If so, then no."

He waited again. She glared.

Finally he said, "Okay, then," and moved to get back into his truck.

There was no way she was letting him continue the carnage. "You've ruined my design," she snapped.

One foot on the running board of his truck, he paused and gave her a comically puzzled look. "Your what?"

"My design."

"Look, lady, I don't have time for . . . whatever it is you're talking about."

"That greenery you're murdering was important to my garden. You've ruined it." Gillian knew she needed more words than she was using, but she didn't have the mental capacity to be more erudite at the moment. In fact, it was taking every ounce of willpower she had not to simply launch herself at him and start flailing. And not in a sexual way at all.

"Killing? Ruining? I'm . . . not . . . what . . . ?" Noah spluttered, his expression growing wilder the longer Gillian kept blocking his way and glaring, immovable. "Jesus." He raked stiff fingers through his hair, then swiped his hand over his mouth, muttering, "Got me arguing about a bunch of damn junk plants."

Gillian started to protest but was startled into silence by the steadying breath he let out, as loud and labored as a dragon's. She half expected smoke to billow out of his nostrils.

"Let's get one thing straight right now, okay?" he snapped, obviously fighting to maintain control. "I don't *care* about your *garden* or your *design* or whatever it is you're on about. This is *my* house, this is *my* yard, this stupid *hedge* is *mine*. I've got enough problems in my life without some pain in my ass trying to tell me what to do with my property. You want bushes, get your own. These are mine, and the rest of them are coming down. Right now."

CHAPTER 4

Noah steered the small motorboat closer to the island. He'd rented the boat at the marina, quietly, without letting on who he was. After his near panic attack the other day, he still couldn't bring himself to strut into the store and announce that the new owner had arrived. Not yet. From what he'd been told by the attorney, the senior managers had been keeping the marina running during Jerry's sudden health crisis and unexpected death. Noah taking over could wait a couple more days without the place falling apart, he was sure.

Noah was grateful for that, because he needed a minute. He wasn't adapting to his new life well at all, if his meltdown after talking with Corinne was any indication. In fact, he could draw a direct line from his devastating phone call with her to the purchase of far too much cheap beer, which was then consumed in the privacy of his new home, among the doilies and artificial plants. That had led to a wicked hangover, culminating in his *Hulk smash* morning, which featured the absolute pinnacle of his week: his argument with the captivating—no, scratch that—infuriating blonde who was now his next-door neighbor.

Stellar.

But it was a brilliant day, which he appreciated, even if the breeze off the water had been cutting as he'd made his way halfway across the massive river. The chill wasn't as vicious now that he'd docked at one of the many islands in the middle of the St. Lawrence that gave the region its name. If he recalled correctly, there were actually more than a thousand islands between the United States and Canada—large, small, and minuscule, as though someone had taken a hammer to the mainland and splintered off pieces from the edge like fragments of peanut brittle.

His uncle Manny lived channel-side, facing the American shore, on a medium-sized island with homes large and small huddled along the shore and a chunk of wilderness in the center. While there were private islands nearby with a single multimillion-dollar house on each one, this was not one of them, and Manny was definitely not a multimillionaire. His house was a modest beige ranch that would have looked at home in a landlocked Midwestern suburb. Instead of power boats, Jet Skis, and other water toys, only a modest old outboard motorboat was tied to Manny's dock, along with a two-story pontoon boat bobbing in the deeper water.

Noah climbed out of his rented craft and made his way across the neatly clipped lawn. Manny's house was set back from the water on a large patch of land surrounded by trees. Ghosts of summers past flickered at him out of the corner of his eye—the firepit had been there; the dip in the land at the water's edge had been where they'd always dumped their inner tubes and boogie boards; the volleyball net had been there, closer to the house, until a wayward ball had cracked a window. They had always planned to move the net, but after it came down, it never went back up. By then he and his cousins were young adults, and they never all gathered at Manny's house at the same time after that.

After a while, they stopped going to Manny's altogether.

Noah had visited his uncle occasionally on his own, only staying a few days at a time, just to make sure he was doing okay, but then he'd moved across the country and only stayed in touch by phone. He hadn't actually seen Manny in years. At least he could try to rectify the situation now.

"Manny?" Noah knocked on the side door that led directly into the small house's living room. Nobody came to the door. "Manny!" he called, drawing out the second syllable like he used to—*Man-nay!*

He tried turning the door handle. Of course it was unlocked. Whoever locked their doors around here? The house was neat, if plain, and deep in shadow except for a patch of sunlight coming in through the sliding door facing the river. Noah heard a sound from the hall leading to the bedrooms, and his uncle shuffled into view, tall but stooped. The older man turned his head toward Noah, and his pale blue eyes, at first unfocused, seemed to clear a little as he stared at his nephew.

"Jamie?" he rasped. "Jamie, is that you?"

Noah sucked in a sharp breath. Manny was looking even older than Noah had expected.

"Manny," he whispered as his uncle shuffled across the carpet toward him. "Jamie's my father. Your brother. I'm Noah."

God, what had happened to Manny? How long had he been like—

Then Manny's expression cleared, his eyes brightened, and he barked a laugh. "Ah, you're too easy, kid. Way too easy."

"Wh–what?"

"About time you showed up," he said, tucking in his shirt and smoothing down his hair. "How long has it been? Give your old uncle a hug."

"Manny? What the hell!" Noah squeaked, as his surprisingly strong uncle grabbed him in a tight embrace. He coughed when

Manny gave him a few affectionate hard thumps between his shoulder blades.

"Just pulling your leg, kid. Mother Nature's gotta work harder than that to bring me down."

"Oh my God. You suck!" Noah exclaimed, trying to calm his lurching stomach. "I thought something happened to your . . . your head!"

"I'm fine. How's *your* head?"

"Exploded, thanks very much. Jesus."

Manny chuckled. "Come on in, kid. Let me look at you." He stood back and studied his nephew. "You're skinny. You eating enough?"

Noah followed him into the small kitchen, and Manny pulled open the ancient, gold-colored refrigerator, its door covered with flyers from nearby towns advertising church spaghetti dinners and restaurants' and bars' extended hours for the summer months. "Something to drink?"

"Sure."

"Move go okay? How's the house?" His uncle paused and squinted at him. "And why do you look like somebody dragged you through a hedge backward?"

Noah had thought he'd gotten a grip on his irritation that seemed to be constantly simmering just below the surface these days, but now it rose to a rolling boil again. "Do *not* say the word 'hedge' to me ever again."

"Okay, obviously there's a story there. How about 'beer'? Is that a better word?"

At Noah's curt nod, Manny fetched two bottles from the fridge and unceremoniously walked out to the patio, expecting Noah to follow the alcohol. Which Noah did.

Once they were settled in two chipped red metal chairs that bobbed gently on their S-shaped supports, Manny swigged his beer and waited for Noah to go off.

Noah did, in fact, go off, and in spectacular fashion. "My neighbor is *nuts*!"

"Huh," was all Manny said in response. It wasn't a question, but instead a word—okay, noise—of encouragement to continue.

"She's picking a fight because I cleared some crap out of my yard. *My* yard. But she's making it *her* business."

"Mm, not a good thing to feud with folks around here. Place is too small for that." Manny made a little sucking sound through his teeth before asking, "Who's your neighbor, again?"

"Some blonde. I don't know." He refrained from tucking "gorgeous" or "luscious" or "sexy as hell" into his description because, no matter what he'd thought when he first saw her, he had a distinctly different opinion of her now. "She was bitching about her garden or something."

"Garden? Bet that's Gillian Pritchard." Manny thought for a moment. "Oh, that's right—you bought Retha's house. Definitely Gillian. So you don't like her, huh?"

"She's bizarre."

"She's spectacular."

"Manny, please."

"Don't act so delicate. She's an exceptional woman—lot of people around here respect the hell out of her. So what's the problem?"

Noah hitched one shoulder, reluctant to explain. With a bit of distance, it all seemed so ridiculous. "There was a line of ugly bushes between my yard and hers. I got rid of 'em, and she pitched a fit."

Manny laughed so hard, so suddenly, that he choked on his beer and started coughing. "You dumbass," he said when he recovered. "Everybody knows Gillian enters the garden competition every year. You just ruined her design."

Noah absolutely didn't expect Manny to echo Gillian's words

so closely, or to take her side. "So . . . you mean . . . this gardening thing is a big deal?"

"The biggest. You just made your first Willow Cove enemy, son. Congratulations." He toasted his nephew by tilting the neck of his beer bottle toward the younger man, then tutted, almost to himself, "Making an enemy of Gillian Pritchard, of all people."

"Great."

"Better make amends, if you know what's good for you." At Noah's bewildered look, Manny added, "Buy her a plant or something. There's a nursery on the east side of town that's good. But don't even *dare* to buy something for her garden. Get some potted thing for her house. Understand?"

Noah nodded, chastened.

Manny downed the rest of his beer, stretched, and said, "I'd invite you to stay for lunch, but, ah, I've got a date."

"A *date*?"

"Well, don't say it like *that*."

"Like what?"

"Like you think I actually have lost my mind."

"I didn't mean . . . it's just, you know—"

"I'm old?"

"You ain't young."

"That's your opinion."

"Your birth certificate states it as fact, more like."

"And this should stop me from spending time with beautiful women? The nerve of you youngsters." A ping sounded from Manny's pocket, and he pulled out his phone, glanced at the text, and smiled.

"From the lady in question?"

"A very nice lady, I'll have you know."

"Pics or I'll think you're hallucinating."

Manny sighed, held the phone at arm's length, and looked

down his nose at the screen while he tapped and swiped for a few seconds.

"There you go. Feel free to be envious."

Noah took the phone from his uncle and found himself looking at a photo of an age-appropriate woman—thank goodness, because he'd had a fleeting fear Manny was chasing women Noah's age—with silver hair, a fresh face, and a kind smile. "Very nice. How did you two meet?"

"Well." Manny said slowly, rubbing the back of his neck just like Noah did. Now that Noah thought about it, he'd probably picked up the gesture from his uncle years ago. "Kind of a funny story. I knew her, of course, from way back. Way, *way* back. But I didn't know she was interested in dating again since her husband died a few years ago until I came across her profile on a dating app. You ever use those? Pretty handy." Before Noah could answer, Manny squinted at him and said, "Nah, bet you never have any need for that nonsense, do you? All you've gotta do is flash those pearly whites at some pretty young thing and she just follows you home. Too handsome for your own good, that's your problem. Always were. You dating now?"

"Manny, I just got here."

"Meh. You're not getting any younger, you know."

"Is that a cheap shot because I called you old?"

"How'd you guess? All right," Manny sighed with finality. "Time to get out of my way and let me get ready for my date. This ugly mug needs all the help it can get."

His uncle pushed himself out of his chair and gave Noah a warm, affectionate smile. "I'm glad you're here, son. Don't be a stranger." When Noah nodded, Manny nodded back and headed into the house. "But don't hang around too much," he called over his shoulder. "You'll mess with my mojo. Call first."

Noah smiled fondly at his uncle's back, now ramrod straight. The bastard. "Get some," he called.

As Noah crossed the river again, he studied the mainland across the sparkling water. Although he wondered for the hundredth time what he was doing here, he couldn't deny it was a breathtakingly beautiful part of the country. The desert had been striking, of course—and his allergies were nonexistent there—but something about this softer landscape spoke to him.

Or maybe it was just his fond memories of the place, vacationing here in the summer with his extended family. Now the cousins were scattered across the country, and here he was, coming back to the smallest, but warmest, place he remembered.

Making a mental note to check in on Manny frequently, Noah edged the motorboat back into a slip in the marina, tied her off, and reached for the ladder, when a powerful sneeze nearly pitched him into the water. Well, this was going to be a problem. Even though the pharmacist had said to give the meds a chance, they didn't seem to be working for more than a few hours at a time. He was going to need bigger guns if he was going to survive the summer.

∽

Noah rang Gillian's doorbell and knocked on the frame of the screen door in quick succession. The situation really wasn't urgent, but his energy was high and he wanted to get this over with before he thought the better of it. He wondered if he should have gone to the front door instead of lurking here at the side door, which seemed way more informal and friendly . . . and then wondered if he was overthinking things. He knocked vigorously one more time before wiping his hands on the thighs of his jeans, one at a time, switching the package he was carrying from one arm to the other.

Before he could analyze exactly why his palms were damp and his stomach was twisting as though he hadn't eaten in days, the inner door flew open, and there was his neighbor on the other side of the screen, staring at him suspiciously.

That was fair. He hadn't exactly inspired confidence in her the last time they'd spoken. Was it only several hours ago? How time flies when you're irritated as hell.

Gillian didn't say anything, just glared, so he said, oh so eloquently, "Uh, hi."

Still no answer.

"Uh, I don't know if you remember me? I'm your new neighbor."

Eyes squinted. She was not amused.

"Just kidding. Of course you do. Look," he rushed on, "I . . . about this morning . . ."

Arms crossed. More squinting.

Okay, why was he finding it unusually difficult to dredge up an apology? Normally he had no problem at all talking to beautiful women. He could charm their panties off whenever he wanted. He needed to get this woman into that mindset or die trying. Not like he wanted her panties off. He didn't think. No, he *didn't,* because as gorgeous as her backside was—and he remembered it vividly—she really did seem testy, and he wanted no part of that.

And now here he was, on Gillian's doorstep, his courage ebbing away, trying to undo the damage from earlier in the day with a few mea culpas—which, he realized, he still hadn't uttered—along with . . .

"Here. I want you to have this."

Noah fumbled the package a little but managed to unroll the brown paper from the gift and hold it out like he was one of the magi presenting the frankincense in a church Christmas pageant. He added a hopeful little smile—always a sure way to win people over, especially women. They couldn't resist his smile.

Gillian's frown only deepened. A gift and one of his winning smiles didn't even get her to soften? What the hell, was she a robot? Made of wood? What?

"What is *that*?" she spat, and it sounded more like a flat statement than a query.

"It's a little . . . you know . . . friend. For your yard."

He'd picked up the oversized gnome at the garden center. Yes, Manny had told him to buy her a houseplant, but Noah was sure this little guy, with his silly grin and jutting paunch and . . . pet raccoon, apparently, peeking out from behind his leg . . . would be a welcome addition to Gillian's elaborate garden. The way she was eyeballing it, however—there was definite venom in that look—made him recall how Manny had warned him not to get her anything for her garden. His caution was supposed to apply to ornaments as well as plants, apparently, judging by the hostility radiating from Gillian right now. She certainly didn't throw open the screen door, embrace the gnome, and thank Noah profusely, that was for sure.

More silence.

Oh yeah. He hadn't said he was sorry yet.

"I . . . I wanted to apologize for messing up your yard. I didn't know you were using the hedge in your . . ."

"Garden design," she filled in for him.

"Yeah, that."

"But I *did* tell you, and you pulled the rest out anyway."

Oh. Yes, he had done that. "I can be a little . . . impulsive . . . sometimes."

"You don't say."

"I was having a bad morning." *Bad week. Bad several months.* "I am sorry. Really."

"Okay."

One flat word. She wasn't forgiving him; she just wanted to get rid of him.

"Your garden is really nice, by the way," he said, in his best *I'm interested in your interests* way.

"Thank you."

Two more flat words. Pancake flat. Florida flat. Salt flats flat. Roadkill flat.

Before he could stop himself, he added, "It's just . . ."

"What?"

Oh crap, here came an opinion she didn't ask for. "Kinda . . . fussy."

"Oh my God."

"I mean, I'm sure it's nice and all, but it's not *my* taste, you know?"

Gillian livened up now. The only problem was that she didn't spark with interest, but with a different emotion altogether. "Oh, forgive me for not creating something to *your* taste. On my own property. Starting five years ago. If I'd known you were moving next door to me five years from when I started my garden, I would have consulted you before planting anything. Wait—let me go fetch my time machine."

Noah was surprised the mesh screen between them didn't melt from the nuclear power of her sarcasm.

"Okay, well, I don't know what you want me to say, here. I said I was sorry."

"Fine. Mind if I go now? I'm busy reworking my entire design."

"Oh! Yeah, no problem. So . . . ?" He held out the statue again.

Gillian slammed the door in his face.

On his way back to his own house, he said to the gnome, "Well, little weirdo, you just weren't charming enough, I guess." Noah flipped up the lid of his wheeled garbage tote and held the statue high, ready to toss it. The gnome just smiled cheerily at him, oblivious to its fate. "Ah," he sighed, "I just can't quit you. And this isn't over yet."

Noah let the lid of the tote fall back into place, cradled the gnome again, and looked around at his handiwork from earlier in the day. Dirt everywhere. Raw bare spots where the bushes had been, like a gash in the flesh of the landscape. A wide-open view of Gillian's yard that now felt like an intrusion, like something private had been laid bare. He'd done that, and he regretted it now, but he couldn't undo it—the shrubs were broken and already withering at the curb.

He placed the gnome on the edge of the grass, in the empty spot where the first plant had come out, twisting the statuette this way and that to settle it in the loose dirt. He gave it a pat on the head and hoped eventually it would charm Gillian the way he'd intended. But he wasn't holding his breath.

CHAPTER 5

"Here." Gillian leaned across the pharmacy counter to hand Delia her phone. "Take a picture of me for my dating profiles. I don't like the one I'm using."

Delia looked at Gillian's proffered phone in horror. "Are you serious right now?"

"What? It's quiet in here. Just take a picture quick."

"Take a photo of you under fluorescent lights? And in your lab coat? I am *not* aiding and abetting such a crime. It's fine if you're taking a picture for your PharmaCon badge or whatever convention you guys whoop it up at, but a dating app? No way."

"A *dating* app? Now, why would you want to do something like that?"

Delia stepped aside to make room at the counter for an older man who approached, his straight posture belying his stiff, slow gait. Tim Warner, eighty-eight, cholesterol medication, blood thinners, but for a man his age, surprisingly little else.

"Hi, Mr. Warner," Gillian said with a smile. "Got two prescriptions ready for you today."

"I keep telling you, call me Tim. Now, what's all this about dating apps?"

"Well," Delia started to explain, "it's when you meet people using this thing on your phone—"

"Oh, I know what a dating app is, young lady. I want to know why this beautiful woman feels she needs to use one. It seems Gillian here would have men lined up around the block for a chance to spend time with her."

Delia shot Gillian a look from behind the elderly customer, and Gillian had to bite down hard on the inside of her lip to avoid laughing.

"Well, that's awfully kind of you, Mr. Warn—uh, Tim," she said as she rang up his prescriptions, "but it's just the way things work nowadays."

"Mm." He shrugged as he accepted the bag Gillian handed him. "Well, if you're going to take a photo, you'd better undo one more button on your shirt."

"Timothy!"

Undaunted, the old man said, "Men like women with a little meat on their bones. If you've got it, flaunt it."

At this point Gillian was speechless and couldn't quite bring herself to excuse him because of his age. She started to retort, but was distracted by a shopper glaring at her from the shoe-insert display. Gillian didn't even bother to nod in greeting. She didn't waste her time with Louise March (fifty-seven, no medical history on record, not a single prescription or pharmacy purchase besides the occasional painkiller), a woman who always seemed to carry her own personal storm cloud over her head.

She was sure Louise had heard Mr. Warner's comment, and she was even more certain that Louise had thoughts of her own about the topic. She always did. Gillian had found that out pretty quickly back when she and her family had moved to town when Gillian was fifteen years old. Louise was their neighbor and her first boss, at the recreation center, and she had made Gillian's life a living hell. Whatever possessed a grown woman to feel perfectly comfortable criticizing a teenager's looks was a mystery for the ages. But Louise had done just that. All the time. Gillian didn't care what had made Louise the way she was; what she needed to worry about was protecting herself. So Gillian had grown up quickly, thanks to her hypercritical neighbor and boss, and she learned that the only way to protect herself was to ignore the older woman. She never forgave Louise, though. As far as she was concerned, there was absolutely no forgiving an adult woman who thought it was her God-given right to comment on a young girl's appearance. And even though Louise didn't make her snide comments to her face very often anymore, the woman made sure Gillian knew she didn't approve of her looks or her lifestyle, even if it was just via a squinty glare like the one she just served up from aisle three.

Although Gillian had learned not to care what Louise thought of her—which wasn't much, she'd learned over the years—she couldn't help but consider what this conversation with Tim Warner sounded like from Louise's point of view. It made her cringe a little. Talking about her dating life while on the job was a bit unprofessional, sure, but this was Willow Cove, where everyone knew everyone else's business. No, the problem was with the way Louise viewed Gillian: unworthy of having a well-rounded existence, including a love life. And Gillian didn't want to give her any fodder for her gossip.

Gillian pointedly turned away from Louise, saw Mr. Warner off, and smiled at the next person who stepped up to the counter: Maria Di Genova (sixty-nine, thyroid hormone replacement, water pills).

The woman huffed, "Well! What Tim said . . . that's just . . . I don't even know what."

"Hi, Mrs. Di Genova," Gillian said. "Don't worry about Mr. Warner. He—"

"Any man you date should like you just as you are, no matter what you weigh." Before Gillian could think of how to respond to this, the woman went on, "So is this true? You're dating again?"

"Just a bit, yes."

"How wonderful. Really, it's wonderful. It's about time too. You've been alone far too long. A nice girl like you, single. Unthinkable. Did you hear that, Anthony? Gillian's dating. You've met my Anthony, haven't you, dear?"

A snort from Delia nearly set Gillian off once and for all.

"Yes, Mrs. Di Genova, I have." A thousand times, if once. Yet Mrs. Di asked her every time they ran into each other.

It was as though she hadn't even spoken. The woman reached her arm out sideways and, like a magician pulling an ungainly rabbit out of a hat, produced her son, forty years old if he was a day, still living with his mom and, as his mother often pointed out, extremely unattached.

Maybe it was the hangdog posture, maybe it was the dress shirt/overlarge cardigan/shorts/white socks/Adidas slides combo, maybe it was the absence of any discernible personality, maybe it was . . . well, Gillian knew for a fact that his mother still did his laundry and made him Fluffernutter sandwiches for most meals. And it didn't help that Anthony followed his mother everywhere. Ev-ery-where. Yeah, it was pretty plain to everyone in Willow Cove why Anthony was still very single.

"You two should have dinner some evening," Anthony's mother suggested.

"Oh . . ."

It wasn't like Anthony was a bad guy. And Mrs. Di was nice. Gillian didn't want to hurt their feelings.

"I could cook," Anthony's mom suggested eagerly.

Delia mimed eating a sandwich, likely Fluffernutter.

"You know, Mrs. Di, it's just . . ."

Gillian was unable to complete her thought, because at that very moment another customer stepped up beside the Di Genovas, inadvertently nudging them out of the way.

Of course only Noah West could be that rude.

"Noah," Gillian said, barely glancing at him, using every ounce of energy she had to keep her voice steady. "If you could just wait a moment, I'm helping—"

Mrs. Di Genova raised a judgy eyebrow. "Young man, I was here first."

"Oh, I'm sorry, ma'am. Go ahead and get your prescription. I'll wait."

"Well . . . I mean . . . I don't have a prescript—"

"Getting medical advice?"

"N–no."

Noah raised his eyebrows, which produced three horizontal lines running across his forehead. Gillian found herself fascinated by this for some reason, caught herself staring, and forced herself to focus on Delia instead. Delia was making her *yikes* face but was also drinking in the handsome sight of All That Was Noah.

"Purely a social call, then?" Noah asked disingenuously. When Mrs. Di didn't respond—and naturally Anthony wasn't about to, as he never did—Noah said, not unkindly, "Would you mind, then? I have a medical issue. Thanks so much," he added as they moved away.

"Rude," Gillian hissed at Noah when they were gone.

"What? I do have a medical issue. I mean, if there's another pharmacist who can help me . . ."

"Believe me, if there were, I'd hand you off in a heartbeat." Something about the combination of "hand," "off," and "heartbeat" made her flush as vivid images from *that* dream clamored for attention in her head, and she looked away again. "What do you want?"

"Talk about rude. Don't you treat customers better than this?"

"If they deserve it, sure."

"I'll rat you out to your manager."

"I *am* the manager. Now, quit wasting my time. What is it? STI? Foot fungus? Warts in your nether region? Rampant body odor?"

Noah turned to Delia, who was leaning on the counter, enraptured. "Is she always like this?"

"Never."

Then Delia giggled. The traitor.

"I'm serious," Noah said to Gillian. "I can't stand these allergies one more minute. This stuff"—and he tossed a half-empty pack of antihistamines on the counter—"doesn't work." Placing one fist on either side of the box, he leaned toward Gillian and said earnestly and evenly, "I need relief."

Gillian felt herself blushing again and took a clumsy step backward. He had to stop saying things like that. Even if his words were completely innocuous. To everyone but her.

"All right." Going into professional pharmacist adviser mode helped her get a grip. "Do you have a doctor in the area? If not, find one, get an accurate diagnosis of what, exactly, you're allergic to, and get a prescription if it turns out you need one. In the meantime, I can recommend a few things."

She unlocked the gatelike half door and stepped down onto the floor, breezing past Noah without looking at him.

As she made her way to the aisle with the allergy meds, Noah came up behind her, leaned close, and murmured, "Okay, look, I'm sorry about the gnome, all right? Hindsight, bad idea, all that."

Gillian didn't say anything. She couldn't. His warm breath

on her ear drove any rational thought right out of her head and made her struggle to remember what words were, exactly.

"I already said I was sorry about the bushes. Which I really didn't need to apologize for, by the way, since they were mine in the first place." He paused. When Gillian didn't answer, he went on impatiently, "Look, how many apologies do you want?"

She took a breath to get her head straight. "All of them."

Gillian stopped in front of a shelf about halfway down the aisle, and Noah leaned in again. "It wasn't really about the gnome, was it?"

Gillian stiffened. He was so close she could feel his body's warmth through her lab coat. As she caught a trace of his scent, clean and soapy, the throbbing that had woken her up in the middle of the night after her unbidden dream about him made a return appearance. She moved away, putting at least three feet of space between them, and turned to face him. "Try this," she said, pulling a box off the shelf. "It's a stronger medication." She tossed it at him, and he effortlessly caught it overhand. "And use this."

Noah accepted the second, larger box she presented to him. He frowned. "What the hell is it?"

"A neti pot. You tip your head and pour warm saline solution into one nostril, and it comes out the other. Cleans out the pollen or whatever irritants are lodged in your nasal cavity. People swear by it."

"You're serious?"

"Also, some people say they've had luck with herbs like stinging nettle."

"What do I do, shove the plant up my nose?"

"I am *so* tempted to say yes right now."

He snorted. And then sneezed.

"Whatever you do, don't try to pick your own—you might end up with poison ivy or something," she went on. "And don't buy the supplements we carry. God only knows whether those commercially produced herbs have any potency left. Your best bet is to go to The Witch on Warsaw Street, and she'll make up some capsules for you. Or maybe tea. I don't know."

"Is she, uh, really a witch?"

"Well, she knows better than to advise you to shove the plant up your nose, so no matter what, she's got one up on you. Now, is that all? Can I ring you up?"

"Trying to get rid of me?"

"Yes, I am."

Noah followed her back to the counter, examining his items. "Did . . . did you hand me the most expensive neti pot on purpose?"

"Yes."

"Is it any better than the others?"

"No."

Gillian forced herself to look him in the eye, unapologetic. He stared back suspiciously, and their standoff went on far too long. She was thrilled he caved first. Even if it was only because he sneezed.

~

"I don't understand," Delia said, breathless, as she tried to keep up with Gillian's quick pace down the sidewalk. "You hate this guy why?"

Gillian stopped walking to give her a look.

"Okay, okay, you've told me about the bushes. I get it. But you said he apologized, so what's the big deal?"

Gillian started walking again. Stomping, more like, because she still had a lot of rage to expend.

"Maybe you're being a little harsh?" Delia suggested.

"Whose side are you on?"

"Just a minute, ladies," a deeper voice cut in. "I'm detecting a little negative energy here. Gotta leave that shit outside."

Despite her mood, Gillian found herself smiling at their friend Gray as the muscled man comically blocked the door to his gym like it was an exclusive club and she was wearing knock-off Louboutins. Delia brightened even more. Of course.

"Mr. Powers, good to see you," Gillian said, feeling her irritation start to melt away at the sight of her friend. "Maybe I shouldn't be taking yoga tonight. You wouldn't happen to have a boxing class scheduled, would you?"

"Feel the need to beat the crap out of something, eh?"

"I don't think she should indulge her violent tendencies any more than she has already," Delia spoke up. "She's in a *mood*."

Gray held open the door to his gym. "A little frustrated, are we? Excess energy you need to burn off?"

You have no idea, Gillian didn't say.

"I thought working in your garden nonstop this time of year took care of that."

"I'm taking a small break for a day or so to regroup. There's been an . . . incident."

"Pest invasion?"

"Of the worst kind. Delia can fill you in while I get some juice."

Gillian didn't really need juice; she just wanted to give Delia and Gray some time alone. Because even though Gillian was cynical about her own love life, she was endlessly optimistic about theirs. So was Delia . . . most of the time. It wasn't easy, because Gray seemed oblivious to the heart-eyes Delia sported whenever he was around. No, scratch that—he was quite aware of Delia's feelings, he just wasn't inclined to risk their friendship for something more. Plus Gray's favorite activity in the world, besides being athletic, was dating anyone and everyone he could. Some people built model trains, some people climbed mountains,

Gray dated. And everyone knew Delia would never content herself with being one entry on the long roster of Gray's prospects.

Gillian stayed at the juice bar for as long as she could, fondly watching her two friends from a distance as they chatted and, yes, flirted. *Someday,* she thought. *Someday.*

But apparently not today, because even though Delia was still talking, Gray's eyes drifted over to a strapping young man entering his gym. The new arrival was definitely Gray's type but, to his credit, Gray stayed where he was and returned his attention to Delia. Gillian could tell he was more than a little eager to introduce himself to the guy, though. Poor Delia. Maybe Gray was a lost cause and she should try finding someone else instead of waiting around for him. Gillian had half a mind to invite her to try the dating apps too, but she had to think more of them than she did right now before dragging her friend into the meat grinder with her.

"So. Anthony Di Genova, huh?" Gray called to Gillian as he came over with Delia, his arm slung over her shoulders.

"Not in this lifetime. Unless he's secretly Superman under that unassuming demeanor."

"Is that all you've got—Anthony? After . . . what's it been . . . a couple of months, at least?"

"Five weeks. Not that I've been counting."

"She's had other dates," Delia said. "She just won't tell us about them. I've been begging, but she won't talk."

"I have nothing to hide. I just don't want to bore you."

"You wouldn't."

"Give us a little something," Gray said, "or Delia won't be able to sleep tonight because she'll be scheming to find you a guy some other way. Because apparently you can't meet them at work either."

"And why shouldn't I?" Delia retorted. "We all should want to help Gillian. She's gone too long without someone special."

When Gillian rolled her eyes, Delia said, "We worry about you and want you to be happy."

"I *am* happy."

"And it's nearly summer. The perfect time for a romance."

Gillian refrained from giving her a significant look regarding the guy who was cozied up to her at the moment and said instead, "There's really nothing to tell. I'm using two different apps. Lots of guys, nobody really floating my boat. Sometimes I wonder why I even try online stuff in the first place."

"What about that one guy . . . Preston? He sounded promising."

"Mm," Gillian agreed, taking a sip of her juice. "Very promising. Too bad that after a few preliminaries he turned our date into a pitch for a multi-level marketing scheme. *That's* an hour of my life I'm never going to get back. Then there was Alex. He was gainfully employed, which was a plus. Owned his own lawn care business. When I told him I was into gardening, our conversation turned into a high-stakes pop quiz about yardwork. Tons of fun."

Gray snort-laughed. "Did you at least pass?"

"I was doing really well. When I got too many answers right, Alex turned into a big manbaby and changed the subject, so I'll never know my actual score. Then there was Dave. Nice and normal, manages an appliance store. Divorced, so I thought if we started out bonding over our bad marriages, maybe we'd find something else we had in common along the way."

"And did you?" Gray asked.

"No idea. Our conversation was actually a Dave-centric monologue. I got to listen to him complain about his ex-wife for about, oh, three or four hours."

"It couldn't have been that long," Delia scoffed.

"Well, you know, your perception of time gets kind of skewed in a hostage situation. I'm sure Dave is a nice guy and all, I just think he'd do better with therapy instead of dating at this point in his life."

"So he's a little bitter," Delia said. "Understandable if he's recently divorced."

"Yeah, but then he started talking about how all women are gold diggers out to force him to spend money on them and then ghost him. Never needed the 911 rescue more, and thank you for that."

When she'd decided to start using dating apps, Delia had volunteered to be her fake emergency escape call, bless her.

"Happy to oblige," Delia said. "But I'm sorry you had to use it."

"I could have used it on Oontsy, but I was too amused. I kind of felt like sticking around."

"What kind of a name is Oontsy?" Gray asked.

"Well, that's just what I called him. I can't remember his real name, and it doesn't matter. I met him for coffee. He kept his earbuds in the entire time, bopping his head to some electronica. It was so loud I could hear the bass—you know, *oonts, oonts, oonts*. The people at the next table in the café could hear it too. Couldn't even hold a conversation with him. He invited me to go clubbing. I politely turned him down."

"So he likes music. Better than having taxidermy as a hobby," Gray said.

"Met one of those guys too."

"Ouch."

"Ooh, Gray should hook you up with one of his clients!" Delia looked up to the gym owner, beseeching.

Wincing, Gillian tried to find a nice way to say *Please, no muscleheads.* Not that every guy in Powerhouse was a steroid-pumped gym rat. But, as at any fitness center, there did seem to be a certain number of individuals who were overly invested in their workouts. Quite a few of them were in her line of vision right now. And each of them, in turn, only had eyes for their own form in the mirrors.

"Maybe," she hedged. "If a guy has got more on his mind than the best brand of protein powder, sure."

"I'll see what I can do."

While Delia beamed at him, Gillian surreptitiously raised one eyebrow at Gray and shook her head slightly. Gray nodded in understanding. The musclehead train was officially shunted onto another track. Good ol' Gray. If Delia brought it up later, Gillian would think of some way to deflect. That was a tomorrow problem. Today she'd just enjoy a good yoga session with her friend and worry about her dating prospects another time.

CHAPTER 6

The invasion was beginning.

Noah sighed and shook his head when he spotted the petite elderly person on his front porch. He wasn't surprised. He'd been living in the house for a week and a half already. It was about time a neighbor showed up with a casserole.

When the doorbell chimed, he set down the box he was carrying and went to greet his well-intentioned inquisitor. It was the woman from across the street who had waved at him on his first day in town.

She was smiling at him brightly through the screen door and holding a plastic container. "Hello, there. I'm Carol. I wanted to welcome you to the neighborhood."

"Noah. Please, come in."

"Oh, thank you." She stepped over the threshold, peering around. "My goodness, this looks almost exactly the same as when Retha lived here."

"The house came with all the furniture. And, well, everything else."

Noah hadn't expected the real estate listing's description

"includes entire contents of house" to mean *everything*-everything. He'd thought he was going to find a few pieces of furniture and the appliances left behind. But every curtain, towel, and matchstick was still here. The house was clean and neat, as though the true owner had just stepped out for a minute and told him to make himself comfortable till she got back. Really, he always half expected this Retha person to walk back in the door any minute.

Maybe he should change the locks, he thought.

"Imagine leaving everything behind and taking off for a new life, just like that," Carol murmured. "It boggles the mind."

Noah knew a little bit about that.

"Well," his new friend said in a perkier tone, "Retha is enjoying Florida, and you have bought yourself a lovely house. Are you, er, going to be the only resident?"

Noah didn't answer; instead, he waited just a moment to tease out the rest of her question. Carol didn't disappoint.

"No . . . wife and children joining you? Or husband?"

His lips twitched, and he allowed himself a small smile. "Nope. No wife, no husband, no children. Just me."

"And you're going to be taking over Spencer's Marina?"

Small-town gossip at work meant Carol had a lot of information on him already, and he didn't much mind. He was proud that he was getting used to the new dynamic. Probably had a good, firm grip on it by now, he thought.

"That is true, yes." He did not, however, feel like feeding the gossip machine, so he decided to focus on the food. "Can I take that from you?"

"Oh! Of course." Carol handed over the Tupperware. "It's just a little goulash for dinner. I hope you like it. People do rave about my goulash."

"I'm sure it's great. Thank you."

Just as Noah was wondering if he should invite Carol into the kitchen while he put the food away, the doorbell rang again.

"I'll just . . . get that."

Another one of the neighbors was on his doorstep, also carrying food.

"Hi, I'm Arnette. I just wanted to welcome you to the neighborhood."

Before she could hand over her container, another shorter and wider woman elbowed her out of the way. "Judy," she said. "Brought you beer."

True to her word, she held out two clinking six-packs.

"Judy," Arnette admonished her, "you couldn't bake something?"

"Not if you want the boy to live. And who doesn't like beer? Uh, you gonna open these?"

Noah decided he liked Judy best of all. "Come on in, ladies."

Arnette paused on the porch, leaning back and looking to her right. "Ooh, doesn't Gillian look nice. Hello, dear!" she tootled, waggling the fingers of her free hand. "Why don't you join us?"

It took everything Noah had not to rub his face and groan. In fact, he pretty much failed, eliciting a sharp look from Judy, although she didn't say anything. He steeled himself and leaned out the door, ready to invite Gillian in. If he had to.

Judy held up one six-pack as a lure. "We've got beer!" she called.

Noah didn't even bother trying to hold back his relieved breath when Gillian said, "Sorry, ladies. I have to go. I'm already late."

Arnette gasped. "Do you have a date?"

"Yes, I do," she admitted, smiling gamely.

"The computer thingy?"

"Through one of the dating apps, yes. Just coffee, no big deal."

"Good luck!" Arnette called.

Noah stepped back to let Arnette and Judy in, but then he muttered, "Excuse me a minute. I'll be right back."

A little voice in his head started *Hey, whoa*-ing, but he couldn't help himself. Ignoring that voice of caution, he jumped down his porch steps and crossed his driveway as Gillian opened her car door. She did look nice—summery fresh, in a floaty, flowery sleeveless blouse with a neckline that dipped quite low, with some ruffles hiding any excessive amount of cleavage (yet prompting curiosity about what was under those ruffles) and a knee-length skirt.

"Hey." He shouldn't have been out of breath after running only a few yards. Then he realized it was nerves.

"Can I help you?"

Ouch. Frosty. He dropped his hands onto his hips and stood on the other side of the open car door. Looked like she wanted that hundred pounds of metal between them. "I was just—"

"Are the meds working?"

"The what? Oh. Yeah. They're actually . . . better than the other ones," he admitted.

"I'll bet you haven't tried the neti pot, though. Or gotten any stinging nettle."

"Come on, cut me some slack. I've got to ease into this."

"Then you're going to keep sounding as stuffed up as you do right now. Sleeping okay? Not enough? Too much? I want to make sure the meds aren't having any adverse effects."

He shook himself, refusing to be distracted by the change of subject. "I'm sleeping fine. Look, did you just say you were going on a date?"

Gillian didn't answer, just cocked one eyebrow. Green. Her eyes were green. The first time he'd seen her, through the window, he'd wondered. Then she'd pissed him off so much on the day of the shrubbery war he didn't even notice. In the pharmacy, she'd barely looked at him. But now he could see they were a brilliant, deep green. And cold as marble as she watched him suspiciously.

"A date with someone you met through an app?" he prompted.

"I don't think it's any of your business, but yes. Why?"

"Nothing. Just . . ." Suddenly he felt extremely awkward. What was he doing, interrogating her about her personal life? "It can be, you know, dangerous."

Gillian actually laughed. "Oh my God."

Noah persisted. "Do you have someone . . . I mean, does anyone know where you're going? If you need . . . help?"

"Are you really assuming I'm that much of an idiot?"

"Wait, I didn't mean—"

"Of course you didn't. Now, if you're through? I'm going to be late."

He stepped back. "Oh. Right. Yeah. Have . . . have fun."

"I don't answer to you." She hesitated. "But thank you," she said primly.

As she pulled out of the driveway, Noah nearly shouted, "Be careful!" but he forced himself not to. He would have sounded ridiculous.

He went back inside to find his three neighbors clustered around his kitchen counter, drinking the beer Judy had brought and eating oatmeal raisin cookies, Arnette's contribution. If it were dinnertime, he'd have expected Carol to put the goulash in the oven to warm. Judy handed him a beer as soon as he entered the room.

"I hope you like it here, dear," Carol said. "This is a lovely house. So much light."

He nodded brusquely and took a pull of his beer. "Does, uh, does Gillian do that a lot? Online dating?" He could hear the agitation in his voice, but he couldn't let it go. "It seems kind of . . . sketchy."

"She's been dating for a little while, on and off. I do hope she meets someone nice," Carol said. "She's been alone so long. Ever since the"—she paused before whispering the last word—"divorce."

"Does she have a contact, someone she can send an SOS text to?"

"Are you volunteering?" Arnette asked with an indulgent smile, her honeyed voice warm with a ready affection.

And then the ladies all shot one another significant looks.

Oh no.

"No, no, of course not. I'm just . . . concerned."

Concern Troll wasn't fooling anybody. The significant looks got more pointed.

"I mean, you hear things . . ."

"Honey, this is Willow Cove," Arnette reminded him. "Gillian will be fine. But yes," she added, "she has a lovely group of friends who look out for her. Don't worry."

"I'm not—"

"It's okay," Carol said, beaming at him. "We won't tell her how you feel if you don't want us to."

"Tell . . . who . . . *what*?" Noah could feel his hackles going up. "No, no, there's nothing—"

"You're kind of defensive right now. Don't want to talk about dating? Had a bad breakup recently? I'm a little psychic," Arnette said. "I can pick up on these kinds of things."

Judy snorted. "Who needs magic powers? Anybody can tell this guy here has some baggage."

"Baggage? I don't—" Noah tried to protest, but Judy stomped on his weak attempt immediately.

"Single guy shows up in town out of the blue, no wife, no husband, no girlfriend, no boyfriend, no mention of anybody special, no mention of any interest in meeting anybody special? Come on, son."

Yep, he definitely liked Judy. Even if he intensely disliked how she was brutally poking this particular bruise at the moment.

He chose to charm his way out of the predicament. With a wink and a conspiratorial smile, he said, "Ah, it's complicated, ladies. You know how it goes. I . . . may have left a . . . situation behind in California."

"Ah-*hah*!" Arnette burst out. "We knew it."

"You knew what?"

"You have that . . . hunted look," Carol explained. "No," she corrected herself, "*haunted*. Haunted." *Hic.* "It's quite attractive."

Apparently Carol was succumbing to the strong alcohol content in Judy's choice of beer.

"I thought you said it was his muscles that made him attractive."

"Judy!" Arnette snapped.

"And it seems like a shame to waste all those good looks hanging around with a bunch of old ladies," Carol went on. "Now, my stepdaughter—"

"Oh, lay off your stepdaughter," Judy groaned.

"What about Kara?" Arnette mused.

"Nah. She's weird," Judy said.

"Nadine, then."

Wait, what? Were they trying to find a date for him? "Uh, ladies? Do you mind—?"

"Too soon, dear?" Carol asked, her voice warmly sympathetic.

Was it? Noah rubbed his face wearily. It had been months.

"Hush up, both of you," Judy said, helping herself to another beer. "Can't you see the kid isn't interested in meeting anybody?"

As if his body had been taken over by aliens and he was a mere bystander, he heard himself protest, "I didn't say I wasn't interested in meeting anybody."

Carol brightened. "Really? Because Gillian—"

That snapped him out of it. "*Not* Gillian."

Startled, all three women shut down a little, their expressions suddenly impassive.

"And what's wrong with Gillian?" Judy demanded.

"And don't give us any song and dance about it being awkward because you're neighbors," Arnette said. "She'd never hold a grudge if it didn't work out. Sweet girl."

He let out a snort. "Sweet. Okay."

"She is!" Carol insisted.

"Ladies, she ripped me a new one over a ridiculously trivial matter and has hated me ever since, so I hope you'll excuse me if I politely disagree with you."

"Trivial?" Arnette prompted.

Noah related the Saga of the Boxwoods. They were all buds now; he figured he could get some sympathy out of them over this ridiculous situation.

"Oh dear," Arnette gasped when he finished his tale of woe. "Not her garden."

Noah sighed. "I know, I know. I've heard."

Without a word Carol hustled out Noah's back door to see the destruction for herself. Everyone else trailed after her, Noah last. He braced himself for the fallout.

As the women stared at the open space where the hedges had been, cooing in dismay, Noah sighed deeply. "I tried to apologize. That just made it worse."

"Did you buy her something nice?" Carol asked. "Like a fruit basket?"

"I did! I got her a . . ." Suddenly even getting ready to voice the words made him realize his mistake. ". . . garden gnome."

There was an ominous silence.

Then it was shattered by three senior citizens laughing so hard he was afraid they were going to fall over and break multiple hips.

"What?" he asked. "It was a really nice gn . . . okay, never mind."

"Oh, gno, honey," Arnette said, wiping tears of mirth from the corners of her eyes. "Gnot a gnome."

"Gnever, ever," Carol added, "give a serious gardener a gnome. Gnever."

"All right, all right, I get it." He hesitated, then asked, "Does this mean you're taking your goulash back? And your beer?"

"Gnah," Judy said. "We still like you, Gnome Boy."

As the ladies succumbed to another round of laughter, Noah noted the empty space in the dirt where the gnome had been. Gillian must have thrown it out. Of course she had.

∽

While Noah could have spent the rest of the afternoon getting drunk with his new neighbors—and Judy had offered to go for more beer—he'd gently extricated himself after a short while. Not that he didn't want to spend more time with them, but he had work to do.

If he was officially the owner of Spencer's Marina, he needed to act like it—check on his new business, introduce himself to the staff, get the lay of the land. The employees welcomed him as he personally shook everyone's hands and apologized for not coming in sooner. He thought he detected a glint of recognition from Parker, but the boy didn't say anything, thank goodness. He wasn't sure how he would have explained that he'd tried to enter the place earlier but chickened out.

Now, however, he was ready. At least that's what he told himself. And it wasn't so difficult. The familiarity of the marina helped calm him, and everyone was so friendly that there was very little awkwardness. They all bonded over the loss of Jerry, and Noah promised to have a plaque made up honoring the original owner, with a nice framed photo on the wall in a prominent place. The staff loved the idea.

Noah spent a couple of hours in his new office, which was just as Jerry had left it, only with a stack of recent bills in the center of the desk blotter. Although the managers had kept the place running, it was now Noah's job to dig deep and make sure everything was in order before the boating season started in earnest. It didn't take long, once he started reviewing the marina's accounts and vendors and service schedules and town regulations, before he had a raging headache from information overload.

Food would help. Carol's goulash was waiting in the fridge, but he didn't feel like going home to an empty house just yet. He seemed to recall a certain neighborhood bar he'd visited with his friends once or twice years ago. He hoped it was still there and hadn't been turned into yet another twee tourist spot.

It was still there, on the main road in town, at a distance from the more popular wine bars, pubs, and microbreweries illuminated by strands of fairy lights and strings of Edison bulbs stretched across outdoor patios that drew tourists, their numbers growing as the weather got warmer, like moths.

Dickie's, as it was now called, was not appealing. To say the least. It never had been, if he recalled correctly, even under its previous name, which Noah had forgotten. If he ever knew it in the first place. No matter—a mangy, no-nonsense, brick-front, dank little hovel in the shadows of a burnt-out streetlight was exactly what Noah was looking for right about now, so he yanked on the door and entered the gloom of the dive bar. Just as he remembered, the place was fairly busy, its patrons all locals. Now he was a local. This was now his spot too. So he settled on a barstool and waited for the bartender to get to him. It didn't take long.

"Noah West," Dickie declared, slapping a white square napkin down in front of him.

He blinked in surprise. "You, uh, you know me?"

"Word gets around. Beer?"

"Apparently I'm going to need several." He pointed out his

choice of draft and then asked, "And you're Dickie?" The man nodded once. Noah recalled seeing him behind the bar when they were younger. And now he owned the place. Time certainly did fly. "What have you heard about me?"

"New owner of the marina, nephew of Manny."

"Does that make me okay?"

"Remains to be seen. So what brings you to Willow Cove?"

"You haven't heard all my sins?"

"You got some?"

"Nothing special, but sure. Do I get to confess to the bartender?"

"Ah, the myth of the bartender as therapist. You wanna talk? Be my guest, just be aware I might not be listening. Not really in the job description, no matter what everybody thinks."

"That's one bubble burst."

"There are worse ones. So go ahead."

"Kinda don't want to now."

"And yet you look like you've got so much to say."

"*That* you can tell?"

"Years behind this bar, so yeah, I can. Try me."

Noah scrubbed his face with his free hand and heaved a sigh. "Well. Broke up with my girlfriend, traveled thousands of miles across the country, haven't been here in nearly a decade. Bought a marina I haven't worked at in fifteen years, bought a house that doesn't feel like home, been accosted by an old-lady neighbor gang, made a mortal enemy of my neighbor. Things are totally going according to plan. Embracing imposter syndrome more and more with each passing day."

"Yeah, most of that doesn't interest me, but I gotta circle back to one thing. Old-lady gang?"

"Those busybodies, the ones that are always deadlier in bunches. They live in the neighborhood, they talk about you, they drop by with casseroles and oatmeal raisin cookies—"

"Oh *no*, not casseroles and cookies!"

"Trojan horse. They just use 'em to get their foot in the door. Then they come in and tell you the history of the house you just bought and everything about the previous owner and they want to know every detail of your life story. And then—*then* they start talking about introducing you to their granddaughters—"

"Uh, dude? How young do you think you are?"

"Daughters, then. Nieces. Whatever. Not the point."

"Since when is living in a nice house on a nice street with nice neighbors in a nice town such a horror story?"

"They're not all nice—not by a long shot."

Noah paused as he edged over to make room on his left for a muscular man who was leaning in to get Dickie's attention. He and Noah nodded to each other, and Noah continued while Dickie pulled beers for the guy.

"I really pissed off my neighbor by making a few minor changes. 'Ruined her garden,' she said. Wow, was that a shit show."

"Ouch. Which neighbor?"

"This blonde . . ." Noah stopped and corrected himself. He knew her name; he should use it. "Gillian?"

"No. Come on, now."

Noah rubbed his eyes as he hunched over his beer. "I know, I know, I heard it from Manny—how could I make an enemy of her, of all people, blah, blah, blah—"

"Okay, first of all, your uncle is right. She's great."

Noah persisted. "Yeah, well, she completely overreacted and was all kinds of bitchy when I tried to apologize."

"Uh . . ."

"I don't know what her problem is, but it's way bigger than me and a couple of bushes I pulled out. Which was within my rights, by the way. I think she's—"

"Dude."

Dickie's voice was so sharp that Noah looked up from his beer to find the bartender eyeing Noah and shaking his head almost imperceptibly.

"What's the matter with y—"

Dickie's gaze shifted to Noah's left.

Oh, great.

The good-looking muscular guy was glaring at him . . . and it seemed, like a lizard fanning out its neck frills to appear threatening, he'd gotten larger since the first time Noah had glanced his way. Two men had joined him—a taller, dark-haired guy and a dark-skinned, bearded guy—and they were giving Noah the same look. Noah recognized the tall one from the marina.

"Hey, Gray, Eli, Ben," Dickie said, "this is Noah. He's, uh . . . he's new."

It was a paltry excuse for Noah's bad behavior, but Eli softened a bit, apparently recognizing Noah too. However, the first man, Gray, didn't take it down even half a notch, despite Dickie's code for *Cut him some slack*. When Dickie finished filling their beer glasses, they scooped them up and moved away with a few last dirty looks at Noah.

"Nice work," Dickie muttered once they were gone, but he was laughing. "Those guys are all good friends of Gillian's. And now you're on their shit list."

Christ.

"Don't screw up again. It's also not a bartender's job to save your ass a second time."

CHAPTER 7

"Any sign of him?"

"I shouldn't be on the phone. I should be looking alert and eager, ready to engage in a scintillating conversation. Or something."

Gillian was sitting at a table in the middle of a country diner outside of town, optimistic about this new date despite her previous disappointments. Delia was waiting with bated breath on the other end of the line, almost more invested in this whole dating thing than Gillian herself. But then again, Delia had always been more of a hopeless romantic, Gillian a proud cynic.

"Hold up," Gillian whispered.

A good-looking man had entered the diner alone. Was this her date? Could she be so lucky? The man's photo on the dating app had been a little shadowy, and he had been wearing a baseball cap and sunglasses, so she hesitated. This guy was tall, dark-haired, sharp-eyed, and had a commanding presence. For that she could overlook the camo pants.

"I think it's him. I've gotta go."

"Wait! What's he like—"

Gillian ended the call and put her phone down on the table as she watched the man scan the diner. He quickly zeroed in on her and strode over.

"Gillian?"

She thrilled a little at the rumble of his deep voice. "Max, hi."

"Mind if I sit down?"

She watched him—subtly, she hoped—as he settled at the table. He didn't appear to be as circumspect. He studied her openly, almost as though he were assessing her. Which, she supposed, was warranted. Gillian knew anyone involved with dating apps entered a face-to-face meeting comparing the real person in front of them with what they'd seen online, trying to figure out if their date was hiding anything. It was only natural. She certainly hadn't been hiding anything, so she had no worries there. What Max saw on the app was what he was going to get right now.

If he was lucky.

Gillian sat up straighter and smiled. She definitely had nothing to hide.

"Glad you found the place okay," he said.

It was a little off the beaten path, Gillian had to admit, a mostly empty diner outside of a little blink-and-you'd-miss-it hamlet she'd never spent time in, even though it was only ten miles or so inland from Willow Cove.

"Is this a favorite place of yours?" she asked.

"It's close to my home."

"So you come here often?"

"Not really, no."

Max's responses were all uttered with a flat delivery and a face devoid of expression, and Gillian felt like she was working twice as hard to make up for his lack of animation.

"Well, tell me about yourself, Max."

"No, ladies first."

He definitely was polite, though, which was a plus. There

were too few true gentlemen in this world. Her mind flitted back to her fight with Noah over the bushes. *He* had certainly been rude as hell. Annoying man.

Why was she still fuming over Noah?

Gillian shook herself and smiled in what she hoped was a friendly fashion. Max squinted at her distrustfully. She dialed it back.

"Well, let's see . . . I'm a pharmacist in Willow Cove, I really enjoy gardening—"

"You grow your own food?"

Suddenly her date seemed very attentive. Maybe they had something in common after all. "I'm more into flowers. Do you garden?"

A server appeared at their table with a coffee carafe, and Gillian turned over her cup to be filled.

"I believe in getting your own food," he said. "It's a necessary skill."

"Oh, you're into organic?"

Max held up a hand to decline coffee. "You ever wrung a chicken's neck?"

The server let go a tiny amused breath at Gillian's shocked expression before moving to another table.

"N–no," she stammered, not sure if Max was joking or not. But he sure looked as deadly serious delivering this blunt question as he had since he'd walked in. Now that she thought about it, his profile picture had also been expressionless. She'd shrugged it off, since she knew firsthand how difficult it was to take a good photo. But now she felt like she needed to see if Max could laugh. "Is that a deal breaker?" she asked with a laugh of her own. She had a sparkling personality, dammit, and she was going to make it dance like a show pony until this guy was charmed.

"Let me see your hands."

"My hands?"

He said nothing more, so she hesitantly extended her hands toward him. He took hold of them, flipped them over, and examined her palms. She had to admit it certainly would be a plot twist if this country dude was into palmistry.

Max grunted, still looking down. He turned her hands this way and that, not too much, but enough to make Gillian curious.

After a moment he said, "Well, they're not as soft as I thought."

"I beg your pardon?"

"You've got calluses." Before she could defend herself, Max added, "That's good."

He released her hands, and she pulled them back immediately. She was starting to feel like he was appraising her the way he would a cow he was considering buying. The server was standing over a nearby empty table, and Gillian was sure she was eavesdropping. Those silverware bundles definitely didn't need that much straightening.

"Seems to me," Max went on, "you're not afraid of a little hard work." He paused, wiping the corners of his mouth with his thumb and forefinger. "You sew?"

"No."

"Hunt?"

"No."

"Shoot?"

"No."

"Can?"

"Can I what?"

"Do you know how to can food?"

"Are you looking for a date or a housekeeper?"

"The right mate *is* a housekeeper."

Mate? This was going south quickly. Gillian sighed. "Uh, Max—"

"You're smart, I could tell from your messages. You're strong. You can do hard work. That's good. I don't want some lightweight twig."

"For what, exactly?"

For the first time since he'd entered the diner, Max's face almost took on an animated expression. He leaned forward again. "I've been working for three years on my property."

"How nice."

"It's better than nice. It's completely self-sufficient. I've got windmills, I've got my own water source, I've got animals. I grow food. I hunt. I'm looking for a partner who can ride out the coming end times with me, who can provide for the home and fight off the alien invaders when the time comes. Now, you said you don't shoot, but I can teach you. Would you like to come see my compound?"

Oh God.

~

"What was this Max guy's last name?"

Gillian wiggled her toes as Alyce settled a cool washcloth on her forehead. She was stretched out on a sofa in the Masterson matriarch's house, embracing the nondrug approach to her raging headache—a shadowy room, a cold compress, and a mom's TLC, even if the mom actually belonged to Jenna and Eli. She'd known Alyce for twenty years, ever since she moved to Willow Cove and became fast friends with Alyce's kids, so she might as well have been her mom as well.

"Hutchinson?" Gillian ventured after a moment.

"Oh, well now, there's your problem. Any Hutchinson around these parts is just batshit."

"How did I not know this? He was around my age, so shouldn't we have gone to school at the same time?"

"Homeschooled," Alyce replied. "All the Hutchinson kids were. Apparently their parents wanted them to study a few extra subjects the public school system just couldn't provide."

Gillian croaked a laugh. "Like doomsday scenarios, I guess. I should run any potential dates past you to get their family histories before I agree to meet them in person."

"I'd be happy to take a look."

"*If* I ever have another one of these dates. I'm back to thinking online dating isn't really the greatest idea."

"Oh, I don't know about that," Alyce murmured, and Gillian heard her settle into a nearby chair. "I think you'll find somebody nice if you keep trying. You're a catch, Gilly, and don't let anybody tell you any different. The problem is you have to kiss—"

"—a lot of frogs before you find your prince," Gillian chorused with her. "I know it's going to take some time. I thought the app would help me filter out the weirdos, but I think it's collecting them instead."

"Oh, you're bound to meet some odd ones, there's no point in lying. But wade through those and you'll find someone great. I have faith in you."

"Where's the prepper?" a new voice bellowed.

Gillian adjusted the washcloth as Jenna roared in, flinging her overstuffed messenger bag into a corner before peering down at her friend.

"Well, now, Miss Homesteader, almost ended up chained in somebody's root cellar, did we?"

"Thank you for your concern and your sympathy."

Jenna laughed and plopped into the chair opposite her mother. "I had no idea Max had gone that far 'round the bend. I thought he was just, you know, kind of a loner."

"That's how they always describe serial killers," Gillian groaned, wriggling slightly to get her phone out of her pocket without moving any more than necessary. "Alyce, would you mind?"

The older woman accepted the device and opened up the dating app Gillian had been using the most. "Okay, let's see here . . ."

"Hey," Jenna said, nudging Gillian's foot with her own, "if that's tea in your mug on the coffee table, that's not going to help one bit. Let's go to Dickie's for wings and a few adult beverages. It's trivia night."

"Not that one," Alyce was muttering as Gillian groaned again, wondering if she had any stamina left to deal with beer, wings, and a trivia contest after her spirit-skewering encounter with Max. "Oh dear, no, not him . . ."

Alyce's pet cockatiel, Bryce, swooped in and landed on the back of her chair. Alyce murmured to him, keeping her eyes on Gillian's phone, and Bryce responded by diligently plucking at the hair on the crown of her head.

"Maybe I'll get a pet instead," Gillian said, pulling the washcloth off her forehead and heaving herself into a sitting position.

"You can borrow Fredo," Jenna offered immediately. She was always trying to give away her dog, but Gillian knew she was never serious. "One fart from him will chase that thought right out of your head. Now, are we hitting trivia night or aren't we?"

"Can't. I've still got a couple of hours of daylight left, and I want to do some work in the garden."

"You gonna plant some of those pickling cucumbers? I hear they store well over a nuclear winter."

"Oh, don't tease," Alyce said, giving Gillian her phone back. "I think Gilly's garden is the most beautiful, romantic place in Willow Cove."

"You're sweet, Alyce." Gillian checked her list of potential dates. It was shorter, but not by much. "Thanks for keeping an eye out for me."

"I wish I knew about more of the men on your list. I'm afraid you're on your own for weeding out the unacceptable ones from out of town."

"Yeah, it's riskier, but I figured I'd have to cast a wider net, since I know pretty much everybody around here." She opened one of her dating apps. "For instance, this guy. I know him. I also know his wife and kids, since they come into the pharmacy all the time."

She sighed and pocketed her phone. She'd rather be gardening. Plants didn't cheat.

"You know what'll solve your problems . . . ?" Jenna started in a singsong tone.

"Beer and wings and trivia questions do not solve problems," Gillian retorted.

"But they do make them go away for a while. Come on, freshen up your lipstick and let's go."

CHAPTER 8

Noah sat in his office in the marina and randomly neatened piles of papers on his desk. He had work to do, he was sure of it. He wasn't seeing any of it, of course, since the managers still handled the day-to-day needs of the place. Not that he couldn't pitch in if he was asked to. His art gallery back in California had been a success, and the marina was just another business, right? Except with boats. But business was business, and he knew how a business functioned. He knew how this business functioned. And he knew boats. At least, he used to.

Restless, he pushed away from the desk and made his way through the building, exiting through the back door to the docks. He loved this spot by the boat slips, where on clear days he could gaze out over the river's mile-wide expanse, imagining he could glimpse the Canadian shore in the distance. Today was not one of those days, however. A cool mist hung over the water, moisture seeming to cling to every surface along the shore like a clammy hand, and the vessels out in the shipping lanes were ghostly shadows.

Noah wondered if he would ever get used to this weather

again. Everything felt so *wet* all the time. The ground, the plants, even the air . . . everything was soft with moisture. He'd thought he'd be fine with it, that he'd remember what it was like living in the Northeast, but after years in the desert of California, a little bit of humidity made him feel like he was being smothered with a ten-pound wet towel on his face.

"Hey, boss?"

It took Noah a few seconds to realize the person behind him was talking to him. He was the boss now. Right. He turned around to find a young woman—her name escaped him at the moment, but he was working hard to learn who everyone was—leaning out the back door.

"What's up? Need me?"

"Mr. Masterson is here."

Noah raised his eyebrows, waiting for more information.

The girl clarified: "Eli Masterson? He's here for his kayaks?"

Oh. Uh-oh. That Eli? He followed the employee back into the building, through the work area, and into the storefront.

The tall man turned around, hands on his hips, and squinted suspiciously.

Noah heaved a sigh, straightened his shoulders, and marched up to him. He'd been in weirder spots. He knew how to be professional. "Eli, good to see you. What can I do for you?"

"Noah, right?"

Not exactly friendly, but on the other hand, Eli didn't punch him, so that could be considered promising. Still, Eli was scrutinizing Noah like you'd watch a sketchy-looking insect, wondering if it's going to go on its way and not bother you or if you should straight-up smash it with a shoe before it flies at your face. This was no way to do business, and Noah knew it. He needed to get this guy to put the shoe away.

"Look, Eli, I've been hoping to run into you. About that night at Dickie's . . ."

Noah trailed off. Eli said nothing. Noah didn't pick up outright hostility from him, but he didn't seem overly receptive either.

Noah went on, "I understand you heard me talking about my neighbor, and she's a friend of yours—"

"A really good friend."

Part of Noah's rapidly firing brain went rogue and started to wonder if Eli and Gillian had dated, and if they had, what had gone wrong, what had driven her to the murky waters of dating apps after being with Eli. Noah would bet the best boat in the marina it was some failing of Gillian's, because Eli seemed like an upstanding kind of guy.

The logical part of Noah's brain quickly fashioned a lasso of nerve axons to rope in his wayward imagination and lock it up. This was not the proper time to speculate on Gillian's dating life. Actually, *never* was the proper time to speculate on Gillian's dating life. Dear God, he was losing it.

"What about Gillian?" Eli prompted, and Noah jumped.

How long had he been checked out of this conversation because he was fixating on that infuriating neighbor of his?

Noah did his best to recover. "It's just . . . I said some things . . ."

"You did."

"And I'm sorry if I offended you."

"This isn't about me; it's about Gillian. She's been like a sister to me for half my life, and I know she's too good of a person to have people talking behind her back."

"You're absolutely right."

"So you should apologize to her, not me."

"I will, I promise. I'm not like that." And yet somehow Gillian managed to reach into his psyche and find the worst of him lurking there all the same. He didn't say that part out loud, though.

"Look," Eli sighed, "whatever is between the two of you—"

"Nothing," Noah said, way too fast. "Nothing is between us. I mean—"

The other man gave him a strange look, and Noah gurgled himself into silence. It was his only method of survival at this point.

When he felt safe enough to speak again, he decided to focus on business. "Let me help you load up those kayaks, okay?"

To Noah's surprise, however, Eli said in a far kinder voice, "You new to the area, Noah?"

"No, no," he answered, lowering his guard a little bit. "I used to come here nearly every summer when I was a kid."

"But you've never lived here."

Ah. There was a distinction between being a resident and being a summer person. Even Noah knew that. "Not lived here, no. I grew up downstate. Moved to California about fifteen years ago."

Eli nodded. "You need time to settle in, then. Come on, let's go have a beer at Dickie's. That is, if you and Gillian weren't planning on spending the entire night lobbing grenades at each other across your driveways."

Noah let out a small breath of relief when he saw Eli's grin.

∾

"You know, this place," Noah said, pushing away the remnants of the chicken wings he'd decimated and wiping his fingers on a napkin, "is probably one of the most perfect bars I've ever been in."

"I'd agree with that."

Eli, however, wasn't speaking of the glory of the dive bar as a whole; he'd caught the eye of his girlfriend, Leah, and winked. As she passed them on the way to the kitchen, she whacked Eli on the back of his head with her order pad. Eli's smile only brightened. Noah could see why. Leah was a beautiful woman with a kind vibe—even her head-whacking was gentle—and she obviously had Eli's heart.

Eli had introduced Noah to Leah when they'd first walked in. After a blink of surprise, she had greeted Noah politely but distantly. It was quite clear his reputation had preceded him. However, with a whisper in her ear from Eli, Leah looked Noah up and down, assessing, and then nodded and gave him a polite smile. Whatever Eli had said was hardly an endorsement, Noah was sure, but he got the feeling that anything even close to *He's not that bad, really* and/or *Give him a chance* was about as good as he was going to get at this point. And he was grateful for it.

"I'm serious," Noah went on. "It's nothing much to look at, of course," and here he dropped his voice as Dickie himself walked by behind the bar lugging a fresh keg, because he'd learned his lesson about speaking out of turn in a public establishment, "and neither is the owner . . ." Eli snickered into his beer. "But . . . I don't know . . ."

"No, I know what you mean. There's a lot of pretense out there." Eli vaguely waved his glass toward Main Street. "For vacationers. And they're, you know, essential to our way of life, don't get me wrong. We need tourists. I know I do, or I don't eat. But this place here is—"

"Blessedly devoid of twinkle lights and 'curated' hipster cocktails." Noah swung around on his barstool and leaned back, putting his elbows on the bar. "If you don't mind sharing it, I could see this bar being a haven, my . . . happy place . . ."

But his last words were anything but happy, as the door flew open and two people entered.

"Or maybe not," he amended, because one of them was Gillian.

The other, a tall, intense woman, narrowed her eyes at them. Noah froze when she marched over.

"Traitor!" she snapped at Eli.

Eli groaned. "Jenna . . ."

"Fraternizing with the enemy," she hissed in his face, tossing a death glare Noah's way.

"Noah, this is my sister, Jenna." Eli said it like an apology.

"Nice to meet—"

"Don't bother. I've heard about you."

"Oh, I'm sure you have," Noah said smoothly, but with a tight smile.

Gillian came up behind Jenna and tugged on her arm. "Okay, stand down. Let's not cause a scene."

"Why not?"

"Because we wouldn't be able to cope with being banned from Dickie's, for one."

The owner in question leaned on the bar between Eli and Noah. "I'd never ban you, Jenna."

Although Noah didn't know Dickie very well, even he was startled by the dopey look on the man's face, as it was so obviously unlike him.

"How many times, Dickie?" Jenna said. "How many times do I have to point this out? You, me, ancient history. Beyond ancient. Happily married." She flashed her wedding band. "Let it go."

"You're cruel, Jenna."

"Not cruel enough, apparently, because you still don't get the message."

Noah had no idea why Dickie was pining over Jenna. She was an intimidating powerhouse of a woman, which was fine, but quite plainly married, which was not. And she was adept at doing "angry," Noah noted. He could feel his balls shriveling up even though she was directing most of her ire toward her brother for daring to have a beer with him.

"Jenna," Noah ventured cautiously, sitting up straighter on

his barstool and turning his entire attention to the woman, "Eli's been telling me all about you. I understand you're the vice principal at the high school."

"No cracks about my nice long summer vacation. It's not that long, and I earn every minute of it."

"Wouldn't dream of it. I was just going to say . . . thank you for your service."

Noah said this with as straight a face as he could muster, holding still, remaining serious. He watched Jenna's lips twitch, and he had to fight the urge to laugh. She fought down the smile and grunted instead. But she softened. He could see it. Progress?

Gillian had drifted slightly out of view, off to his left, and Noah found himself sneaking a glance at her. She looked tired, and he wondered if she wasn't feeling well or if she'd had a hard day. Maybe her foray into Dickie's on a weeknight with Jenna implied the latter. While he was lost in thought, he noticed Gillian was obviously trying very hard not to look at *him*. Which was fair, all things considered.

From behind Noah, Dickie said, "Hey, Gillian, I hear you're dating, finally."

Gillian colored a little. "I guess so. Not sure how well it's going just yet, to be honest, but I've only been on a few dates."

"Using a dating app," the bar owner scoffed. "You should meet someone in person."

"Where? Like here, you mean? I'm in here all the time, and I haven't been swept off my feet yet."

"Ah, you're just not looking close enough." Dickie's voice was a little louder and a little clearer when he said, "For instance, the perfect guy could be right under your nose."

Noah stiffened. After going eight rounds with his neighbors about why he didn't want to date Gillian, he didn't want to have to explain his disinterest to Dickie too—and with Gillian present, no less.

Then Dickie said, even louder, "Gillian Pritchard, I would be honored to take you out to dinner sometime."

That got everyone in the group to focus on the bar owner, Noah included. Jenna, however, wasn't stunned into silence for long.

"Nice try," she drawled. "But you can't make me jealous by asking Gillian out."

"What if I *want* to date Gillian?"

"Do you? Really?" Jenna challenged him, arms crossed.

Dickie's glance skittered over to the other woman. "Why not? I like Gillian. She's great."

Apparently unfazed that Dickie obviously didn't actually have romantic intentions toward her, Gillian threw him a lifeline immediately. "I'm honored, Dickie, but I'd be forced to turn you down anyway," she said.

"Right," Jenna agreed. "Goes back to not wanting to be banned. You know, if things didn't work out."

"No, I just don't think I could compete with the memory of you, honey," Gillian said to Jenna.

The wicked smile that accompanied her words did unexpected things to Noah's nerve endings.

"See?" Dickie said to Jenna. "Everybody gets it but you!"

"I hate you so much right now," she hissed at Gillian, who only started laughing.

Seeing her unguarded and joyous like that wrecked Noah even more. What was happening to him?

And—worse—Gillian caught him staring. Her sparkle vanished immediately.

"What?" she demanded.

"Nothing. It's just . . . interesting to see you with your squad."

Gillian's eyebrows flew up. "My *squad*? What are we, sixteen?"

"Friends, then. Close friends, obviously."

"You know what? I think I like 'squad.' Let's go with that. But this isn't my squad."

"It's not?"

"It's only *part* of my squad. I have more out there. So watch yourself."

"Duly noted."

She paused and studied him for a moment. "What about you?"

"Me?"

"Your friends. You do have friends, don't you?"

Hm. He'd left all of his friends behind in California. Gillian was waiting for an answer, so he blurted out, "Sure, I have friends. I mean, hey, I've got . . . Eli."

"You do not have Eli," Jenna snapped.

"I do not have Eli," Noah amended immediately.

"Dickie, wings and a pitcher for the table," Jenna ordered, and Dickie rushed to comply. To the men, she said, "Well, come on, then. You might as well sit with us. Even you," she said to Noah.

Noah brightened. His charm still worked. He hopped off the barstool . . . and caught a glimpse of Gillian. Even though a moment ago she had seemed to be relaxing in his presence for the first time, now Noah could feel her holding her breath as she looked at him, her expression tight, the tension coming off her in waves.

She didn't want him there.

And it hurt more than he wanted to admit.

Jenna went back to the table in the middle of the room and everyone followed, including Noah, but his guts tied in knots at the thought that his joining them would make Gillian uncomfortable.

So after he pulled out a chair for her, he remained standing and said, "You know, I appreciate the invitation, but I've really got to go."

Jenna blinked, surprised. "Something wrong?"

"No, no," he insisted, trying to keep his voice mild. "I've just . . . I've got a lot of things to do. Eli, thanks for the drink. Have a good night, everyone."

Noah spun around to beat a hasty retreat, nearly knocking over Leah, who was crossing the room to take some patrons' orders. Of course he couldn't make a smooth exit. That would have been too much to ask of the universe.

CHAPTER 9

Gillian let out a shaky breath as she watched Noah march straight out the door of Dickie's (after he bumped into, caught, steadied, and apologized profusely to Leah) without even a backward glance. Which was fortunate, because Gillian wouldn't have known where to look if he had. She was grateful nobody at the table was paying attention to her, as she needed a moment to process what was going on with her nerves. When she'd walked into the bar and spotted Noah—her eyes had locked on him immediately—her stomach had done this weird flipping swoop, as if she were on a roller coaster and the car had gone into free fall down the first, tallest rise. Desperate to get herself under control, she'd quashed that feeling with her usual snarkiness. But when Jenna invited Noah to join them, those nerves of hers had taken over once again.

Several observations came crashing in all at once: First, Noah made her nervous. Her? Nervous? Around a guy? Unthinkable. If Gillian were in some Viking movie where people dressed in furs and talked in a stilted cadence, she'd be the one lounging on the chaise, shattering her wineglass on the flagstones and shouting, "Pah, I fear no man!" So yeah, those nerves of hers were entirely unexpected.

Noah had noticed her hesitation too. That look on his face . . . she'd never seen it before. His level of confidence—egotism, really—usually blew hers out of the water, but just then he'd looked *hurt.* The fact that she'd frozen up for a moment, thanks to those sudden nerves, had made him think she hadn't wanted him there. And it had hurt his feelings?

That made her heart hurt. She actually felt bad for Noah West. She really should have taken a moment to poke her head outside to see if the four-legged residents of Sam Wrigley's Hog Haven Farm had taken flight and were winging their way to Canada.

Then that thought got pushed out by the final, stunning blow to her already addled cranium: He'd left, but not because his feelings had been hurt. He hadn't joined them for drinks because he thought she didn't want him there. Had he left to spare *her* feelings?

Gillian had no idea what to make of this, if it was even true.

And if it was, it certainly didn't help clarify her muddy view of her new neighbor. She'd been so sure he was arrogant, rude, and obnoxious. And selfish, judging by the way he'd brazenly continued to rip out the hedge when she'd asked him not to. Well, when she had yelled at him not to. But then he'd apologized. Twice. Clumsily, and bracketed by more rudeness, but he'd said he was sorry nonetheless. He'd even given her a gnome. Which she still didn't know what to do with. It was standing in the corner of her mudroom, smiling away, rescued from the ugly bare strip of dirt that still looked like a World War I trench. Stupid thing. But she could tell he'd meant well.

And despite the fact that his fury had gone to eleven when she'd confronted him about the bushes, he seemed more normal, overall, than pyramid scheme Preston or angry divorcé Dave or—shudder—alien invasion prepper Max. What did it say about her dating experiences for Noah to appear more appealing than anyone she'd allegedly matched with after throwing her likes and dislikes into those fancy algorithms?

Wait. Did that mean she was a natural match for weirdos?

Nah.

She was fine. She was great. She was in the "kissing frogs" stage of dating, that was all. And any warm, fuzzy feelings she thought she was developing for Noah were the result of her raging hormones, which even dragged an imaginary, idealized—and naked—Noah out of her subconscious and into her dreams.

Stupid hormones.

And now they were getting her all hot and bothered again because the false memory of that idealized, naked Noah had set up shop in her brain and wouldn't go away.

Then Delia, Gray, and Ben came charging into the bar and Leah stopped by the table to perch on Eli's knee and all her friends were around her, reliable and supportive, and among all the chatter and conviviality she didn't have time to think about Noah West anymore.

"Gillian!" Delia exclaimed, plopping into the chair next to her and grabbing her friend's arm. "Did I just see your hottie neighbor leaving?" She fanned herself, a goofy expression on her face. "Why didn't you tackle him and make him stay? I would have."

Gray frowned at Eli. "Is that the guy . . . ?"

"Yeah. But . . . just now, we talked, we had a beer," Eli said in a placating tone. "He's okay. Really."

Ben snorted. "You're a saint."

"Of course he is," Leah said, kissing her boyfriend on the cheek before going back to work.

"He wants to make amends," Eli added.

"I approve of the boy," Jenna said. "Sorry, Gillian."

"Since when?" Delia marveled.

Gillian did her best to focus on her friends and said, "My new neighbor appealed to Jenna's sense of martyrdom by implying serving as a vice principal is tantamount to doing time in a war zone."

"Well, it *is*," Jenna declared.

"Uhh . . ." everyone else chorused uncomfortably.

"Okay, maybe a little less intense. But just a little." At their skeptical looks, she insisted, "It's a matter of perception!"

"*Any*way," Gray interjected around Dickie, who was delivering their order of beer and a bucket of wings. "Who's doing the Summer Solstice Fest 5K run with me this year? Anyone? Anyone?"

Jenna waved a chicken wing at the fitness fanatic. "No. These are my religion, not sweat and pain."

"Ah, you disappoint me."

"I can't renounce my faith." She pulled another wing out of the bucket in the middle of the table and cooed to it, "Come to me, my sweet."

"Come on, don't make me do this alone."

"Don't look at me," Ben said, holding up his hands. "Unless you want to scrape me off the pavement around the first half kilometer."

"Sorry, I'll be busy. I've got a booth on the green," Delia said.

"Do you really?" Gillian was truly excited for her friend, a fledgling jewelry designer. "Why didn't you say something?"

"I didn't want to jinx it. But I think I'll have enough pieces ready, so I figured . . . why not?"

"You've been busy, then. When was it, a couple of months ago you said you had nothing . . . ?" Gillian trailed off, distracted, her attention caught by the door opening again.

For a moment she found herself hoping Noah had changed his mind and come back to join them. Then she gave herself a virtual slap for wasting her time worrying about hurting his feelings. She reminded herself of all the run-ins they'd had up to now that proved he obviously had none. And as for that fluttering in her belly he incited once in a while, well, the sight of some muscles and some stubble might cause those inner gyrations, but so would some day-old sushi. So. Enough about Noah West. There were other men out there—normal, likable men—to be found just about anywhere.

Even in Dickie's, apparently, no matter what she'd said earlier.

A group of men came in and made their way to the bar. Jenna elbowed Gillian, but there was no need. She'd spotted them. Once upon a time, she recalled, people didn't rely on dating apps. They flirted across a crowded room, maybe sent over a drink, and things progressed from there. She remembered how that worked. She'd done it before and she could do it again.

The group stood near the bar while one of the men gave their order to Dickie, who nodded. The stranger propped one foot on the rail, rested his elbows on the bar, and looked around. He had a fresh face, so young looking he could have been twenty-five, forty, or any age in between. Slightly floppy brown hair that he pushed back once or twice added to his youthful appearance. As he glanced around the room, an easy smile danced on his open face, making him look approachable. He clapped eyes on Gillian, who jumped a little as she realized she'd been staring. And also because of a second jab from Jenna. The man smiled wider, this time a bit bashfully, then turned back to Dickie to collect the five beer bottles.

"Girl, if you don't—" Jenna started.

"On it."

A beer sent his way lured him to Gillian's table, where he squeezed a chair in next to her and chatted until the trivia contest started. His name was Jeremy, and his smile was a sight to behold as he grinned, ducked his head, and glanced at her sideways. The cynical side of Gillian wanted to write off the move as a carefully cultivated affectation, but even if it was, it worked. By the third time he did it, she didn't really care if it was on purpose or not. It was cute, and it was flattering.

Jeremy was in the area on a fishing vacation with his friends, he told her, and they decided to participate in trivia night instead of spending another evening around the fire at their riverside campsite just outside of town, "re-creating the baked beans scene from *Blazing Saddles*," he said.

"Good knowledge of vintage movies," Ben noted. "That'll come in handy tonight. What's your team name?"

"The, uh, Walleye Wranglers," Jeremy said, and he actually colored a little when he uttered it. "Stupid, I know, but we came up with it at the last minute. To be honest"—and here he leaned over to Gillian conspiratorially—"I'm pretty sure we're going to come in dead last. It's going to be so embarrassing. How's your team?"

"We don't do too badly," she said, happy to lean in as well. He smelled good. "Then again, we play pretty often all year 'round."

"So you live here? How interesting."

Gillian realized the information wasn't actually that interesting, but if Jeremy was going to be engaged in their conversation, she was all for it. Another drink and she was thoroughly enjoying how he hung on her every word.

"A pharmacist. Wow," he murmured, resting his chin on his hand and gazing at her with what appeared to be open adoration, and she was fine with that as well.

A sudden whisper in her ear from a certain film phantom who had decided to drift over to Dickie's—a rare journey for her—nearly undermined her self-confidence. *Oh, please,* Inner Bette whispered. *What a con man.*

"Go away!" Gillian whispered at her.

Jeremy blinked and drew back. "I'm sorry. Am I bothering you?"

Crap. Had she said that out loud? "No! No, not at all." Gillian cast around for an explanation. "I just meant . . . it's nearly time for the competition. You should get back to your team, right?"

"I'd rather defect to yours, if you'll have me."

Jenna overheard. "Limit of five to a team. Gillian, you and Jeremy should be your own team. Over there, in that nice intimate corner booth."

Gillian flashed her a fake smile. "Gee, you're so subtle, Jenna. Love you."

But if Jeremy had noticed Jenna's ham-fisted approach to throwing them together, he was too polite to point it out. "I'll sign us up. How's G and J Force for a team name?"

Ugh. Inner Bette sighed heavily and lit a cigarette. Gillian refrained from talking back this time, but she did shoot Bette the stink eye when Jeremy left the table to add their team to the roster.

Gillian willed Inner Bette away, and she vanished in a swirl of taffeta skirts and cigarette smoke, likely to haunt her properly later, in her own house. She didn't care what Inner Bette said. Jeremy was pleasant, polite, charming, and easy on the eyes. She was going to enjoy her evening and see where things went without putting too many expectations on him. However, she was already daydreaming about deleting her dating profiles.

~

"Oh, come *on*!"

Gillian leaned back into a shadow and for once in her life tried to make herself smaller while Jeremy bellowed at the emcee.

Now she remembered why it wasn't a great idea to pick up men in bars.

"You can't seriously say the Taj Mahal isn't one of the seven wonders of the world. I know for a fact—"

Gillian reached for his sleeve, but he yanked his arm away. So much for the bashful, polite guy from an hour and a half ago. Evidently Jeremy had a bit of a competitive streak. And also didn't listen closely to trivia questions.

"Jeremy," she hissed. "It doesn't matter. Seven wonders of the modern world, seven wonders of the ancient world—they're easy to mix up—"

"I want a recount! And I want that question thrown out! It wasn't clear! Was it clear? It was unclear! And another thing—!"

Gillian caught a glimpse of five identical horrified looks on her friends' faces across the room just before she closed her eyes, groaned, and let her forehead hit the table.

~

Gillian had never wanted to see the inside of her house more in her entire life. Especially the magical spot between her duvet and her mattress. Dealing with the Mr. Hyde portion of Jeremy's personality had wrung her out. Spending the rest of her life in a convent was looking more and more like a viable option. Never mind that she wasn't even religious. She wanted to hold out hope for the male half of the species, she really did. But this latest run of disappointing dates was really chipping away at her optimism. She'd tried the apps, she'd tried picking up men in bars—what else was there, really? Was she going to have to start going to swap meets?

She pulled into her driveway. Noah's house was dark, although his pickup was there. She eased her car forward, the headlights illuminating their conjoined stretch of property all the way to the back lot line . . . and she slammed on her brakes, stifling a scream.

Her heart hammering, she sat behind the wheel for a moment, a hand on her chest. After taking one deep breath, then another, she composed herself and slipped out of the car.

"My God," she called, hoping her voice sounded confident and not shaky. She sauntered down her driveway, shaking her head. "You looked like a mole rat just now."

Noah—and it had taken her a second to realize it was her neighbor, not some terrifying sci-fi creature rooting around in the dirt—straightened up and jammed his shovel into a mound of freshly turned earth. "I resent that."

"I calls 'em as I sees 'em. What in the world are you doing?"

He didn't answer her question. "How was your night?" he asked instead.

"I think the more important question is how was *yours*?"

Noah shrugged. The closer she got to him, the clearer it was he must have continued indulging after his beers with Eli at Dickie's. He was swaying blearily, and his jeans, T-shirt, and bare arms were dusky with soil.

"You know, I would be remiss in my professional duties if I didn't ask you whether you're having some sort of reaction to the antihistamines I recommended."

"Of course I'm not. Why would you think that?"

"The mole rat impersonation. Why are you digging up our yards in the dark?"

"I'm fixing things," Noah answered, as if that made perfect sense.

It probably did, a few beers back. Gillian glanced over at the stack of empties nearby. She sighed and shook her head. "Whatever you're doing, Noah, it can wait till morning. Why don't you go inside and sleep it off, okay?"

He started digging again. "Made a mess. Gotta fix it."

"Noah."

"Nope. Gotta. You . . . you're unhappy. My fault. But I can . . . I can fix it."

Gillian decided not to argue. All she said was, "Daylight's better for that. Come on."

She took a step forward and gently took the shovel away from him. Noah looked down, and Gillian realized he was studying her shoes, which weren't made for tromping through turned earth. Her spike heels sank into the soft dirt, and even if she didn't care, he looked concerned.

Then he scratched the back of his head and squinted at her, asking vaguely, "What happened to the gnome?"

"He's in a better place, Noah. Do you need help getting inside?"

Noah snorted. "'Course not."

"Okay." She hoisted the shovel and stepped back. "I'll take this for now. For safekeeping. Have a good night."

She walked away, glancing over her shoulder to make sure Noah did indeed leave the midnight yardwork behind. He was taking great care to walk normally as he made his way to his back door, and Gillian fought back a smile.

"Idiot," she whispered, but almost fondly.

Noah wasn't proud he'd needed to hunt down the best hangover cure in Willow Cove, but it was a good bit of information to have at his disposal—just in case his life in town continued its current downward trajectory. He wasn't sure how low he could go, but so far he'd made a permanent enemy of his neighbor, her friends were still on the fence about him, and he didn't even know what he was doing at his new business. All that meant he had been drinking far too much, far too frequently, which was not like him at all. The way his body was rebelling at the moment, though, "never again" would be a good mantra to adopt.

It was all Noah could do to drag himself out of bed. He got up at pretty nearly the time he'd set for himself, since he wanted to be at the marina bright and early each day to inspire confidence in his staff. He did have to pause in the shower, however, to see if turning up the water temperature to near-boiling would help wake him up and eradicate his headache. It did neither of those things, so he made a small detour to a popular café on the river in search of better coffee (it would be better, he figured, as long as he didn't have to make it himself) and something greasy to soak up the rest of the alcohol sloshing around in his stomach.

The café did not disappoint. The coffee was strong, the egg sandwich's grease was soaking through the wax wrap *and* the paper bag—always a promising sign—and one of his patented roguish winks got a blush out of the young lady at the counter as well as a free blueberry muffin tucked into the bag. Heartened, he had planned to gobble the breakfast sandwich during his short drive to the marina, but a familiar someone out on the patio caught his eye.

Maybe he should take a moment to sit and eat his breakfast slowly, he thought. After all, it wouldn't be very wise of him to get grease and hot sauce all over the cab of his truck, would it? No, of course not. And oh look, there were quite a few tables free outside. Or maybe his neighbor would like some company. He could at least ask. He didn't know what impression he'd left her with the night before, but he was pretty sure it wasn't good. However, he was nothing if not optimistic. Most days, anyway. Whatever he did last night could be undone if he played it right: a little casual stroll past her table. No rush. Dig deep to locate the ol' Noah West saunter. No looking at Gillian right away, and then just "happen to" notice her. Ask to join her. Again, casual. No sudden movements. No desperation on display.

Noah kept his eye on the boats on the river as he stepped down onto the patio. Gillian was to his left, seated at a table abutting the sun-splashed wall of the establishment, nearly around the corner of the outdoor eating space. He aimed for a table far enough away from hers, at the outer edge of the patio, closest to the water, but one where he'd have to walk past her and be able to act surprised to see her there. Perfect.

When he came alongside Gillian, he started to veer toward her . . . until he saw she wasn't alone. Her companion wasn't one of her friends he'd met the night before, but a man he'd never seen. Oh lord, was she on a breakfast date?

He was tempted to feign innocence, walk up to her table and greet her, introduce himself to the guy, even join them without being invited—drag over an extra chair, slap his breakfast sandwich on the table, and start chowing down—but to what end? He'd risk pissing her off even more, ruin their date, and look like even more of a jerk, which was the exact opposite of what he was trying to accomplish. Because no matter what he told himself about not caring what Gillian thought of him, deep down he was desperate to spend even five normal, calm minutes with her to prove he wasn't the spiteful ass she so obviously thought he was.

Which was probably a futile goal. And yet it seemed to be one he refused to give up on. What else would have made him get that drunk and dig up their mutual property line in the middle of the night trying to make things right, trying to win her over?

Yeah, this was an uphill battle, and he wasn't sure it was one his hangover-addled self was prepared to take on today.

So Noah turned away from Gillian, sat down at an empty table, and tried valiantly not to look over at her and her date.

It didn't last.

As life-affirming as his egg sandwich was, it didn't hold his attention. Not when Gillian was mere yards away. He couldn't help but glance over at her. Repeatedly. She was captivating. Like a spotlight was shining on her at all times. He couldn't look away if he tried. Perfectly dressed and made up as ever, her posture so flawless that royalty would do well to emulate it, Gillian sipped her coffee delicately and focused all her attention on the man across from her as he talked.

At length.

Gillian was mostly silent, Noah noticed. Her date, apparently, did not notice.

So that's a love connection from an app, Noah thought. Interesting. Actually, not interesting at all. Gillian may have felt the same. Yes, she was paying attention, but Noah thought he detected a slight glaze to her beautiful eyes, a bit of immobility in her impeccable posture that revealed she was there in body but not in spirit.

Noah found himself feeling sorry for her, and yet . . . he was also feeling something else. Kind of . . . pleased. That the date wasn't a success.

What?

Had to be the hangover talking.

By the time he'd inhaled the egg sandwich and entertained the idea of going back for a second, his body was well on its way to returning to normal, and he decided he could be a little late to work if it meant drinking in the sight of Gillian in the sun.

Too bad she looked so unhappy.

No, she wasn't unhappy. Noah was projecting that on her, he was sure. Until he saw her sigh—an exhale barely more than her usual breath, but somehow Noah could tell the difference. She dropped her gaze to her phone on the table. Was she thinking of messaging a friend for an escape route? Suddenly Noah desperately wished he knew her phone number. He'd have been happy to call or text a fake emergency from his observation spot at his table, just to be able to see her brighten up.

Gillian didn't touch her phone. She rallied instead, and broke up her date's monologue with some words of her own. It was only a short respite. The man answered what seemed to be a question from her, not with a short reply, but instead another tangent, punctuated by him waving his fork around for emphasis. A bit of egg flicked off the tines and landed on Gillian's blouse. She patiently wiped it off.

This was hopeless. Why didn't she just leave?

Because she was polite? Or maybe optimistic her date would, what, run out of breath? Give himself laryngitis?

Noah cast around for a distraction—for himself, for her, he wasn't quite sure. He picked apart the blueberry muffin the cashier had given him. Not one of his favorites, but he wasn't going to quibble.

A gull landed nearby and eyed his food. Why sure, he could share. He tossed a chunk of the muffin, but with some distance. It landed right next to Gillian's date. The gull flapped over to grab it, and the guy flinched. Noah always forgot how impressive a gull's wingspan was up close. One gull took up a lot of space. One gull plus more who'd figured out the first one was on to something good and wanted their share of it? That was a true crowd.

Well. Couldn't allow all those birds to fight over one measly bit of food. Noah tossed another chunk of muffin over. And another.

There sure were a lot of gulls around, all of them more than ready to swoop in and fight over a couple of scraps of food.

Gillian figured out where the food was coming from and caught his eye. Noah covered the rest of the muffin with the empty paper bag and shrugged innocently. It looked like she was hiding a smile, but he couldn't be sure. Meanwhile, the guy was swearing up a storm, edging his chair away from the birds and shooing them. They just flapped back, looking for more food.

When Gillian returned her attention to her date, who now seemed to be quite agitated, Noah tossed more pieces of muffin, aiming for an open spot directly behind the guy's chair. All the crumbs landed exactly where he wanted them. As did even more gulls.

Finally the man stood up, shoving his chair about two feet behind him, swearing a blue streak as the gulls scattered but regrouped and descended again, not to be denied their free breakfast.

Gillian looked over at Noah again. And this time she flashed him a genuine, bright smile. He thought there was no better sight in the world.

~

Noah only stuck around long enough to watch Gillian try to placate her date, who was clearly about to storm off, most likely because Gillian was laughing and didn't seem to be able to stop. His work there done, Noah got a second cup of coffee to go and drove to the marina to start his workday.

It consisted of chatting with his staff, going over the summer calendar of important river-centric events the marina participated in during high tourist season, like PaddleFest and the regatta, and sorting out Jerry's convoluted accounting system.

Noah was going over the books when the office phone rang.

"Yeah," he said curtly, distractedly scrolling through a spreadsheet.

"Mr. West?"

"Speaking."

"I'm calling on behalf of Louise March."

The name meant nothing to Noah. "Okay?"

"She would like to speak with you."

"Regarding?"

"I don't ask Louise's business. I'm only calling to tell you she would like to speak with you." There was a pause. *"Now."*

Noah actually held the receiver away from him and looked at it. Whoever this fussy-sounding man was, and whoever Louise March was, they were being awfully presumptuous.

"Much as I would love to speak to this Louise person about this mystery topic, I'm a little busy right now. Why don't you tell her to call me directly—"

He was cut off by an indignant strangled noise on the other end of the line. "Louise doesn't make direct calls."

"Then I guess she's out of luck. Have a nice day."

And Noah hung up.

The phone rang again—the same phone number that had appeared on the caller ID moments before. Noah answered with a sigh. "Yes?"

"Mr. West—"

"Look, I don't have time for this cloak-and-dagger stuff. Who is Louise Match—"

"March."

"—March, anyway?"

The name didn't spark any recognition in Noah. He reached deep into his memory for some knowledge of this person from his summers as a teenager in Willow Cove. He came up empty, which wasn't surprising.

"You don't *know*?" The man sounded horribly affronted.

"I would if you told me. And if you told me what she wants."

"It's hardly my place."

Noah shrugged even though he was alone in his office. "Then I don't know what to tell you."

And he hung up a second time.

~

At the end of the day, he exited the building into the early evening summer heat to find a black SUV parked sideways across several spots in the small lot. A tinted rear window lowered.

"Mr. West," came a voice from deep in the shadows of the back seat of the SUV. "Get in."

Noah looked around. Someone had to be pranking him. Granted, he didn't have any friends in the area, so who would? Manny? This wasn't his style.

"Mr. West," the voice prompted as he hesitated.

Well, fuck it. He needed a little intrigue in his life. He

climbed in and shut the door. The window went back up. He found himself facing a severe-looking woman. The dim light in the car made it difficult to determine her age, but she was maybe fifteen, twenty years older than he was. Her skirt was pressed, her dark hair was coiffed, and even her slight wrinkles were perfectly parallel to one another. She glared at him.

Thunder rumbled in the distance.

"Louise March, I presume." He stuck out a hand. "Noah West."

"I know who you are."

She didn't shake his hand. He withdrew it awkwardly.

"You do?"

"Noah West. Emmanuel's nephew. Purchased Retha's house, 44 Whitlock Avenue, for a sizable sum. New proprietor of Spencer's Marina, at which you were employed more than a decade ago."

There was that small-town gossip network at work again. Word did indeed get around. He needed to stop being surprised.

"Ripped out Retha's hedge and made a lifelong enemy of Gillian Pritchard."

"Well, I'd hardly—"

"Oh, no, no, you absolutely did."

Here Louise allowed herself a wicked little smile, the corners of her mouth curling upward, Grinch-like.

"I have a proposal for you, Mr. West. Regarding the town garden competition."

"Oh?"

"I take it you've heard of my gardening club's event?"

"Your—?"

"I am head of the town recreation department, which organizes the competition, and that makes it my event. I would like you to enter the competition."

That was . . . not what he was expecting. All he could manage in reply was, "Believe me, you don't want that. I'm no gardener."

As if he'd said nothing at all, she went on, "I think it's time Ms. Pritchard was given a run for her money."

This woman wanted someone to beat Gillian? "What for?"

"I have my reasons."

"Like?"

"I think we've had enough of all that froufrou nonsense."

"Frou . . . ?"

"I understand she's doing an English garden this year. *Honestly.* Froufrou."

There was that word again. Noah wasn't sure what Louise was getting at.

The woman went on with a sneer, "So much piffle. *Lush* blooms. *Soft* edges. *Mounds* of ground cover."

Noah wasn't sure what, exactly, was wrong with those descriptions. They sounded all right to him. The flowers, shrubs, and trees in Gillian's yard were just starting to bloom, and Noah found himself intrigued by the promise of it. He could only imagine what it would look like in a few weeks. He knew it would be impressive. She'd created something special over those five years she'd been working on her place, he could tell already.

Louise, however, sniffed as though she'd gotten a whiff of some particularly potent manure. "Egregious excess is all it is. Now, *you*"—she looked him up and down with a sharp eye—"*you* look like a man who can take on all that sumptuous excess, who can *dominate* with some proper *hard* lines . . ."

Noah's brain stopped processing what Louise was saying, because suddenly the words "lush," "soft," and "mounds" juxtaposed with "dominate" and "hard" made his insides do funny things. Although he was aware the conversation had been, and continued to be, about gardening, somehow other thoughts filled Noah's head. Incorrect and impure thoughts. Overlaid with the memory of Gillian Pritchard rolling her eyes at him as he made a fool of himself last night . . . laughing at the café this morning . . . dancing in her underwear . . . and suddenly plants were the last thing on his mind.

"Young man, are you listening?"

Louise's waspish tone snapped him out of it.

"I don't get any of this," he said. "So . . . what would happen? I'd enter, I'd lose. How do you benefit?"

"Think, Mr. West. I'm the organizer of this yearly competition. I head up the judges' panel."

The penny dropped. "You'd . . . you'd make me win?"

Louise's face was impassive, but there was an affirmative glint in her eye.

"Seriously? You're looking for a ringer to make sure Gillian doesn't win? And you're in charge of the contest? That's the most unethical thing I've ever heard."

"Do you have a problem with it?"

"Yeah, I do."

Because despite what he initially thought of Gillian and how infuriating she could be, he'd seen another side of her lately, and although it surprised him, he realized he didn't actively want to hurt her in any way, least of all by joining forces with Louise.

"Pity," she said. "I thought we had the same opinion of Ms. Pritchard."

"And what for, anyway? Besides the 'froufrou' claim. It's like you hate Gillian or something. Mind if I ask why?"

"You may ask. I don't have to answer."

"Okay, well, look, you've tapped the wrong guy. Find someone else to do your dirty work."

"We'll see."

And the car door swung open, seemingly of its own accord. Noah was dismissed.

Gillian was going to be late for work. She was never late for work. Granted, she still had time, but there was one task she had to take care of first: a new photo for her dating profile. Apparently Delia had been right—the pharmacy's fluorescent lights hadn't done her any favors. Although her profile had been generating a fair amount of interest, she still hadn't attracted anyone she felt a spark with. She had to up her game, connect with the more interesting men, and an easy way to do that—according to all the online tips for making the most of dating apps—was to try a new photo that reflected her personality and interests. Otherwise she was going to be doomed to match with men she had nothing in common with.

Case in point: the dullard she'd had a breakfast date with yesterday. What was his name? She couldn't even remember. It had been as forgettable as his stories of his adventures as a middle manager in a widget factory—whatever the company manufactured was also something her brain had wiped. He wasn't awful like Preston the pyramid-scheme guy or Jeremy of the ill-fated trivia contest. He wasn't even entertaining in a weird way like Oontsy, bopping to electronica while she was trying to find out details about his life. Her date yesterday had been perfectly pleasant . . . and utterly mediocre. Just like so many other men she'd matched with. Widget had somehow made it to the next level of dating, meeting in person, when so many of her other less-than-promising matches never went further than chatting by text, but darned if Gillian could remember why she'd agreed to it. Desperation, perhaps. She'd interacted with so many uninspiring men, the human equivalent of background noise, and that had to change. Hence the new photo, to attract someone more interesting. Not for the first time, and likely probably not the last, the only thing Gillian wished for, as she'd said to her friends not too long ago, was someone remarkable.

She hated to admit it, but the best part of yesterday's breakfast date had been, shockingly, Noah West, who'd rescued her even when she didn't know she needed rescuing, ridding her of her date with some accurately tossed muffin crumbs. His ridiculous *Who, me?* expression denying he'd done anything, when he quite obviously had been the one flinging the food that had summoned the gull invasion, had made her laugh for the first time all morning.

She found herself laughing again at the memory as she studied her reflection in her full-length mirror, holding up one shirt and then another as she tried to determine which neckline would look best in a photo. Inner Bette, striking a languid pose in the bedroom doorway, raised a strong, arched eyebrow. Of course Inner Bette could read Gillian's mind. That was where she lived, after all.

"Stop," Gillian said to the phantom. "I don't like Noah West. He just amused me. One time. It doesn't make up for how annoying and . . . and . . . repellent he is. And no, I don't care what he looks like either."

Inner Bette scoffed and took a drag of her cigarette, tilting her head back to blow a plume of smoke up toward the ceiling, then the phantom faded away.

Bette had made her point. Gillian had to wonder why, exactly, she was now taking the time to peer out her window to see if there was any movement in Noah's bedroom across the way, if not to catch a glimpse of those ridiculous muscles or the wicked glint in his hazel eyes, bracketed by crow's feet that made the wickedness a touch more dangerous. More enticing.

Dammit. It was those kinds of thoughts that got her into trouble.

His blinds were down and snapped tight, which was a good thing.

But when she made her way outside into the brilliant, intense morning sunlight, she saw Noah was already back at work on the yard, finishing his project from the other night. The trench was gone, and he was raking the loose dirt into a level grade. Even though her brain told her to just get on with her own business, her feet had other ideas, and before she knew it she was standing over him, arms crossed.

"Well, someone's looking more functional today," she said.

"Than what?" he grunted over the scraping of the metal tines on stones rolling up from the loosened dirt.

"You have to admit you were in pretty dire straits the other night."

Noah snorted derisively. "Ancient history."

"If you say so. I'm just glad to see you vertical this week." If Gillian were closer to him, she'd have patted him on his arm in as patronizing a manner as she could muster. As it was, she contented herself with resettling her purse handles in the crook of her arm, adjusting her posture, and giving him a serene smile before she turned to go. Still, she couldn't resist asking, "Um, what exactly *are* you doing, by the way?"

"Oh, I don't think it's any of your business." Scrape, scrape.

Gillian bit her lip at his throwback to the afternoon when he questioned her about one of her dates. She decided not to acknowledge it. "Just making conversation." She paused. "Think you'll be done soon? You're going to get in my way when I need to work on my own garden."

"As long as some people stop wasting my time. Don't you have somewhere to be?"

He was right. She really did have to get moving. She let him have the last word and, without a backward glance, crossed to her own yard and started scanning for a spot that would make a good background for her profile photo. She preferred not to do this with Noah nearby, watching her every move and sniggering. Wait, was he a sniggerer? Probably not, but he would definitely mock her given half a chance. *That* she was sure of. She had to make this quick.

Once she decided on a nice spot—sitting on a bench in the far corner, with a lovely flowering dogwood behind her—Gillian made a valiant effort to smile cheerily into her phone's camera lens. The first few attempts—okay, first dozen—weren't great, but really, it couldn't be so hard to figure out, could it? If she just . . . shifted her shoulder, maybe . . . or raised the phone higher . . .

"By the way, are you going to give me my shovel back or what? And what are you doing?"

Out of the corner of her eye, she could see Noah standing nearby, rocking back on his heels, his hands stuffed in his pockets.

"Brokering world peace with the leaders of the free world. Macron says you're blocking my light."

"I never took you for the selfie type," he said.

"You don't know anything about me at all. Or hadn't you noticed?"

There was a pause. Gillian continued to ignore him. She adjusted her posture, raising the phone once more.

"You sure you want to do it that way?"

She stifled a sigh. "If I give you your shovel back, will you get back to digging your tunnel to Australia and leave me alone?"

"I'm just saying—"

Gillian lowered the phone and glared at him. "Did I ask for your input?"

"No, but you should. Here."

Noah stretched out his hand for her phone. Gillian yanked it out of his reach. He actually growled, a dangerous rumble low in his throat. She knew he was expressing frustration, but it communicated a different thing entirely, at least to her ears. She told her ears to knock it off.

"Are you kidding?" he snapped, with a touch of incredulity. "What do you think I'm going to do with it, throw it in your fountain? Give it here."

Reluctantly, she handed it over. "What do you want with it?"

Noah let loose a labored, irritated sigh. "I'm going to take your picture. You don't exactly look comfortable doing the whole selfie thing."

"I admit I don't spend hours a day on social media."

"Good for you. But it means you don't know your angles—that was obvious from the way you tried to take your own picture just now. I, on the other hand, happen to know a little bit about photography." When she didn't express any interest in his comment, he held up the phone, peered at the screen, and asked, "I assume this is for your dating profile?"

Gillian shifted on the bench. "Maybe."

"It's a simple yes-or-no question."

Fidget. ". . . Yes."

"Kinda scraping the bottom of the barrel with Birdman yesterday."

Gillian sniffed disdainfully.

"I thought I'd at least get a thank-you."

"For what?"

"I sacrificed my blueberry muffin for you."

"Nobody asked you to."

"Bet you were glad I did, though." When she didn't answer, Noah said, "So Birdman didn't turn out to be your Prince Charming?"

Whir-click.

"At least warn a girl before you take a photo," she protested.

"Answer the question."

"Maybe I don't want to."

Whir-click.

"Why don't you want to talk about it?" Noah pressed as the phone *whir-click*ed several times in succession. "You stayed there a lot longer than you looked like you wanted to."

Gillian gaped. "You were *studying* me?"

"Don't flatter yourself. I finished the book I was reading and had nowhere else to look."

She narrowed her eyes. "You didn't have a book with you."

"You were *studying* me?" he parroted. "You'd think you'd have spent more time paying attention to your date. Or was he so boring you nodded off every time you tried?"

Wow. Her approval of Noah West had lasted all of about two minutes, and now here he was annoying her again. If her temper was timed like an explosive device, the little digital numbers' countdown speed would have been blinding. Who did he think he was, judging her date? Even if he was right.

"Okay," Noah said, "you need to look more—"

"Accessible. I've heard."

"I was going to say look more to the left of the camera." Noah lowered the phone to frown at her. "And don't look *too* accessible. Unless you want to end up dead in a ditch somewhere."

"Apparently you don't have a very high opinion of dating apps."

"I have a brain."

"You're implying I don't?"

"I didn't mean it like that. In fact, I'm surprised you're doing this. You don't seem the type. Too smart, I mean," he was quick to explain, before she went off on him. "Seems you could find someone to date without the need for all this nonsense."

"It's not as easy to meet people as you'd think."

"Why not? You seem . . . personable. When you want to be."

"Gee, thanks. Let's just say a particular man in my past might have given me the gift of a few trust issues before I used a crowbar to get him out of my life."

Noah grunted in a commiserating tone. "Is he buried in this flower bed here or the one on the other side of the yard?"

"I just mean it was a bad relationship and an even worse breakup."

Gillian stopped herself. The last thing she wanted to do was share details of her personal life with Noah West.

"What are you doing over there?" she huffed. "Reading my text messages?"

"Couldn't be less curious, don't worry. Just trying to . . . okay, look this way a little." He held his right hand out, and she did her best to focus there. "Look friendly, but like you could kick the guy's ass if he tried anything."

"You're paranoid."

"You're a sucker. Smile."

"How can I, when I'm looking at you?"

"Pretend I'm Ryan Gosling."

"Now you're just asking for miracles."

The *whir-click* of the camera sounded, and Noah examined the result. "Ugh. No."

"Thanks a lot."

"It's not your looks. You're too stiff. Try again."

Gillian shook out her hair and tried to relax. *Whir-click.*

"Meh. Again," he ordered.

"You're not as good a photographer as you think you are."

"You're not making this easy. Relax. Think of something else."

"Like strangling you?"

"Whatever floats your boat."

Whir-click.

"Better," Noah muttered. "Your hatred of me at least brightens your eyes a bit. But I don't think it's really the look you want to go for in an online dating profile pic."

"What look?"

"Murderous."

"Accurate."

Noah glanced around. "What's that leafy thing over there?"

"What do you care?"

Whir-click.

"Yep," Noah confirmed. "Madness in the eye. Try again."

"Shut up. Give me my phone back. I'll do it myself."

"Not a chance. This is a challenge now. And if you haven't figured it out, I was asking about the plants to distract you, maybe get you to ease up with the squinty look you've got going on."

"I do *not* . . ." Gillian trailed off as she realized how many of her facial muscles were tense. "Look . . ." she started again, but trailed off when he stopped peering at her through the phone and approached her instead. She stiffened. "What are you doing?"

"So suspicious," he tutted, crouching in front of her. "I'm arranging the subject. That's you."

He reached out a hand, and she flinched.

"Seriously?" he marveled.

"Sorry," she muttered.

"Permission to approach?"

Gillian rolled her eyes. When he didn't budge, just left his hand hanging in midair, she reluctantly said, "Granted."

"Thank you." He settled onto his knees, put her phone on the bench beside her, and reached out. "Don't slap me."

"Come on, I haven't got all day."

"Neither do I."

He inched closer and gently tugged on the short sleeves of her wrap-style top, then smoothed out the fabric along her shoulders and collarbone, adjusting the neckline with the lightest of touches. Gillian didn't know where to look while he did that. Watch his hands? Stare blankly over his shoulder? She didn't have a clue. Gillian could feel her breath grow shallow as the heat of his hands warmed her skin through the light fabric. Her eyes were drawn to his face no matter what common sense warned her not to do. He kept his eyes down, and she was grateful for that. Her breath nearly stopped altogether when Noah reached out again, his hand slowing hesitantly. Was he going to touch her cheek? Cup his hand behind her neck and pull her to him? And if he did, would she go?

His fingers gently scooped up a lock of her hair and brought it forward over her shoulder. He arranged it a little, smoothed it down. "That looks good there." His voice was rough, and if she didn't know better, she'd say his breathing was as shallow as hers.

Then he looked at her, and everything seemed to stop—the birdsong, even the breeze and the rustling of leaves. All her awareness had telescoped to one thing at the exclusion of all else: Noah.

He was inches away; now she could see his eyes weren't one uniform hazel color, but mottled brown and gold. She was getting lost in them, falling into them, into him. He reached out once more, again slowly, and ran his index finger along her hair that grazed her forehead, moving it out of her eyes carefully, almost reverently. She shivered a little despite the warm sun.

Noah's gaze dropped to her mouth.

There was a pulse at his throat beating rhythmically, hypnotically. Dimly, she realized they were much too close, their foreheads nearly touching, their lips inches away from each other. Somehow she couldn't pull away.

"Noah . . ." she breathed.

Mistake. His eyes snapped up to hers again, and he seemed to come back into himself. His face reddened as he sat back on his heels, and the moment was over. The birdsong and breezes and noises of the neighborhood returned. Noah picked up her phone again. Without another glance at her, he stood up and stepped back, concentrating on the screen.

"Smile."

She tried her best, but she wasn't sure what her face was doing.

He took one more photo, brusquely said, "Good—use that one," and handed her phone back to her.

Gillian wanted to thank him—say something, anything—but he wasn't looking at her now. In fact, she got the feeling he was making sure he looked anywhere *but* at her. Without another word, he marched across their driveways and into his house. She was still sitting on the bench, immobile, when she heard the back door slam.

It took her a minute to realize she wasn't moving. She wasn't able to—not while one overwhelming thought consumed her: Noah West had been about to kiss her.

And she'd wanted him to.

But he was gone—disappeared as soon as she'd said his name and brought his attention back to her. He'd looked at her, realization dawning, and then he'd walked away. Just like some other men in her life, she noted. The memory of that first date she'd made through one of the apps, the guy who had taken one look at her and walked out of the café, filled her head and made her heart race in a very unpleasant way.

Gillian shook herself. She was reading way too much into what had just happened with Noah. So he'd walked away. Big deal. Maybe he had a cramp. Maybe he was expecting a phone call.

Maybe he'd realized the last place he wanted to be was alone with her.

Gillian stood up and smoothed out her top, pushing away the memory of Noah doing the same thing a few minutes ago. At the time his touch had felt sensuous, intimate, promising. And maybe it had been. But if Noah had stopped himself without an explanation, Gillian knew exactly what to do with the moment: throw it on the trash heap with all the gestures from other men who were too afraid to act on their feelings.

At least that's what she told herself as she worked hard to ignore the pain in the vicinity of her heart.

No. Not pain. She refused to let another man's rejection determine how she felt about herself. She was better than that. She was better than all of them put together, and far better than Noah. Her blood started to boil, and she welcomed the familiar feeling. Hating on Noah West fed her soul, with a white-hot intensity only his egotistical, cold, callous behavior could incite. Who did he think he was, anyway? She was a snack, and she knew it. No, she was far more than a snack. She was even more than a whole meal. She was an entire buffet. On a luxury cruise. How dare he not see that? She snatched up her phone and purse and marched out of her yard, casting one last scathing look toward the house next door. Noah West could rot for all she cared.

No. No, no, no, no.

Noah took a breath and ran the numbers again. And again.

Dammit.

For the first time in days, something besides the ghost of Gillian had finally occupied his thoughts for more than five minutes. Too bad it was something as ugly as this.

Of course, his last interaction with his neighbor was pretty gnarly too. Not that he'd intended any of it, but being so close to Gillian had nearly wrecked him, almost made him do something massively stupid. He'd come close to kissing her. Gillian Pritchard! Of all people.

He couldn't understand how he'd gone from desire at the first sight of her dancing in her bedroom, to loathing as he sparred with her over greenery, then back to . . . what was it? Desire, of course—he hadn't had such an overwhelming urge to pull someone to him and . . . and . . . well. Not in a long time. But what frightened him was the inkling that it could be more than a physical thing. He was starting to realize he might, just might, actually like Gillian Pritchard. Self-possessed, confident, smart, funny, and sexy—it was only natural that, when he found himself in the moment, close to her, breathing in her scent, looking into her sparkling green eyes, he'd wanted . . .

Well. It didn't matter what he'd wanted. He'd made his choice. He'd walked away. That was growth, wasn't it? Not acting on impulse? Granted, walking away was too much like running away, but in his defense, when he was that close to Gillian, all common sense left him, so it was a matter of self-preservation. And she probably was grateful that it had ended the way it did.

Wasn't she?

No, of course she was. Being annoyed was her baseline when it came to him. The last thing she wanted was for him to kiss her, he was sure. The next time they ran into each other, they'd happily go back to their sparring and sniping and that moment in the garden would be history.

For the hundredth time, he forced the memory of Gillian out of his mind and focused on the screen in front of him. Maybe this discrepancy in the marina's finances wasn't what he thought it was. Maybe there was some mistake. Of the accounting variety? That was all he needed.

But yeah, if he was reading these calculations right, he had a bit of a mess on his hands.

"Shiiiit," he muttered, frantically calculating again.

Something didn't add up. No matter how he finessed the numbers, it was quite clear the marina had a much tighter profit margin than he'd expected—one that barely allowed the place to pay its bills. Noah could have sworn the marina had been doing much better financially years ago, when Noah had worked there, and maybe that had been the case. Now, though . . . the place needed a boost, to put it mildly. Noah cursed himself. He was the one who'd bought the marina without doing his due diligence and examining the books beforehand. He had been in a rush to get away from Corinne, and now he was paying the price. Probably literally.

"Shit, shit, shit," Noah hissed.

He took a deep breath and forced himself to look at the situation critically. This was fixable. There were a dozen ways to right this listing boat: reallocate funds, even reduce his salary for a while. Naturally his first priority was to keep paying the employees, and it hurt his heart that the raises he'd planned to give them would have to wait, possibly till the end of summer. But he had to do what he had to do: Pay the immediate bills. Keep the lights on. The numbers in front of him showed he could do that if he persevered through the profitable summer season. He'd have to have a little chat with the taxman soon, though, because that was a big red number on the spreadsheet, and there was nothing on reserve for such a large amount. He just hoped the town's summer events would fill those empty reserves fast, and if he could come up with other, new ways to make the marina some money, all the better.

He needed someone to brainstorm with, someone to offer up suggestions, someone he could bounce ideas off, but he had no one. Noah had never felt more alone in his life, in fact. For a nanosecond he thought about phoning Corinne. She'd always been the one he'd consulted when he had a problem with his Palm Springs gallery. Now that door was closed to him. Manny? No, Manny was a great many things, but he wasn't a businessman. His new neighbors? What would a bunch of long-retired seniors know about managing a business these days? And he sure couldn't talk to Gillian, although he found he desperately wanted to. She had the most level head of anyone he'd met here. He had to face it—he was on his own.

Think, West, think, he admonished himself. *Think like a mini-mogul.*

His inner mini-mogul apparently marched on its stomach, because it responded with the advice, *Get a burger at Dickie's.*

Which wasn't a bad idea, all things considered.

Once he'd fueled his belly, his mind started working better. He knew what to do. Of course he did. He'd cut costs here and there. Tighten the marina's belt just a little, for a little while. Have a big sale, maybe with free food, like a hot dog cart in the parking lot. Announce the sale and some special events by laying out a little cash for advertising. What he spent would surely come back in profits from increased attendance. Hell, he'd even enlist the help of his teen employees, get them to talk up the marina on social media. Soon enough there'd be more black than red in those spreadsheets, he was sure of it.

Noah even had enough confidence to stop at the town hall to address the tax issue, certain that arrangements could be made.

When Noah was directed to the treasurer's office, he was brought up short at the sight of a familiar name on the door. Couldn't be. But the town was only so big. There couldn't possibly be two of them.

"Ms. Louise March," he declared, burying his surprise as he leaned on the doorjamb, feigning nonchalance.

"Mr. West." Louise steepled her fingers in front of her, resting her elbows on her massive desk. "I take it you've changed your mind about the garden competition. And just in time—the deadline to enter is at the end of this week."

"I absolutely have not changed my mind about the garden competition. I've come to talk to the most powerful person in Willow Cove's government about a different matter."

"I'm not the mayor."

"Yet," he supplied and watched her Grinch smile curl upward. "Still, treasurer *and* head of the community center? And that includes being in charge of the gardening club? That's a lion's share of town responsibility."

"We all do what we can. There aren't many stout hearts that can survive in local government, so some of us are forced to multitask. Fortunately I'm able to wear multiple hats without buckling under the strain. Now, if you're through paying me compliments, may I ask why you're here, if not to discuss the garden competition?"

"I've come to talk to you about some financial issues related to the marina that may have been . . . overlooked for a while."

"I take it you're talking about your little tax conundrum."

"Right."

"I can't forgive those back taxes, Mr. West."

"Of course not. But maybe a little forbearance. That's not too much to ask, is it?"

Louise relaxed into her high-backed office chair, her dark hair blending in with the leather, giving the illusion that Noah was staring at an oval face rising from the blackness like it was surfacing from a scrying mirror, evil Disney-queen style.

She was silent for a few moments, her lips pursed as she considered his offer. Noah's high hopes rose even further, as he was certain he'd found a way out of this financial mess. He flashed her his most charming smile to close the deal.

Louise smoothed out a nonexistent wrinkle in the calendar page of her desk blotter, then looked him in the eye. "No, I'm afraid not."

Noah could actually feel his confidence deflate like a punctured tire. "I'm sorry, what?"

"I can't do that. Of course not. It's out of the question. You have to understand, Mr. West, I was quite lenient with the previous owner, but now I feel as though Spencer's Marina is taking advantage of the town of Willow Cove. As treasurer, as tax collector, I can't let that continue indefinitely." Louise cocked her head. "You seem puzzled, Mr. West. Were you not aware of this substantial financial issue before you took ownership of the establishment? I'm sure the tax liens were listed quite clearly—?"

Noah didn't have the time or the inclination to explain what he'd willingly overlooked when he'd bought the place. Buying Spencer's Marina had provided an escape from his life in California when he so desperately needed one, so perhaps his judgment had been a bit clouded and he'd taken the risk of purchasing a business with a tax lien on it. He just didn't think it was going to be this much of a problem so soon. And being the tax collector's pawn in some long-standing vendetta against another Willow Cove resident? Definitely not on his bingo card when he was grabbing the marina like a drowning man grabbing a rope.

Louise was immobile, staring at him placidly from behind her vast desk. Noah was certain she had no reason to refuse his offer of an extension or a payment plan except that she was getting back at him for refusing to go along with her vendetta against Gillian. The scrying mirror he'd conjured up wasn't lying. Louise March was pure evil.

And Noah hated people who preyed on others' weaknesses.

"I should have known you didn't have a compassionate bone in your exoskeleton," he snarled. "Thanks for the welcome to Willow Cove. It really makes a guy feel at home."

"Mr. West—"

"No, forget I said anything." He was suddenly far too loud. He could hear it. He just couldn't seem to stop it. "You want to seize the marina? Because you and I both know that's the only way a situation like this ends. You don't give me time to pay the taxes, the town gets to seize it. And then the town profits. I know. Well, go ahead. I hope you choke on it."

Noah didn't calm down one bit on the drive home. Granted, he didn't try very hard. He was too busy seething at the memory of that self-satisfied harpy who wouldn't give an inch to help a guy out. He could barely think straight, he was so furious. Turning into his driveway at top speed, he flung himself out of his pickup and slammed its door with far more force than was necessary. He caught a glimpse of Carol tending her yard across the street, straightening up like a meerkat at the sight of his violent gesture. He knew if he hesitated even for a moment, she—and likely the rest of the neighbors—would descend, wanting to know what was wrong, and he didn't have the stomach for that right now. He needed to hole up in his new home, even though it felt nothing like home to him, and reevaluate . . . everything.

He charged around the back of his vehicle, only to nearly run smack into Gillian, who was making her way to her own car. Despite his dark mood, he was happy to see her.

"Hey," he muttered, still irritated by his run-in with Louise, but suddenly feeling a glimmer of hope, however irrational, that Gillian might cheer him up. Because, he realized, even when they were bickering he preferred her company over anyone else's.

Gillian didn't even answer him, though, just dodged him and walked to her car. She was usually more polite than that, but Noah shrugged it off.

"Going out?" he asked, following her.

"Mm."

"Another date?"

"None of your business," she answered in a cruelly friendly tone, fiddling with her keys and reaching around him for the door handle.

It was May, right? Because Noah could have sworn it had just started to snow.

"Something the matter?"

"Well, first of all, I don't owe you a blow-by-blow account of my whereabouts at all times, Noah."

He felt his hackles rise. "I wasn't—"

"Move."

Gillian elbowed him out of the way, and he took a step back.

"What the hell is going on?" he snapped.

In a patronizing tone, Gillian said, "Nothing is going on, Noah. Nothing at all. Not a single, solitary thing."

Yeah, that meant something was definitely going on. He just couldn't figure out what. She was acting annoyed with him, but they hadn't even spoken since . . . oh. Oh no.

He intercepted her again. Because he had a self-destructive streak like that. "Is this because of what happened the other day?"

She stiffened, but she still wouldn't look at him. "I have no idea what you're talking about."

Yep, just as he suspected. Gillian realized he had nearly kissed her, and she was angry about it. Well, why couldn't she just say so?

"Really?" Noah felt overly warm—irritated and agitated. It seemed it was in Gillian's very nature to piss him off. Maybe it was because he was feeling guilty for nearly kissing her—and that she'd realized it—but he was going to bury it all by going on the offense. That self-destructive thing again. "That's the way you want to play it? With some passive-aggressive bullshit?"

Gillian remained coldly calm. "No bullshit about it. *Nothing* happened the other day."

"Come on."

"You gave me a hard time, you insulted me, somewhere in there you took my picture." Now she looked at him, and Noah found himself wishing she wouldn't. "What's there to discuss?"

Christ. First the marina, then Louise, now Gillian. It was like the universe was pulling out all the stops to give him a shit day. And it was doing a really, really good job.

"You know what? You don't want to talk about it? Don't. I don't care."

Before he could turn to go, she blurted out, "Fine. Let's talk about it."

Gillian rounded on him so suddenly he took a step back. Noah couldn't help but note it seemed he was always backing up and she was always advancing. She took a step closer. He forced himself to stay where he was and not retreat for once, which brought them perilously close. Not as close as that morning in the garden, but close enough to make him uncomfortable. Or maybe it was the way she was bearing down on him.

"You first," she prompted, and it was more of a dare than an invitation. "Go ahead."

"*Me?* What—"

"I mean, it seemed there was quite a lot you wanted to . . . *discuss* . . . the other day. Until you didn't, and you walked away instead. But I'm all for second chances, so please, do go on now."

"Gillian—"

Her name stopped in his throat. In the silence, his phone buzzed in his pocket. He couldn't move to answer it. He didn't have the wherewithal to even look away from Gillian. The buzzing seemed to go on forever and still he didn't reach for his phone, nor did he speak as she had commanded.

"Let's cut to the chase. Do you want me or not, Noah?" she demanded. "Did you want to kiss me that day?"

Noah's stomach clutched. This woman certainly didn't mince words. He wanted a lot of things, most of which he couldn't have or shouldn't have. Which was she? Probably both. He heard himself swallow heavily. He prayed Gillian couldn't hear it as well, but no such luck. She watched his Adam's apple move, and she raised one eyebrow and almost smirked. Now he was confused, embarrassed, still angry, and underneath all that, somehow, kind of turned on.

"Speak up," she prompted. "It could be your last chance. And a bit of advice—if you're smart, you'll start with an apology."

Now they were getting somewhere. This was something he

could respond to, and easily, and clear everything up once and for all.

"Fine! I'm sorry I thought about kissing you. Happy?"

Gillian, however, was evidently not happy. She exploded. *"How dare you!"*

Noah had had enough. He exploded back. *"What the hell are you talking about?"*

"You . . . *coward*!"

"Ex*cuse* me?"

"You heard me! You're a coward! I thought you . . ." Here she faltered, but only for a moment, barely giving him enough time to wonder what it was she was on the verge of saying before she rallied, more combative than before. "But it turns out Mister Tough Guy is too scared to take a chance!"

"Scared?" Noah was incredulous. Scared of what? What was she accusing him of? What "chance" was she . . . no.

Couldn't be.

She was mad because he *didn't* kiss her?

What was even happening right now?

The entire world was tipping on its axis, that's what was happening.

"I am not *scared*," he spit out through clenched teeth, "I am exhausted. I am annoyed. I am desperately in need of some peace in my life. Which you, may I point out, do not grant me. Ever. And for your information, I've been doing nothing *but* taking chances for months. I've upended my entire life, and you know what happened? Everything got entirely fucked up. So no, I was not about to 'take a chance,' because if you haven't noticed, I. make. bad. choices. And you, my friend"—and here he laughed a little maniacally, startling even himself—"*you* would be a *massively* bad choice—one I do not need or want in my life."

"I don't believe you," she snapped.

"I don't *care*," he snapped back, incensed. "Stop putting

words in my mouth and deciding what's going on in my head. You want an answer but you don't wait long enough to hear one. I tell you the truth, and you don't accept it. Well, listen up: I want no part"—he pointed a finger first at her, then at himself, and then back again—"of this. I do not want—any part—of *you*."

Gillian actually smiled, but it was more like she was showing her fangs. "Liar."

"Oh my *God*—!"

She was so smug, so certain she could see right through him. But no matter what the more primal parts of him demanded, he *didn't* want her. That was his story and he was sticking to it.

"Well, don't worry," she said brusquely. "You definitely *won't* have any part of me. Now or ever."

Then Gillian bumped him out of the way and, without another word, got into her car and drove away.

Noah stood alone in the driveway, fists on his hips, still seething long after she was gone. Any remnants of attraction to Gillian were quickly buried under the avalanche of his fury. He hated the way she always knocked him off-balance. Hated the way she poked at him till he cracked. Hated the way she always seemed to win every argument. Hated the way she always had the last word. Hated the way she influenced his life even when she wasn't trying to. Hated the way she made him lose control.

He just wanted to get the better of her for once—just once.

Today would not be that day, apparently.

His phone rang again. Noah dug it out of his pocket, desperate for a distraction. Maybe the marina needed him. But the caller ID showed an unfamiliar number. Of course nobody at the marina was looking for him. They were never looking for him.

"Yeah."

"Mr. West, this is Louise March."

He couldn't take much more of today. He really couldn't.

Heaving a sigh and scrubbing his scalp with his free hand, he grunted "Yeah" again.

"I've been going through the marina's record of tax payments. I have to say I'm surprised this tax issue has been going on for as long as it has. I'd quite forgotten."

Wait—could something good be happening? Noah's hopes rose for the first time since leaving the harpy's office. Maybe she'd had a change of heart. Maybe her heart grew three sizes today. Hell, he'd be fine with her growing any heart at all.

Noah held his breath.

"While I'm sympathetic to your challenges with the marina, Mr. West, I'm calling to inform you that the town of Willow Cove is hereby demanding payment of all back taxes due from Spencer's Marina, in full, by the end of the week."

What?

"I will be sending a formal demand letter by mail and email, of cour—"

"I don't have that kind of money!" he cried, hating the frantic edge to his voice, but he couldn't seem to tame it.

There was a silence, then . . . "I know."

Oh, that self-satisfied purr curdled his innards.

"Then what's possessing you to want the money this week, as if—" He stopped himself abruptly, realizing. "Don't tell me. Let me guess. I enter the garden competition and you waive the taxes?"

"Of course not," Louise answered crisply. "That would be against garden competition rules. And unlawful. However, I would consider granting you an extension on collection of said taxes and reevaluating your situation in July, which would just *happen* to coincide with the time period in which the garden competition takes place. At that time, if you prove yourself trustworthy, I would entertain the idea of a payment plan. But the timing would be *purely* coincidental."

Of course it would.

This stupid garden competition. Such high stakes that Louise would use it as a weapon against Gillian. Such high stakes that Gillian nearly murdered Noah when he "ruined her design." Noah felt like he'd fallen down the rabbit hole. He thought back to how readily he'd turned Louise down the last time she'd floated the idea of his entering the competition. Back when he'd been hopeful that everything would work out as he started a new life. Back when he'd thought everything would work out fine with the marina. Back when he'd believed himself to be a moral, ethical sort of person. Back when he hadn't skated too close to the edge with his beautiful neighbor.

"Are we reconsidering, Mr. West?"

"What would I have to do?"

"Simply create a garden. Submit the entry form and nominal fee by the end of the week. Naturally your entry would have to meet the gardening club's standards. After all, I have a certain reputation to uphold in this community. And in the gardening club especially. I can't award the first place trophy to just *any* garden. It would have to be respectable, worthy of the prize. But the gardening club does welcome all entries to the competition, and because we like to encourage new participants, there might be a certain amount of . . . *lenience* on the judges' part. Do we understand one another, Mr. West?"

This offer from Louise . . . it would save the marina, yes, but it also was not lost on him that it would give him the upper hand over Gillian for once. Plus it would pry her loose from his thoughts every waking moment—where she'd taken up residence slowly, and had been firmly lodged ever since—once and for all. If he did this, she would hate him for the rest of his life. But hey, she kind of already did. This, however . . . there would be no coming back from this. If he agreed to go along with Louise's plan, he'd have no chance of any sort of relationship, even a friendship, with Gillian Pritchard. He certainly would never have another chance like he'd had that morning in the garden. Which was exactly what he needed. It would be better this way—for his blood pressure, for his sanity. For his heart. Before he lost it.

"Fine. You have a deal."

CHAPTER 13

"You . . . you spend weekends doing *what*, now?"

Gillian realized her eyes were narrowing and she was flinching a little, which was sending the wrong message, but she couldn't seem to help it. She wasn't necessarily against camping—what this pleasant man, Trevor, sitting across from her at dinner, was gushing about—but the stuff that went *with* the camping. Which, as it happened, was what Trevor was most excited about.

"Jousting," he said, his eyes alight. "Aw, you should see it in person. It's really awesome."

"Jousting," Gillian repeated, as she sat still, letting her food go cold in front of her while she tried to wrap her head around this concept.

"Yeah."

"But not with horses."

"No."

"With . . ."

"Four-wheelers, yeah. It's epic."

"That is . . . epic. For sure." Gillian tried to sound enthusiastic, or at least actively interested, but she wasn't quite able to manage it.

Too bad, because Trevor was very nice. Except for the jousting-on-four-wheelers part. She even might have been willing to check out his hobby—it was unique, at least, so he got points for that—but she couldn't picture herself out in the wilderness for days at a time, watching a bunch of grown men knocking one another off all-terrain vehicles with poles.

Gillian leaned in and murmured earnestly, "Do . . . do you wear armor?"

"Yeah! We make it ourselves, out of old car parts. You know, some people wear, like, foam pads and stuff? But fiberglass and metal? That's the tits."

Gillian bit the inside of her cheek to keep from laughing, and then found herself thinking about how this moment beat Birdman for ridiculousness, and Noah would be the only other person who could appreciate it.

Noah?

Absolutely not. She was not going to get derailed thinking about him, of all people, and in a positive light. She was still mad at him, after all. No, livid. She refocused on Trevor.

"It's even more fun after it rains and everything is all muddy and shit."

Yeah, no. She was out.

Gillian smiled politely. "You know, Trevor, I'm not sure—"

"Hey, are you done with your dinner? I kind of want to get going. I need a good night's sleep. Huge tourney tomorrow, and it's a long drive."

Yes. Yes, she was done.

Maybe, she thought, she needed to be more specific when she asked the universe for someone remarkable. Trevor was remarkable. In a way. But there she was, going *not like that*. So this one was on her.

As she watched Trevor's Jeep pull away from the curb, Gillian actually felt a sharp pang of disappointment. Not regret, though. She hadn't had overly high hopes for Trevor, just modest ones. She hadn't deluded herself that he was going to be the man of her dreams, but after all these dinner and coffee dates, all the online chats and texting, all the probing questions she and these strangers lobbed back and forth at one another in their quest for some sort of connection, she was still trying to find one man—just one—who made her feel . . . well, anything at all. Intrigued. Charmed. Pleased. Enchanted. Happy. Anything.

There was one man, of course, who made her feel all sorts of things, but nothing she wanted to feel. More emotions bubbled up at the thought of the five-minute altercation she'd had with him earlier than from hours upon hours of time with all the other men she'd met recently.

It wasn't right, she knew. Fury, while it got her blood pumping, was definitely not the ideal emotion a man should inspire. And lord, did Noah West make her furious. Never mind that he could be kind, like when he took her photo, or could make her laugh, like when he literally brought the gulls down on her boring date. No, most of the time, like today, he just made her want to set him on fire. The nerve of him, getting her all hot and bothered like he had the other morning, looking at her like he wanted to eat her for breakfast, and then walking away. She could show him the list of men on her phone waiting for a response from her. She was in high demand. She didn't need to lose sleep over Noah's smoldering gazes that were followed up by a whole lot of nothing. What an insult.

So what if Trevor wasn't her knight in shining armor, despite his homemade helmet and trusty ATV steed? The next man she met could be. But it certainly wouldn't be Noah West, she knew that much. She didn't have time for indecisive and emotionally unavailable guys. She wouldn't give him one more thought. She had better things to do.

∽

The next day was beautiful, sunny and mild, perfect for gardening, and Gillian had every intention of spending every single moment of the day perfecting her garden. She was well rested, since Trevor had ended their date so early, and she had a long list of things she wanted to do that were all plant related. Gillian slipped on her Wellington boots and pulled on her sun hat and gloves, all while trying to ignore the presence in the corner of the mudroom. It definitely wasn't Inner Bette, who wouldn't dream of haunting her this early (she was most likely still snoring away in the ether, eyeshade firmly in place). No, it was the friendly, colorful gnome Noah had given her. What was she supposed to do with the thing? She couldn't give it back. She couldn't throw it away. She *certainly* couldn't—well, *wouldn't*—find a place for it in her garden. Even if it wasn't as repellent as she'd thought at first. She had to admit the little guy was kind of growing on her. Unlike the big guy who gave it to her.

Oh look, there was the big guy now, on his knees, digging in an overgrown flower bed running along the back of his house, just past the patio. It was almost like he was gardening, even though he was merely wrestling with foot-high weeds, which was all that had filled the spot for years. And were those new plants lined up on the open tailgate of his truck?

Didn't matter. She still didn't want to talk to him, not even to find out what he was doing.

"What are you doing?"

She saw Noah's broad shoulders tense under his faded T-shirt, but he didn't turn around. "Good morning to you too."

"You're up early."

"It's not that early." He looked over at her. "You look . . . cheerful this morning."

"I'm always cheerful. I'm a ray of bleeping sunshine."

Noah turned back to his weeding. "My mistake, then."

"So . . . ?" she prompted.

"Well, if you must know, I decided it can't be that difficult."

She waited, but he didn't offer any more information. With a sigh, she asked, "What are we talking about?"

"A garden. Try to keep up."

"What about a garden?"

"I mean, how hard can it be?"

What? "Wait. You're . . . you're putting in a *garden*?"

"Yep. Good enough for a trophy, I'd bet."

"Are you *kidding*?"

"Oh, I wouldn't kid about a garden competition." Noah looked at her again, and now he was grinning smugly. "What, you're the only person on the street who's allowed to enter this sacred contest?"

"I never said anything of the sort." He was doing this just to infuriate her, she was sure of it. She wouldn't give him the satisfaction. "Well . . . it . . . it's a free country. I think it's cute."

Was it her imagination, or did Noah start digging more violently? "Cute," he muttered.

"It's a lot of work, you know," she cautioned.

Noah waved his trowel cavalierly. "I'm aware. I can handle it."

"And you have a lot of space to fill."

That was an understatement. Retha's lawn had long been a barren wasteland, just the way the woman had liked it. Gillian had once given her a birdbath—something, anything to break up the large, square, not-very-smooth blanket of green and brown that was the backyard. Retha had thanked her profusely and put it in her shed, and that was the last Gillian had seen of it. It was probably still in there. There was so little ornamentation in the yard that the lawn guys Retha had hired to mow it barreled in once a week and were in and out in four and a half minutes flat, on average. Edge trimming included. (Gillian had timed them. She'd also amused herself by humming lively circus music as a soundtrack whenever she had the opportunity to watch them try to break their land speed record for fastest mowing job.)

Noah was putting in a garden. And was entering the garden competition. The more Gillian thought about it, the more she realized how ridiculous it all was. He didn't stand a chance. This contest was hers to lose, which meant she could take the high road. Because she was classy like that.

"Well, good luck. If you need any advice—"

"Nah. Got it covered."

"But—"

"You're going to give me advice anyway, aren't you?" He sighed, pausing in his digging again to give her an exhausted look.

"No! Never mind! You've got it all under control, so don't mind me. Just don't expect much."

"Don't expect . . . ?"

"I mean, enjoy participating, but don't expect to win a prize or anything. I've been working on my garden for years. Take it from me, you can't just plop a few new plants in some dirt and think it'll be as good as mine."

"It won't be."

"I'm glad you agree."

"It'll be better."

The nerve. "So this is personal."

"You're awfully full of yourself, aren't you? Why would you think this has anything to do with you?"

"You're trying to get back at me. Because of, you know, the other day."

Noah actually had the audacity to snicker. "Don't flatter yourself."

"Fine," she snapped. "This isn't personal. You just woke up this morning with a sudden urge to become a master gardener. Wonderful. Good luck."

"Thank you."

"Oh, and that thing you're so carefully working around? It's a weed."

"No, it isn't," he bit out.

"Broadleaf plantain," Gillian declared. "Useful as medicine, but considered a weed in a formal garden."

"Don't patronize me."

"Just ask The Witch on Warsaw Street, if you don't believe me. Oh wait—you never went there for allergy help, did you? Anyway, I'm not patronizing. I'm trying to help."

"I just said I've got it handled, *thank* you."

"Do you, though?"

Noah stopped answering her.

Gillian marched back over to her yard and, fuming, dropped her basket of gardening tools on the grass. She decided to start working on her flower bed closest to Noah's yard. Just because it needed the most work, she told herself, not because she wanted to keep an eye on him. Who cared what he was up to? Gillian stomped over to her composter, gave it a few turns, and opened the lid. Perfect fertilizer, if she did say so herself. She got her wheelbarrow out of her shed, shoveled some compost into it, and pushed it across her yard. It took her twice as long as usual to spread the fertilizer, because she kept spying on her neighbor. She winced as she watched him roughly take hold of the plants he'd bought, yanking them out of their plastic pots by their stems instead of teasing them out gently. He'd bought stalky, root-bound, sad little things, and he didn't even break up the strangled roots to let them breathe before sticking them in dirt, which he obviously hadn't prepped first. Shade plants in sun, sun plants in shade . . . before she even knew what she was doing, she was back in his yard, standing over him, arms crossed.

"I have never seen anyone with less affinity for gardening than you."

"Good thing it's no concern of yours, then."

"You really don't know what you're getting yourself into."

"It's a garden competition, not rocket science. I'll figure it out. There's this fancy thing called the internet now? Loads of information. Now, you go over there and worry about your own plants."

He dismissed her with a flourish, waving her away with a bare-ass gardenia with broken stems, breaking more in the process, and she flinched.

She reminded herself it was his funeral—Louise would bury him in his own flower bed if he wasn't careful—and redoubled her efforts in her own yard. He'd find out, she said to herself. His overconfidence was going to get him exactly nowhere this time. When the judges turned up their noses at his ham-fisted attempt at what was, essentially, an art form, she'd laugh merrily, make sure he got a good look at her first-place trophy, and maybe even raise a glass of some expensive champagne she'd purchase especially to celebrate her victory.

Yes, that would be the perfect way to celebrate Noah's inevitable defeat. Which she was going to heartily enjoy.

Mimosas.

French toast.

Eggs Benedict.

Mimosas.

Noah rolled his eyes and told himself to stop pulling his phone out of his pocket every time his text alert went off. The neighbors were trying to entice him to join them in what apparently was going to be a boozy brunch, judging by Carol's repeated mentions of mimosas.

Judy's got a flask in her purse to remedy any watered-down drinks we get.

Yep, boozy brunch.

Got a place saved for you.

As fun as it sounded—and it was not lost on Noah that he now had no qualms about hanging out with old ladies, as long as it was these old ladies in particular—he had work to do.

"Right. Garden."

Noah surveyed the half-hearted handiwork he'd abandoned a few days ago and tried to envision . . . well, anything. A completed garden. With a theme, ideally. Something award winning, preferably. As Louise had so clearly communicated, he had to make it look like he'd put in some sort of effort. And he had his pride. Somewhere deep down he wanted his garden to legitimately be worthy of the trophy he was about to steal from Gillian.

But all he saw was the destruction he'd gleefully committed in his yard and the various plants, now withering, that he'd frantically grabbed at the garden center, hoping it would all come together somehow.

He kicked a clod of mud. He was entirely uninspired. But he was smart, inventive, and adaptable. He could learn something as simple as gardening. And he could make something of this crater that was once a lawn. If he moved his ass this century.

When he heard Gillian's side door open, Noah scrambled to look busy. He didn't know if she was watching him, but he refused to risk looking like an idiot. Well, looking more like an idiot than he had already. She knew darn right well he wasn't capable of creating a garden—any garden at all, let alone one that would win a prize in a competition, and definitely not one that could beat hers. But he had to fake it.

As usual, here she came, once again risking her fancy shoes by venturing farther into his dirt-strewn yard. As if she'd picked up on what he was thinking—and maybe she had, if she'd caught him glancing at her feet—she stopped, slipped off her heels, and tossed them onto the driveway before coming any closer.

"Just can't stay away, can you?" he challenged her.

"Here," she said, holding out the shovel she'd confiscated when he was drunk.

"I was wondering if you were ever going to give that back."

Gillian stuck it in the lawn and turned to go, then turned back. "Too much water."

"Excuse me?"

"You've watered your plants too much. See those yellow

leaves on your rhododendron? Which is going to be done flowering in a few days, by the way; it'll be spent by the time the competition rolls around."

"Did I ask you for—"

"And no wonder it's waterlogged. What is that? A moat?"

"A what?"

"There," she said, pointing at the circular ridge of soil under the plant. "Looks like a moat."

"To retain the water."

"What *for*? We get too much rain as it is. You've got to let the excess run off, not trap it near the roots, or they'll rot."

Noah started to retort, but he stopped himself. She was right. In California they did everything they could to preserve what little moisture they had, but there was no need for that here, in this sopping wet, humid climate. They'd gotten almost half an inch of rain in one go just yesterday, thanks to some torrential thunderstorms. Noah wondered if he'd ever truly feel dry again.

"What you've already planted is going to die. The little sprouts over there, under the gutter? They're going to get swamped as well—"

"Don't worry about me. I've got it under control," Noah growled, even though the more he talked to her the less confident he felt about having anything at all under control. And he wasn't only thinking about his garden.

"I'm not worried about you. I'm worried about the plants. They don't deserve this kind of abuse."

"Don't you have someplace you need to be? Obviously you wouldn't dress up so nicely just to come over here and bother me again."

"You think I look nice?"

Ah, shit.

Noah said nothing, just pulled another thing out of the ground, hoping desperately it was a weed.

After another moment's awkward silence, Gillian let him off the hook. "I do have to get going, actually."

Noah nodded toward a suitcase sitting on the driveway behind her. "A weekend away with a new beau?"

"You know," she sighed, "I do have other things going on in my life besides dating."

"Sure. You've got your garden."

"I also happen to have a career, remember? I'm going to New York this week. For a conference."

Noah couldn't help himself. "An entire week talking about pills? Isn't that overkill?"

"I'm not even going to go into how misguided you are about my profession. And not that I need to share my whereabouts with you, but I'm visiting my parents first. My point is, don't sabotage my garden while I'm out of town. I'll know it was you."

"What do you take me for?"

"A garden saboteur."

Noah shook his head. "I'm offended."

"You're a lot of things. Good luck with the garden."

Before he could stop himself, Noah followed her. She popped the trunk of her car. Noah grabbed the handle of her suitcase and lifted it. "Jesus," he fought out, "what's in this thing? A dead body?"

"None of your business."

"Yeah, you say that a lot. It's shoes, isn't it? Gotta be shoes."

"That's stereotyping. And sexist."

"If it matters at all, the dead body theory is more believable when it comes to you." He took a breath, heaved the suitcase into the car, and slammed the trunk closed. "Have a good trip."

Once she was gone, Noah stretched, and with the freedom granted by her absence—as empty as their little corner of the neighborhood suddenly felt without her in it—really looked at her yard. Some whatsits were blooming mightily; other ground cover seedlings she must have planted recently had taken root and were filling out. The small area of grass in front of the beds was trimmed and green. Trees and bushes were shaped nicely, and no wonder. He'd watched her gently and carefully clip each branch, one at a time, stepping back and examining the whole effect frequently. She was building up her garden the way an artist built up a painting, one small brushstroke at a time, with an eye on the big picture from a distance.

He surveyed his own handiwork, trying to picture his empty yard awash with flowers, trees, and plants, like Gillian's. Who was he kidding? There was no way that was going to happen, especially in the small amount of time he had to learn all there was to know about gardening and then put it into practice.

Well, he'd told her he could look up anything, even how to plant an entire garden, so that's what he was going to do. Noah pulled out his phone, sat down on the back step, and started a search. *How to . . .* what? *How to create a garden. From scratch. For beginners. But prize winning.*

Even Google got confused.

Noah looked again at his own lackluster effort and sighed. He really didn't have any talent for this, nor any desire—or time—to learn. He had to try another tack.

~

"That's cheating!"

Noah used to think only cats could jump straight into the air from a standing position until he did it himself. "What the *hell*!"

He spun in a circle in his driveway in the dark, looking for Gillian. He knew her voice, and he knew that tone—he'd heard her rage far too many times in his life already. There was no mistaking it.

Noah saw movement in the shadows on her front porch, and

then Gillian was down the steps, across her front lawn, and in his face.

"I said, that's cheating."

Noah leaned back and growled a little. "Welcome back. When did you get in?"

He had reminded himself at least a dozen times last week how blessedly quiet it was without Gillian around to judge him—and his garden—but, in fact, he'd sort of missed her.

Maybe. Now he couldn't remember how he felt without her around, because here she was, cornering him in his driveway late at night after a long day at the marina, pummeling his senses, and not in a good way.

"Don't change the subject," she snapped.

"Well, we weren't exactly getting anywhere with your original subject, whatever it was. Mind telling me what you're talking about?"

Stupid to ask. He knew. Here was the confrontation he'd been bracing for, but now he found himself stalling for time. Turned out he was not prepared for the cyclone of rage that was Gillian.

"*That.*" She spat the word as she pointed toward his property with a rigid arm and accusing finger. "What exactly do you call *that*?"

"A pretty good job, if I do say so myself."

Her eyes narrowed. "You didn't do that. In one week, while I was gone? Please."

"I didn't say *I* did it."

"You'd better not. Because I heard all about it." She didn't name Carol, Arnette, and Judy, but of course she didn't have to. "You hired Kennedy and his lackeys to put in an entire garden *for* you."

Noah wasn't sure if it was a defense mechanism or what, but he felt like laughing. He absolutely had hired a team to landscape the entire yard. Back *and* front, because he was feeling generous, even though the front yard wasn't in the running for the competition. Using almost the last of his savings, Noah had lured the landscapers away from their regular jobs to get his garden done in record time. Kennedy and his lackeys, as Gillian had put it, had delivered, sweeping in and constructing, in a most professional and skilled manner, sculpted raised beds with concrete barriers painted white, runs of small white marble chips, concrete pathways, and sparse but artfully selected and placed greenery. It wasn't cheap, but it was easy, and best of all, it was finished well ahead of the actual competition date. All Noah needed to do was crack a beer and stand in the middle of it, admiring Kennedy's lackeys' handiwork.

"So what if I did?"

"Wh—?"

Gillian couldn't even complete a single word, let alone repeat what he had said. So instead she reached into her back pocket, came up empty, frantically scrabbled in her other pockets, let out a muted frustrated noise, and hustled back to her house. Noah stayed where he was, arms crossed, hands cupping his elbows, watching the glorious sight that was Gillian in motion. She hurried back soon enough, waving a piece of paper.

"*This* is the big deal." She thrust the paper at him. "Read it," she ordered, when he didn't immediately take it from her.

"Care to join me on my porch? The light—"

"No."

Noah heaved an exaggerated sigh and made a business of locating his phone and turning on the flashlight. He squinted at the paper he accepted from her, recognizing it immediately. "These are the rules for the competition. I've seen them."

"Have you really? Number eight. Read."

Noah read. "Oh."

"Yeah, 'oh.' 'All gardens must be designed and executed by

the entrant.' No professional installations. Which yours clearly is. You're disqualified."

Shit.

"Well, hold on a minute." He scrutinized the details of rule eight. "It says *most* of the garden has to be done by the entrant."

Gillian rolled her eyes. "The exception is for something like, say, a water feature with plumbing you couldn't install on your own."

"So? I *couldn't* install this stuff on my own."

"You paid to have an entire, complete garden put in by professionals, in one fell swoop!"

Noah had to admit he admired a woman who could use "one fell swoop" in casual conversation. He might have been distracted by Gillian's unique talent, because suddenly there was some dead air between them.

"Are you listening to me?" she demanded. "You don't qualify for the competition if you don't lift a finger to create the garden yourself."

Noah lifted one finger in front of her face, just to annoy her. Gillian practically stomped her foot in frustration.

"I'm taking this to Louise."

Ah. His ace in the hole. "Louise approves."

"She does not."

Gillian had no idea Louise would approve of anything he did . . . or had someone do for him. He felt a pang of guilt about it, but it was slight, and overpowered by the promise of getting the marina's finances under control.

Noah leaned toward Gillian, just a little. "Do your worst," he murmured in what he hoped was a threatening way, but he feared it just came out warmly.

Was it his imagination, or did she shiver a little? Well, the night air was cool. He didn't want to get his hopes up that he had any effect on her besides utter revulsion.

She retorted, "Oh, you've already done your worst. That"—she indicated his new garden in the shadows—"is damn ugly."

"Ex*cuse* me?"

"It's ugly, I said. It's cold, it's unfeeling."

"It's modern."

"Modern? It's inhuman. Where's the *heart*?"

"In my chest where it belongs. The garden, on the other hand, is a structural marvel."

Gillian laughed outright. "A *what*? 'Structural . . .' okay. Okay, pal. Whatever you need to believe so you can sleep at night. Just know this." And now it was Gillian's turn to lower her voice to a murmur, a hum that thrummed in his bones. "I am going to pummel you in the competition. If you're even allowed to stay in it. Count on it."

CHAPTER 15

"What do you mean, you're not ready?"

Jenna's voice was harsh and accusatory in her ear. Gillian shifted the phone and scrambled to explain.

"No, no, *I'm* ready. But I'm going to be *delayed*. Mick's had a change of heart and offered to drop off the load of bricks he's been keeping for me at the salvage yard."

Nothing but stunned silence on Jenna's end. Then, "That *is* huge."

"Right?"

"Did Ollie drop that iron winch on Mick's head again? Because I can't think of any other reason he'd *offer* to deliver. He usually comes up with a million reasons *not* to."

"I know. It's freaky. But I'm not going to question it."

"We're coming over right now. I need to see this for myself."

Gillian didn't blame Jenna one bit. The opportunity to see Mick actually make a delivery might never come again in their lifetimes. While she waited, Gillian went upstairs to change into shorts. The day was surprisingly warm already, and she didn't want to sweat her way through the day with her friends. As she pulled the shorts' drawstring tight at her waist, she found herself staring out her window at Noah's professionally installed garden for the hundredth time since it had popped up like an ugly mushroom while she was away. What a shock it had been to come home to that.

It was a travesty. Not just that he'd paid someone to do it, but that it was so damn hideous. So much concrete, so few plants. It went beyond austere; it was violence. How was it a garden? It was like someone's idea of a cruel joke. Unless that was what Noah was going for—a way to thumb his nose at her interests, her passion, as well as at the gardening club and all the other participants who took this competition seriously. She wouldn't put it past him.

Then her view of Noah's property was blocked by the arrival of a beat-up flatbed truck, piled high with bricks, rolling down her driveway accompanied by the piercing intermittent whine of its backup beeper. Her bricks. Now, *those* had character, which would in turn add character and depth to her garden. *That* was how you did it.

Gillian slid her sandals on and went outside to meet the newly affable salvage yard owner.

"Mick, thank you so much for doing this," she said as the tall, potbellied, grizzled man rounded the back of the truck.

He modestly brushed her off as he started unhooking tie-down straps and pulling off a dirt-stained, once-blue tarp covering the load. "Never you mind. Happy to."

Happy to? Had Mick been abducted by aliens and a doppelgänger put in his place? It was the only explanation. But she wasn't about to argue. Instead, Gillian stood back and directed Mick and Ollie to where they could stack the materials until she had time to dig her new path.

They finished piling the last of the bricks just as Jenna's minivan pulled up and parked at the curb.

"Threw in a few bags of sand too," Mick told Gillian. "Wasn't sure if you had some already or not, and it always turns out you need more than you think anyway."

"How very thoughtful of you. Thanks."

"Gillian, you sure you're going to be able to do this all by yourself? It's a lot of work."

"It's just a short path. And I'm stronger than I look."

"Yeah, I know. You're, uh . . . you're one impressive woman, I gotta admit."

Gillian wasn't sure what to do with that, so she just said "thanks" again.

"I hear you're dating these days."

"I . . . I am, yes. A bit."

"Give my nephew a shot, then? He's always thought you were a looker."

A "looker"?

"Hayden? Isn't he a little young, Mick?" Hayden was barely twenty years old, she guessed. And she suspected she was being generous with that estimate.

"Gotta start sometime."

"Not with me, he doesn't."

"He could come by, put in the walkway for you, you could see how you get on?"

"Thanks, Mick, but I'm going to say no."

"Well," he grunted, "if you change your mind, you say the word, I'll put you two in touch. Better get going. You have a good day, Gillian. And if you need help with the path . . ."

Gillian put on a smile, shook her head decisively, and waved the truck off before turning to face the friendly firing squad who had heard just about every word of their exchange.

"Go on," she sighed. "You know you want to."

Jenna and Delia wasted no time reverting to their preteen selves, hooting and making kissing noises, while Leah, pure little thing that she was, merely stood by and laughed a little.

After a few seconds of nonsense, Gillian cut them off. "All right, all right. You've had your fun. Aren't we late?"

"There's plenty of time," Jenna said. "Perhaps a round of 'Hayden and Gillian sitting in a tree' before we go?"

"Let's not."

"You're no fun."

"Hey," Delia interrupted, "where's your hottie neighbor?"

"What did I say, woman?" Gillian demanded. "In no way is that man hot. Look at what he did." Naturally she'd told her friends about Noah's gardening transgression, but they hadn't seen it for themselves yet. She gestured expansively. "And he calls *that* a garden. In what universe could I possibly find a man who did that attractive?"

"You do have a point," Jenna murmured. "What was he going for? Postapocalyptic hellscape?"

"You got me."

Leah studied the yard. "It definitely could do with a little something . . ."

"Some flamethrower action? A wrecking ball?" Gillian suggested.

"A little drastic. I was thinking more like some color."

"Oh lord, speaking of color, I completely forgot to show you the pièce de résistance. Hang on." Gillian disappeared into the house and came back out a moment later with the gnome.

"What is *that*?" Jenna gasped while Delia squealed, charmed.

"This is the horrible man's apology gift after I went nuclear on him for pulling out the hedge. He suggested I put it in my garden!"

"Okay, back to hating this guy, right? Are we unanimous on that?" Jenna asked. "I just need our benchmark before I can start planning the proper kind of revenge."

"Cute gnomes count for nothing?" Delia took the figurine and jiggled him in the crook of her arm like a baby.

"Less than nothing," Gillian said. "A garden gnome is neither a compliment nor a gift. It's an insult. It's an affront to beautiful gardens everywhere."

"What are you going to do with it, then?"

"I might take it to the rod and gun club and skeet shoot it."

"You don't know how to shoot," Leah reminded her.

"I can learn. I have motivation."

"I'll adopt your little friend," Delia said, gazing fondly at the happy little face and booping his red-tipped nose.

Although the gnome would have fit right in at Delia's whimsical little Swiss cottage–style home on the water, Gillian surprised even herself when she said immediately, "No, let me keep it."

"You mean you *are* going to put him in your garden?" Leah asked, shocked.

"No, of course not."

"Then what—"

"I don't know. Wait, yes I do." Gillian gestured for Delia to hand it over.

Delia dropped a kiss on the top of the gnome's head before reluctantly obeying. "No dismemberment."

"I'm sorry, Miss Dupree, I make no promises."

Gillian dragged out her ladder from her shed, along with a coil of rope. She steadied the ladder on the precarious gravel path at the back of Noah's yard just under something that looked like an unfinished pergola—only two posts with crossbeams, not a full structure—painted white. She had no idea what the point of the thing was. Now she was going to give it a purpose.

"You wouldn't," Delia said, horrified.

"This is an opportunity I can't waste. Noah could come home any minute." She didn't know where her neighbor was, or when he was going to get back, but running the risk was part of the thrill.

"This is weird, you know that?" Jenna said as she footed the ladder for Gillian.

"It has to be done," she called down as she flung the rope over the nearer of the two crossbeams.

"Does it, though?"

Gillian ignored Jenna, as well as the fretful noises coming from Delia, who stood with Leah in the driveway to act as lookouts for Noah's truck. Of course, by the time he pulled into the driveway it would be too late—she'd be trapped at the scene of the crime—but she didn't really care one way or the other. She wanted to make a statement.

Gillian finished her knotwork in record time and let go of the gnome. He plummeted earthward and ended up hanging upside down by his ankles six feet above the gravel path, twisting lazily on the end of the rope. She climbed down the ladder, booped the gnome's nose like Delia had, and whispered, "Tell your friend it was me."

"You know you're obsessing, right?" Jenna accused her.

"Not obsessing," Gillian said, securing the ladder in her shed once more. "Not in the least."

"It's not healthy to let someone live rent free in your head like this."

Delia was the last to leave the yard, trailing behind her friends and repeatedly glancing worriedly over her shoulder. "For shame, Gillian. How *could* you? All the clay is going to rush to his head."

Gillian waved them off, quite pleased with her handiwork, and was only sorry she wouldn't be home to see Noah's reaction. "Let's go. Don't we have jewelry to sell?"

∽

The Summer Solstice Fest's craft fair on the town green was one of the more popular events of the season, and they had a lot to do to set up Delia's tent—so much so that Gillian's friends almost didn't have time to grill her about her feud with Noah. Almost.

"So, wait. I have some questions," Leah said as they unloaded totes full of Delia's jewelry from the back of Jenna's minivan. "About your thing with Noah."

Gillian puffed up, affronted. "I do *not* have a th—"

"You just spent ten minutes risking your neck on a ladder to hang a garden gnome from his pergola as some sort of inside joke with him. This is not normal behavior."

"Joke? I most certainly do not *joke* with Noah West."

"Love-hate is a thing, you know," Delia said. "I think Leah's onto something here."

"Sorry to burst your bubble, but there is no love-hate anything," Gillian said. "That man is obnoxious, rude, insensitive, a massive grouch, *and* he created that monstrosity of a so-called garden. The only emotion he inspires in me is straight-up hate."

"Mm, I don't know . . ." Leah mused, one finger on her chin. "Sounds like an awful lot of protesting for someone not worthy of being on your radar."

Jenna added, "And somehow none of Gillian's dates, of which she's had plenty, turn into *second* dates. Why is that, Gillian? Hm?"

Gillian valiantly ignored her friends, plonked a tote on a handcart, and started rolling the cart toward the booth. Delia ran ahead of her and blocked her path.

"Yeah, why is that, Gilly? You'd think at least one or two of the men you've met would be worth seeing more than once. Are you holding all these guys to some impossible standard of hotness—your neighbor?"

"Jewelry, ladies. All this has to be put on display."

Gillian steered the handcart around her friend and pushed it into the white tent Delia had been assigned. The others trailed after her, lugging more boxes. For a first-timer, Delia had actually gotten a good spot on the town green, right in the middle of the action, on a main walkway and with a lovely view of the river. There were worse spots to spend a summer day.

Gillian pulled the cover off a tote and scooped up a handful of beaded necklaces. "Now . . . where?"

"I know you're capable of multitasking," Jenna said to Gillian as she passed Leah a compartmented box. "Unpack, and at the same time tell us why you're rejecting all the men you're meeting, *and* whether it has anything to do with the hot guy next door."

Gillian had to get them off the Noah train. Good thing she had a decent distraction ready.

"Fine. *Fine.* I wasn't going to tell you this, but—"

Her three friends leaned in with bated breath. Delia whispered, "I knew it. You already jumped your neighbor."

Gillian pulled a face. "No! Actually, I . . . met someone at the pharmaceutical conference."

"Really?" Jenna exclaimed, overjoyed.

"When do we get to meet him?" Delia demanded.

"Hey, now, we can't scare him off yet. I just met him."

"Very funny. Also accurate," Jenna said. "At least give us some details to tide us over."

"All in good time."

"Don't do this to us," Delia begged. "What's his name? Where does he live? Is he nice? What does he do for a living? Was it love at first sight?"

"Sebastian, Albany, very nice, pharmaceutical rep, and let's not get crazy."

Delia was undeterred. "Tall? Short? Fair? Dark?"

"Think . . . Superman," Gillian supplied, and Delia sighed rapturously.

And she didn't even know the half of it yet. Gillian had been stunned when she'd spotted Sebastian across the crowded convention center foyer and had thought she was dreaming when he'd walked straight toward her, eager to introduce himself. But he'd been real, incredibly charming, and committed to spending as much time as possible with her during the convention. Best of all, he'd made her promise to see him again before they'd parted when the convention was over. It had been hard to keep him a secret, but now Gillian was more than happy to tell her friends about him.

Leah asked, "When are you seeing him again?"

"Soon," she said with a wink. "Okay, back to work. Time's a-wasting." She rattled the handful of necklaces again.

Delia said, "I have T-bar stands for those. You can just slide a bunch of them on each peg. Let me find them . . ."

As she rooted around for her display stands, Leah opened the box Jenna had handed her and peeked inside. "What are these?"

Delia raised her head to see what Leah was holding. "Body jewelry. Mostly lip rings, belly rings, belly chains. You interested?"

Leah's cheeks flushed pink as she put the box down on one of the folding tables that ran along the tent's three walls. "Not really my style."

"They can stay in the box—just take the lid off."

"Delia, when did you find time to do all this?" Gillian asked, marveling at the sheer quantity of jewelry they were unpacking.

Even though the artist was back to digging so deep in the tote it looked like she was going to fall in and end up in Wonderland, her derisive snort came across loud and clear. "I've got time on my hands."

"And whose fault is that?" Jenna asked.

Delia surfaced and patted down her hair. "Don't start bugging me about Gray again. Besides, I'm serious about this business, so I've been spending all my time and energy being, you know, creative. I've been on a hot streak lately, and you are seeing the fruits of my labors."

Jenna snorted. "Sounds like a sexual dry spell to me."

"I'm not talking to you about my sex life."

"Or lack thereof."

"Just sell my jewelry and make me a successful artist, okay?"

The rest of the day was spent flogging Delia's wares. Customers swarmed the tent, enchanted with her necklaces, earrings, bracelets, body jewelry, rings, pins, beaded suncatchers, and eyeglass chains. It was all the women could do to accept payments, wrap up the pieces, send the buyers off with a wish for them to wear the items in good health, and hurriedly shift to the next customer.

"Oh my God, I didn't expect to be this mobbed," Delia gasped, dropping into a chair by the cashbox. "I'm going to nearly sell out if this keeps up."

Gillian squeezed past some customers in the crowded booth and sat down next to Delia, handing over some money she'd just collected. "Well, good. I swear we've seen nearly every tourist around, *plus* every Willow Cove lifer. Everybody loves your work—"

As she reached under the table for more paper bags, a shadow fell over her, and Gillian could have sworn a chill wind swept through the tent. She looked up slowly and found herself face-to-face with Louise March. Great.

Louise cracked one of her humorless smiles. "Gillian Pritchard, I'm surprised to see you here."

"I'm always happy to help a friend, Louise." She refrained from adding a snide remark about Louise not knowing what friends were. High road, high road . . .

"Mm, how nice." She made a move to go but turned back

around. Gillian waited for the knife Louise always wielded, especially when it came to her. Louise did not disappoint. "But you're not going to find many single men in a jewelry booth."

Of course Louise would have kept up with her adventures in online dating. She had innumerable sources for town gossip. Gillian shrugged it off, desperately hoping the woman would move on to another booth. Louise did not, in fact, move on. Gillian decided to ignore her. She had a harder time ignoring Delia, who was kicking her under the table.

"Do something!" Delia hissed as Louise drifted a few feet away to peruse the jewelry on another table, her self-satisfied air polluting the tent.

"Like what?" Gillian practically mouthed, as she suspected Louise had the ears of a bat. And probably the wings too, folded under her cardigan. "Leap across the table and take her down?"

"If you don't, I will."

"She's the head judge of the garden competition. I need to stay on her good side."

"She has never let you be on her good side. If she even has one."

Delia was right. But Gillian had perfected the art of letting Louise's digs bounce off her ever since she became a favorite target of hers years ago, and she was older and far tougher now. She would not let Louise get to her.

"After all, dear," Louise spoke up again, in the same falsely friendly tone, as she held up an elaborate necklace and scrutinized it, "with so many strikes against you, you shouldn't waste any time. I mean, at your age, one failed marriage already, and . . . well . . ." And she looked Gillian up and down, clearly communicating she'd have trouble finding a man who wouldn't mind her size.

"Oh, I swear . . ." Delia muttered.

"Don't do it," Gillian warned Delia, putting a hand on her friend's arm.

"Excuse me."

The melodious, deep voice came from the other side of Louise. Large hands grasped Louise's stiff shoulders and moved her, ever so gently, but ever so pointedly, out of the way. And there he was in front of her: Sebastian Fellows.

Or, as Delia squeaked, awestruck, "Superman."

Gillian wasn't sure if she was beaming because of Delia's reaction or because of the fact that the man who'd swept her off her feet in New York was standing before her once again, just as he'd promised, just as they'd planned.

"I wonder if you could help me."

Although his eyes were twinkling, he kept his distance, speaking formally, pretending not to know her, and Gillian went along with his little game.

"Of course, happy to. Are you looking for anything in particular?"

"I don't know," he mused, crossing his arms. "What's your favorite piece? Or am I putting you on the spot?"

"Not at all. It's right over here."

Her favorite jewelry item was one of the first pieces Delia had created, a gold and amethyst pin. Which was on a table right in front of . . .

"Excuse me, would you, Louise?"

With Louise effectively still sidelined but watching their every move, Gillian picked up the pin and turned to Sebastian, sounding calm, confident, and authoritative as she pointed out how the delicate coils of gold wire were balanced by the substantial amethyst beads. When she glanced up at him, though, she saw he was looking not at the piece of jewelry but at her.

Sebastian murmured, "I'll take it."

"You didn't ask how much."

"Doesn't matter. If you like it."

"What matters is if the, er, recipient likes it."

"Oh, apparently she does."

Gillian held it out to him. "Would you like to look at it more closely before I wrap it?"

"You don't have to wrap it." Keeping his eyes locked on hers, he said, "Just promise me you'll wear it when I take you out to dinner."

Sebastian flashed his brilliant smile, and Gillian heard Delia and Jenna gasp, which made her grin from ear to ear. But it was the strangled noise coming from Louise that made her think life was pretty perfect right about now.

CHAPTER 16

Noah tried not to flinch. It had been what felt like years—okay, it had been a week or two at most—since he and Gillian had had their blowup about his professionally installed garden. That was the last time they'd spoken. The last communication he'd received from Gillian was in the form of a gnome hanging upside down from his pergola. Yeah, he knew it was her. And he knew what it meant. Noah was quite proud of himself that he'd chosen to be the bigger person and ignore the message she was sending. He'd just quietly rescued the little guy and tucked him away in his house for safety, before Gillian could do anything worse to him. Other than that . . . radio silence and total avoidance. Noah didn't shop at her pharmacy anymore, and Gillian had no reason to visit the marina, where he'd been spending most of his time.

But living next door to each other made things difficult once in a while. Like now, when they both happened to exit their houses at the same time to head for their cars.

Noah faced Gillian bravely, jaw set, always mindful to keep his toes firmly on his side of the strip of grass between their driveways.

"'Morning," he said grimly.

"'Morning," she returned, just as stiffly, also not crossing their proverbial line in the sand.

Much as Gillian infuriated him more often than not and engaging with her always ended up in some kind of confrontation, he wanted to say something, have a polite conversation. Perhaps just once it would turn out differently, he hoped. But no, that ship had sailed. His fate had been sealed the moment he'd entered the garden competition.

Which he would be hard-pressed to win, at the rate things were going. His garden was suffering. He didn't know what to do with the plants, sparse as they were. He was just praying they'd hang on till the judges came around. Then they could wither and die for all he cared. In fact, he'd prefer it. The garden was nothing more than a lasting reminder that he was about to screw Gillian over just for money.

What made him feel even worse was that even though he was about to rob her of the one thing she wanted most, she was actually being nice to him. On the down-low, of course. Once or twice during a dry spell he'd come home to find his yard and driveway damp, meaning she must have turned her hose on his garden while seeing to hers. For some reason his heart ached when he thought of this small kindness.

Noah reminded himself that she'd already told him she cared more about the plants than about him. He had to remember that.

Still, he couldn't seem to avoid peeking from his bedroom window into hers occasionally, hoping to see her dancing again. Or maybe he'd catch her eye, and maybe she'd smile, even if it was only at the memory of their window flirtation. In fact, one time he thought he saw *her* peeking at *him*, but he didn't dare believe it. When he tried to get a closer look, nobody was there at all. It had probably been his imagination.

Noah wanted to say something more, even if it was as banal

as a comment on the sunny weather, but all he could think about was how stunning Gillian looked. She was wearing a coral-colored dress with a full skirt that had buttons down the front and short sleeves that rested off her shoulders. Her hair caught the sunlight, and a sparkling necklace glittered at the hollow of her throat. Noah didn't have the words to describe how she looked except . . . beautiful, fresh. Radiant. He wanted to pay her a compliment, but he knew how she'd react, and he couldn't deal with that today.

Then the moment passed, and Gillian was in her car and backing out of the driveway.

~

"Oh *God*."

And sometimes Willow Cove was too darn small. Especially when it came to options for brunch.

Noah stood close beside Gillian defiantly, stuffing his hands in his pockets and rocking back on his heels. "Do you really need to sound so . . . so . . . put upon? So I go to brunch. Big deal."

"Since when? I *literally* never see you here."

They'd both walked into Luca's, a bright and airy restaurant with a bank of floor-to-ceiling windows overlooking the water, at almost the same time, only minutes after their uncomfortable near-monosyllabic exchange in their driveways.

Noah had finally given in and accepted the standing brunch invitation from his elderly neighbors, but he couldn't resist asking why Gillian was there. He feared he already knew.

"What about you? Another first date?"

Noah desperately, desperately hoped it wasn't a date. Even though it shouldn't matter to him.

"No. It's not." Gillian paused for effect. "It's a fourth date."

"Dating apps finally worked for you?"

"For your information, I met him the old-fashioned way. At a work event."

"How retro. Who is this fine gentleman without a dating profile?"

"His name is Sebastian. Sebastian Fellows."

Noah raised one eyebrow.

"*Yes*, it's his real name. And you wouldn't know him. He has a cottage in Alexandria Bay. It's a town up the river—"

"I'm acquainted with Alex Bay, thanks. So where is Mr. Fourth Date?"

"He's on his way. He should be here any minute."

"Why didn't he pick you up? What kind of a gentleman is he?"

"For your information, meeting him here was my choice. I prefer to have my own agency."

"All right, then, Miss Austen."

"I would have thought you'd approve of extra safety precautions."

"So you admit you need extra safety precautions with this guy?"

"What? No!"

"Yoo-hoo! Noah!"

"Your brunch bunch is waiting for you," Gillian said, nodding at the table where the neighborhood ladies sat waving. "And it looks like they've gotten a head start on the mimosas. Better catch up."

Summarily dismissed, Noah slunk down the stairs into the dining area and joined Carol, Arnette, and Judy at their table, dropping into the empty seat they'd saved for him and immediately draining the mimosa beside his plate. The combination of orange juice and alcohol was harsh in his throat.

"Why are these stupid champagne flutes so small?" he muttered.

"Here, have mine," Arnette said, pushing her glass toward

him. "I haven't touched it yet. The server will be by with more any minute."

"They know our rate of consumption and have adapted accordingly," Judy added.

As he downed the second drink, he scanned the room, on the lookout for Gillian and her date. He didn't see them, but he did spy someone he didn't expect: his uncle. And Manny wasn't alone. He was in a corner booth with an attractive woman who seemed to be the dating app match he had told Noah about when his nephew had first visited him.

Noah stood up, intending to cross the room to say hello, but Gillian got there first, hugging the woman and chatting animatedly. Well, he couldn't go over there *now*.

Instead, he sat back down and gulped a third mimosa that had magically appeared, as promised, when he wasn't looking.

"Liquid brunch today? We've all been there," Judy commented. "But you might want to consider a pancake or two to help absorb the alcohol."

"I saw my uncle over there." Noah, grateful his back was to Manny's booth, hitched his chin over his shoulder. He risked another quick glance in that direction and saw Gillian was still chatting with the couple. "I was going to go over to say hi, but . . ."

"Ah," Arnette murmured knowingly, buttering a blueberry muffin.

"I, you know, didn't want to interrupt."

"Mm," Carol hummed, sipping her drink.

"Who's, uh, who's my uncle's date? Gillian seems really friendly with her."

"Oh, that's Alyce Masterson," Judy supplied.

"Masterson?" Noah repeated. "Like—"

"Eli and Jenna's mother, yes," Arnette said. "I had no idea she'd decided to start dating again. Her husband has been gone for years, but I never thought . . . well, it just goes to show you."

"Lucky thing," Carol mused, chin in hand, as she gazed over at the couple. "Reenters the dating pool and immediately snaps up the biggest fish."

Noah really couldn't envision his uncle as a prize catch, but he couldn't argue with the way all the women at his table were staring at him wistfully. Then a strange, unsettling tremor suddenly ran through them, and they went from mooning to squinting suspiciously. Noah looked over again to find another person standing with Gillian by his uncle's booth. This person was ridiculously tall and broad shouldered, with dark hair, dressed impeccably in khaki shorts and a light polo shirt. Like a catalog model. So that was Sebastian.

Noah turned back to the ladies. They were all still eyeing the scene suspiciously.

"What?"

Carol snapped out of it first. "What, dear?"

"You all suddenly look . . . weird."

"That one there," Arnette said in a low voice, indicating Sebastian. "I don't know about that one."

"You know him?"

"No," Judy said, turning sideways in her chair to give the man a full-on stink eye. "It's just a vibe."

Well, he was wearing boat shoes with no socks, but what else about Sebastian would make the ladies take an instant dislike to him, Noah had no idea. Not that he was complaining; it did make him feel a whole lot lighter all of a sudden. Or maybe it was the champagne on an empty stomach.

He shrugged, reminding himself Gillian's dating situation had nothing to do with him. "I don't know, he seems all right."

"There's 'all right,' and there's good enough for our Gillian," Carol pointed out. "I don't think he suits at all."

"Well, who would?" Noah said. "That's an awfully high bar."

He meant his question rhetorically, his comment sarcastically, but suddenly Arnette was studying him intently, one eyebrow raised. "Who indeed?"

Oh, hey, no.

"Look," he stammered, ready once again to get on top of this before the ladies started making plans for an outcome that neither he nor Gillian wanted, "that's completely out of the question, all right? All of you—forget about it. Right now. We're in a place there's no coming back from. Your girl is demanding, egotistical, stubborn, short-tempered, and have I mentioned judgmental? Ridiculously judgmental. So no. Thank you, but no. Never. Not in a million years."

Judy looked at Arnette. "Protesting too much."

"By half," she agreed.

Noah's mouth flapped as, completely frustrated and desperate to convince them, he intended to start over again, when his brunch companions turned their attention to Gillian and waved. Gillian waved back. Noah busied himself looking elsewhere, then was immediately disgusted with himself. Did it matter she had a date? Not in the least. So there was no reason not to stop by his uncle's table, no matter who was also there. Even if—especially if—it was Gillian. And her date. Whom he did not care about.

"Excuse me, ladies. I'll be right back."

Noah stood up, chugged the remainder of his drink, cleared his throat, and crossed the room.

"Noah!" Manny exclaimed with a smile. "Good to see you, son."

"Hi, Manny."

Noah was keenly aware Gillian was only inches away, although her date had gone off somewhere. He was grateful for that. He didn't want to have to do the iron-grip-handshake-look-the-guy-in-the-eye-to-see-who-blinks-first thing. Even though Noah wasn't a rival for Gillian's affections. Not at all.

Manny introduced Alyce, and Noah approved. She had kind eyes and a sweet smile—definitely more like her son, Eli, than her daughter, Jenna. He was glad his uncle had found someone after so many years alone.

"Well, don't just stand there like gateposts, the two of you—sit down," Manny urged.

Noah stiffened as Gillian said quickly, "Thanks, but I really need to get back to my date."

Then she was gone, floating across the room to a table for two by the windows. Noah watched Sebastian stand up, pull out her chair for her, and, while pushing it in, whisper something in her ear that made her laugh merrily.

Noah was staring, wasn't he? Yep, he was definitely staring. Tearing his eyes away from the romantic tableau, he said, "I think I will sit down for a minute," and hauled a free chair over to the open side of Manny and Alyce's table.

He risked another look at Gillian and Sebastian. They looked pretty cozy. Yeah, this was pointless. He was never the type of guy who'd waste away pining for a woman he couldn't have, mainly because he'd never *not* gotten a woman he'd wanted, but that was beside the point. The point *was* he wasn't about to start now. Because he didn't want Gillian.

Manny was talking about the upcoming regatta, and suddenly Noah couldn't think of a topic that interested him more. He leaned in, selected a muffin from the bread basket, and focused on his uncle.

CHAPTER 17

"Everything all right?"

Gillian started as Sebastian, back from the buffet table, set a plate of fruit down in the center of the table and resettled in his chair.

She brightened and said, "Of course! Why do you ask?"

"Oh, no reason. You just looked very, very serious for a minute."

"Well, we can't have *that*." She speared a crescent of cantaloupe, added it to her plate, and said, "Amuse me."

"Did you know FedEx has an arrow hidden in its logo?"

"I did. And did you know the Amazon logo's arrow goes from A to Z and makes a smile?"

Sebastian's own smile looked a little strained.

"Maybe I should be asking you the same question," she said. "Is everything okay? Something wrong?"

"I don't know." His voice was light, but his handsome face was serious. "Care to tell me about the guy you were with over there?"

"First of all, I was not 'with' him," she said, stirring some cream into her coffee, "but if you must know, that was Noah."

"The neighbor you hate?"

"Yes. So trust me, you have nothing to worry about."

Sebastian shrugged and took a sip of juice—plain, no champagne, unlike Gillian's. "It's just . . . you keep looking over there."

"Wh—? I'm not!"

"Okay."

"Seriously, Sebastian, I'm not. If I've looked back at the booth, it's because I'm so shocked to see Alyce out on a date. She's been alone for a long time, and she never said anything to me. I'm not even sure she's told her kids."

Gillian definitely hadn't been looking back for another glimpse of Noah, tanned and charming in fresh jeans and an oxford shirt with the sleeves rolled up, his usually tousled hair tamed, his frequent stubble shaved.

She kind of preferred the stubble, if she were going to be honest with herself.

But no, she shouldn't be thinking of Noah's looks when she had Superman sitting across from her, looking a little put out.

"Hey," she said, determined to change the subject, "the weather's beautiful, and I've got the whole day off. After brunch, why don't we go back to Alex Bay and take your boat out?"

Sebastian hesitated, suddenly focusing all his attention on his food. "I'm sorry, Gillian, I can't."

"No? Why not?"

"It's . . . it's being repaired."

"Nothing serious, I hope."

"No, just some routine maintenance."

"What a shame. I was hoping to see it."

He didn't answer her, just gave her a polite smile as he forked a piece of his omelet.

Sebastian had certainly sounded proud of his boat, and his riverside cottage, when he'd talked about his summer home in

Alex Bay. He hadn't invited Gillian to see either the boat or the cottage yet, and Gillian vacillated between being grateful he was enough of a gentleman not to try to get her alone in his house or on his boat this early in the dating ritual and being a little miffed he hadn't tried.

Gillian turned her attention to her own plate. She didn't want to be the paranoid woman convinced her new man was hiding something, like maybe he didn't, in fact, have a cottage. Or a boat. Or he had another girlfriend. Or even—the classic fear—a wife. Like any twenty-first-century singleton, she'd done her due diligence, snooping on his social media as much as she could. Sebastian was a bit of a Luddite and didn't have many accounts, but what she did glean from them pretty much lined up with what he'd told her: He'd broken up with a girlfriend three months before, and he was based in Albany but of course traveled all over a fairly large territory for the pharmaceutical company. It all checked out, so she had to get over herself and let this dating thing roll out in its own time.

"I've got an idea," she said, waggling a forkful of pancake at him, "we should join the Willow Cove regatta if your boat is ready by then. It's in a couple of weeks. You'd love it—it's a lot of fun."

Sebastian wasn't looking at her. Instead, his eyes were trained on her fork that she still held in midair. A droplet of syrup slowly dripped off the piece of pancake toward her plate. His gaze followed it down. Gillian glanced down as well. A stack of three pancakes. Two slices of bacon. A small pile of home fries. The crescent of melon.

Then she looked at his plate. A large mound of fruit and a veggie egg-white omelet.

Gillian's stomach clenched. She knew what this looked like—a larger woman daring to eat carbs in public. Even worse, eating carbs while sitting opposite a gorgeous, physically fit date who was subsisting on protein, vegetables, and fruit.

She'd done this dance before, with her ex-husband. There was a reason Tucker was her ex. Lots of reasons, actually, but judging her eating habits wasn't the least of them. If Sebastian was anything like Tucker—anything like quite a few men she'd encountered, actually—she knew what was expected of her at this moment. That one glance communicated so much. After years of *You're actually gonna eat that?* and *How about a salad instead?*, she heard it loud and clear, even if Sebastian hadn't said anything.

A wave of nausea washed over her, and suddenly she didn't want any food at all.

Wait a minute. Hang on.

With effort, she took a deep breath. She had no reason to feel guilty about the meal in front of her. It was a bit indulgent, she admitted, but it wasn't like she ate pancakes and bacon every day. She wasn't a glutton and she wasn't an ascetic; she was just a normal human being who liked carbs. She also liked vegetables. Mainly, she was an intelligent woman with a medical degree who definitely did not need lessons in proper nutrition.

Gillian took another breath. Maybe Sebastian had just zoned out. Maybe he'd watched the syrup drip absently, not even knowing he was looking at it. Or maybe he had been worried it was going to land on her clothes instead of her plate. That look of his could have meant anything.

Or it could have meant exactly what she suspected.

Gillian knew she could do one of two things at this moment. If Sebastian was like Tucker, she could push away the pancakes and eat nothing but the melon, and he would smile, relax his shoulders, and they could continue their day. Or she could test her theory by continuing to eat whatever she damn well pleased. Even if it meant finding out Sebastian was not, in fact, Superman, or super anything, except super disappointing.

Gillian caught a glimpse of Inner Bette lounging at a nearby table. She looked Sebastian up and down slowly with a sharp, critical eye that wouldn't have been out of place on an eagle and growled, *Oh, fuck him, darling.*

Indeed, Bette.

Gillian fought down her nervous nausea and defiantly ate the forkful of pancake, watching Sebastian the entire time.

He . . . didn't see her eat it. Putting down his own fork and picking up his juice glass, he said, "Regatta, huh?" His eyes met hers just as she swallowed her food. "I'll see what I can do."

~

"You'd better tell me everything," Delia ordered Gillian.

"I'm most definitely not telling you everything, you freak."

Gillian was helping Delia package the jewelry pieces she had made after taking special orders during the craft fair. Delia, however, was more interested in what getting up close and personal with Superman was like. The only problem was Gillian didn't know how to explain what was going with this new man of hers. If she could even consider him hers.

"He's very much a gentleman," she hedged.

"Oh, I'm sorry," Delia said with a wicked wink.

"I don't know about this guy, Delia," she admitted, pulling another padded envelope out of a box and decorating it with a rubber stamp of Delia's new business logo. "He's great on paper, but . . . it's weird with him. There's something . . . I just can't put my finger on it . . . but something's not right."

Delia tucked a pendant into a box and wrapped the whole thing in bubble wrap. "Give him a chance."

Gillian wanted to, she really did. But the whole situation had her unsettled. Not that she thought Sebastian was a serial killer or anything—far from it. He really was polite, kind, courteous, and thoughtful. And very affectionate . . . but only when they were alone, locked away in her house. And only her house.

"Why do you think he's never invited me to his place?" Gillian mused.

"He doesn't want to make you uncomfortable?"

"We never spend any time in Alex Bay at all, and you know there's more to do there than here in Willow Cove."

"Bite your tongue. We're alive with activity."

Gillian laughed. "No disrespect to the WC, but you know what I mean."

"Gilly, stop looking for trouble. You sound like you're trying to torpedo this before it even gets rolling. Here." She handed Gillian a square of bubble wrap. "Therapy."

Gillian commenced to popping. "And you know . . . Sebastian never touches me when we're in public. No arm around my waist, nothing. No public displays of affection whatsoever. I even tried to hold his hand once, when we were out antiquing, and he pulled *his* hand away."

"Oh, that's not good." Delia grabbed her phone and started texting furiously.

"What are you . . . oh. No, Delia. That's not—"

"You never know."

Gillian heard the swoop noise of a text going out, and after a moment the incoming swoop sounded.

"What does Gray say?" Gillian asked.

"He says, 'How should I know?' He says he doesn't want to presume, since he's never met him. He can't go on just a few details. Says he'd only assess Sebastian if he sees him in person."

"Well, I highly doubt Sebastian's not interested in women. He's *very* physical. Just not in public."

"So maybe he's shy."

"What's he got to be shy about?"

"Gilly . . . are you really giving Sebastian a chance? A fair chance?"

Gillian sighed, seeking out the last of the intact bubbles to pop. She couldn't tell Delia everything. She just couldn't. Sebastian's conditional affection was only part of the story, and it was secondary to what really set off alarm bells for her—how he had glanced at her food at brunch. That never happened to Delia, and Gillian wasn't sure she'd be able to adequately explain why it was such a big deal.

All she said to her friend was, "I certainly don't want to go back to the dating apps, but it's not looking too good for ol' Sebastian right about now."

"I think you're being too hard on the guy. Don't hold him to some standard he doesn't even know about."

"Okay. I will do my level best to continue to find the good in Superman. The dating will continue until I figure this guy out. And I invited him to the regatta, so when he shows up in his fancy boat and sweeps me out onto the water, I will make every effort to maybe let myself fall in love with him. How's that?"

But Delia wasn't listening. She'd gotten another text, and her full attention was on her phone.

"Gray again?"

Delia glanced up, startled, and pointedly put her phone down. "He can wait."

Gillian didn't let on that she saw Delia immediately crane her neck to see what the next text message said when it popped up on her screen.

CHAPTER 18

Noah squinted into the distance across the glittering expanse of the St. Lawrence. It was a downright gorgeous day for the regatta, and the turnout was impressive. He had been a little confused when he'd first heard about it, because the only regatta he'd known about when he was a teenager was the Canadian one solely involving high-powered speedboat races. This regatta, based in Willow Cove, was a new tradition—only a few years old, but very popular. It was more sedate, more traditional, in that people joined in to show off their watercraft and participate in rowing and sailing races. And there were some speedboat races as well. Overall, the marina staff had explained to him, it was less about the races, more about showing up on the river and showing off your beloved craft.

And show up people did. Boats of all shapes and sizes and power sources peppered the water. Not far away, on a grassy verge under the trees, parallel with the finish-line buoys, sat the judges' stand and a table laden with trophies. Lively music blared through the speakers until it was time for race announcements.

After their races, the boats could dock at the marina, and it was only a short walk from there to the food trucks lined up in the narrow parking lot behind the judges' stand. The scents from the trucks were making Noah's mouth water, but he had a lot of supervising to do before he could take a break and investigate them.

He approached one of the workers mopping bird poop off one of the docks. "Hey," he ventured, "can I—"

"Oop, sorry, Noah," another worker called as he dodged him and hurried down the dock, his arms straining from the weight of an extra hose.

"No, my fault," he said, stepping back. "I'm in your way."

"'Scuse me, Noah," the mopper said, since he was getting perilously close to the boss's shoes.

Noah jumped back again, spun around to avoid two more marina workers, and gave up entirely. The last thing he wanted to do was slow down his staff while they were busy prepping for the people who would be coming ashore when their races were completed. So it was a blow to the ego that none of them seemed to require his help. So what? The fact that they didn't need him was a good sign. It meant they knew what they were doing and didn't need direction from him. Maybe he could take a few minutes for a short walk, stay out of their way, let them do their thing.

Noah made his way over to the thin strip of public park that ran alongside the river, enjoying the shade, following the tempting smells of all things fried, when he nearly physically mowed down the person he most—and least—wanted to run into.

"Maybe I need to change my outfit, if I'm that invisible."

Noah stumbled to a halt, speechless. How in the world could Gillian think she'd ever be invisible? A delicate, lighter-than-air shirt, this time over white cropped pants. No skyscraper sandals, as she sometimes wore. Proper grippy sneakers instead, coupled with a pale pink baseball cap and a canvas tote, made it clear she was on her way to board one of the boats. Which one, he had no idea. He had no idea about a lot of things when he was this close to her.

Noah stepped back. "You look nice. Joining the race?"

"I'm going to be a supportive passenger," she said, blushing a little.

And Noah's spirits drooped accordingly. "Alex Bay guy?"

"Yep."

It was a yacht, wasn't it? It had to be a yacht. Or some fast (and expensive) cigarette boat that seemed to hover over the water without touching it. From what he'd seen of Sebastian, Noah was pretty sure a guy like that didn't have a puttering, oil-spewing little dinghy.

Noah looked around pointedly. "Well, where's the boy now? Wait, don't tell me," he said before she could answer. "You're meeting him here."

"Well, it's not like it was more convenient to haul the boat out of the water, put it on a trailer, and drive to my house to pick me up on the way to the regatta."

Noah was losing his edge. Of course Sebastian would come to Willow Cove by boat.

"He's more than welcome to use one of the marina slips, of course. Let me get you one."

"I already have a slip reserved."

"Okay." Noah figured it was better to cut his losses; this conversation wasn't going to be friendly no matter what he tried. "Enjoy the regatta. Hope you win your race."

He watched Gillian stride away, head high, down the dock. Standing in the hot sun, she pulled out her phone, probably to text Yacht Boy that she was waiting. So Gillian would be gliding along in what would probably be an expensive, race-winning craft, breeze in her hair, pretty blouse fluttering against her gorgeous frame, while he toiled on the docks with his staff. Unless his staff kicked him out of the marina entirely, because they didn't need him and he would just be getting in the way.

Was it too early for a burrito?

∽

It was probably a bad idea, but when Noah sauntered back from the food trucks and he saw Gillian still standing alone, he made a detour. She turned around when she felt the dock sway under his weight.

"What's going on?" Noah ventured. He hoped he sounded nice and neutral.

Gillian hesitated, then said, "Sebastian seems to be running late."

"Have you heard from him?" he asked. "Maybe he's having trouble with his boat."

"I texted. No answer. He's probably on his way right now."

"Of course."

It really was hot out there. He stared at the sparkling drops of perspiration on the back of Gillian's neck, under her ponytail.

"Look," he said, "if you want to get out of the sun, come on into the office—"

"He'll be here."

"I'm sure he will. At least sit under the trees over there before you get sunburned."

"I'm wearing sunscreen."

Of course she was. But the heat had made her fair skin pink already. "I just don't want you fainting out here and falling into the water or anything. I'm wearing my good underwear, so I'm not about to jump in after you, you know."

That got a small smile out of her. "Heaven forbid."

Noah waited. She wouldn't even look at him. "All right, then. The offer stands. Come inside anytime."

She didn't answer. Noah retreated into the cavernous pole barn of the repair shop but watched her from the doorway. She never turned around.

∽

"Okay, come on."

Gillian jumped, startled, when Noah took her elbow and led her gently back onto shore. He had told himself to let her boil out there in the heat for the rest of the day if she was going to be so stubborn, but in the end he only held out for about twenty minutes before he marched back down the dock to retrieve her.

"But—"

"I know, I know. Yacht Boy is coming."

"Yacht Boy?"

"I assume he has a yacht. Am I right?"

"I . . . don't know."

"You haven't been on his boat yet? Have you seen it?" She shook her head. "*Pictures* of it?" When Gillian shook her head again, he blurted out, "What kind of a boater is he, if he doesn't even show off pictures of her?"

Gillian shrugged, silent. He could tell she was upset, and for a fleeting moment he wondered if she was embarrassed as well . . . and if his being witness to her embarrassment upset her more. Not like he was going to gloat that she may have gotten stood up. He wasn't that kind of guy. He couldn't possibly take pleasure in her unhappiness.

"Come on inside, into the air-conditioning. It's got to be a hundred degrees out here."

"Eighty-seven. Not so bad."

"You're delirious already."

Gillian didn't resist when he ushered her in the back door, through the repair shop, and into his office.

"Sit." He reached into the mini fridge behind his desk for a bottle of water. "Drink. No dehydrating on my watch."

Gillian didn't argue. She opened up the bottle and downed quite a bit of water. Even in the cool indoors, her skin was still flushed.

"You probably have things to do," she said as she recapped the bottle. "I should go."

"Well, if you haven't noticed, this place runs just fine without me. I sign invoices and paychecks, mostly."

"We both know that's not true."

"You'd be surprised. Have you heard from Yacht Boy yet?"

"Do you have to call him that?"

"You haven't, have you?"

"No. And it's not like him to be late."

"I'm sure he's fine."

Despite the pleasure it afforded, Noah pushed away thoughts of Sebastian flailing helplessly in the jaws of Georgie, New York State's version of the Loch Ness Monster. Granted, the beast was supposed to reside in Lake George, hours away, but in Noah's imagination it was able to travel from the lake to Willow Cove via a series of tunnels under the Adirondacks known only to plesiosaurs. Of course Georgie would be happy to surface in the St. Lawrence on regatta day, solely to snack on Yacht Boy.

Noah sighed. "Try him again."

He watched her text and apparently come up empty once more.

"Nothing?"

"You're enjoying this, aren't you?"

"You have no idea how little," he countered.

Gillian, surprised, stared at him for a moment, until her phone pinged and she jumped. Noah may have started slightly himself. Gillian scrambled to open the text, then her shoulders fell.

"News?" Noah ventured.

"He says he can't make it. That's all. No . . . no reason."

"Ah."

"Well, go on," she sighed. "You may gloat now."

"Wouldn't dream of it. I'm only sorry he isn't going to get to see you looking so nice in your boating finery."

"Are you making fun of me?" she snapped.

"No," Noah said, completely serious. Her crestfallen look was too much to take. He took a breath and slapped the desk with both hands. "Okay, that's it. Let's go."

He surged to his feet and pulled Gillian up as well.

"What are you doing?"

Noah prodded her out of the building. "You can't sit around pouting all day because that lowlife didn't show up. Where's your dignity, woman?" He marched her down a different dock from the one she'd been standing on to wait for Sebastian, all the way to the slip at the end.

"You've got nerve, West."

"Get in."

It was no yacht, that was for sure, but the marina-owned motorboat would have to do. Noah helped her down into the rocking boat, climbed in, handed her a life jacket, and cast off.

Gillian demanded, "Am I being kidnapped?" as Noah navigated the boat out into the open water.

"Shh. Concentrating." He wasn't kidding; there were so many vessels on the water for the regatta, it was like pulling out into heavy traffic on a highway.

"Noah, come on."

"There's no reason for you not to enjoy the day just because Yacht Boy has a hangover or whatever."

"He doesn't drink," she sniffed. "Where are you taking me?"

"Someplace you can get a different perspective."

That place was Manny's island. It was literally a different

perspective—from the shade of his uncle's yard, they could watch the regatta races and view the charming town of Willow Cove across the river.

When they docked at Manny's, the man in question was climbing into his own boat.

He greeted Noah with a brusque, "What're you doing here, boy?" To Gillian he was much more congenial. "Gillian Pritchard, to see you twice in as many weeks is an unexpected blessing."

Noah rolled his eyes at his uncle's cheesiness, but Gillian seemed to enjoy it.

"I thought we'd come hang out with you, watch the regatta," Noah said.

"I," Manny declared, "am meeting Alyce in town, so I don't have time to waste with your sorry ass. Not you, Gillian. I'd be happy to clear my social calendar to visit with you, but I have plans, and I wouldn't dream of making my woman wait."

Noah nodded at Gillian significantly, silently pointing out that even his gruff uncle knew how to treat a woman better than Sebastian did. She pointedly looked away.

Manny went on, "Stay here as long as you like. Got a nice breeze, and some beers are in the fridge. What more do you need? I, ah, probably won't be home at all tonight, so—"

"I *really* don't need to hear this," Noah groaned.

"What? It's a beautiful day, promises to be a beautiful evening. I'm a grown-up—"

"Debatable."

"—and I don't have to ask permission from you, boy." To Gillian, he said, "The nerve of this one. I changed his diapers, you know."

This sent Gillian into gales of delighted laughter, which warmed Noah's heart. It was nice to see her happy again, even if it was at his expense.

However, once Manny was gone, Gillian said, "Noah, we don't have to—"

"I get it. This is definitely a comedown. You were supposed to be out on a yacht with your new boyfriend—"

"I don't think a handful of dates makes him—"

"—winning trophies and everything, and now you're hanging out with the person you hate the most, at his uncle's old shack. I can take you back to the mainland, and you can salvage the rest of the day. I hear Eli's competing in the kayak race. You should cheer him on with your friends."

Gillian hesitated. "I think I'd like to stay here, if you don't mind."

Noah blinked, surprised, and nodded. He led her up toward the house, into the shade, brushed some grit off one of his uncle's lawn chairs, and held the back of it to keep it steady on the uneven ground while she sat down.

"Okay, well," Noah said, dropping into the chair beside hers, "since I've got you here, all isolated and helpless—"

"Rethinking my decision, West."

"What I mean is, I've been meaning to talk to you. I've been thinking, and, to be honest, fighting with you is exhausting."

"You're no walk in the park yourself, you know."

"I've heard. Anyway, I think we should hang up our swords, take a break—or even end the war entirely. I'm willing to be friends if you are. Okay?"

"Friends? That'd be pretty weird."

"Too much, huh? How about frenemies? We can argue all we want but not really mean it."

"That's not what frenemy means."

"I know. But it can be our definition. Nobody's stopping us."

"You annoy me."

"And you annoy me. But I'm tired of being angry at you. Aren't you tired of being angry at me?"

"I kind of enjoy it, actually. Keeps the blood pumping. Better than cardio."

Noah heaved a sigh. "Fine. Forget I said anything."

"No, no," Gillian protested. "You might be onto something, here. I think we can be civil to one another. You've . . . you've been very kind to me today. And . . . other days. The garden competition notwithstanding."

Noah flinched. She didn't know the half of it, and he couldn't even tell her.

"Still," she continued, "you're bound to lose anyway, with such a hideous installation, so you're no threat to me."

Noah decided to ignore her comment. The day of reckoning was coming, but not for a while. In the meantime, he truly *didn't* want to fight with Gillian anymore. It *was* exhausting. Not the way she might have thought he meant, though. He didn't want to just forego the open warfare but continue to hate her silently. He wanted a real truce. He wanted to make her laugh. He'd managed it once or twice, and it was the best feeling in the world, seeing her happy. He realized he wanted to spend time with this dazzling woman without sparring with her. For as long as he could, anyway, until she ended up hating him for good.

"So what do you think—possible? Frenemies?"

He stuck out his hand. Gillian looked at it, then looked him squarely in the eye. He held her gaze, forcing his features into what he hoped was a neutral, friendly expression.

Finally Gillian pursed her lips and, with a bit of lingering skepticism, shook his outstretched hand. "Still weird."

"I don't mind weird. You shouldn't either. Oh no . . . wait . . . I just thought of a potential problem with this plan."

"And what's that?"

"Will calling a truce make you crush on me? Are you suddenly dying to rip my clothes off right this minute? If you think we should roll around naked on the lawn, I'm game. I think those boats are far enough offshore. Nobody on them will be able to see us."

"Stop." Gillian laughed, taking her hand from his and smoothing her ponytail. "You're out of your mind."

"Good thing I'm cute, then."

"Nobody said that."

CHAPTER 19

"Tell me about when you used to visit Manny in the summer."

Gillian kept her eyes on the river, but she was keenly aware of Noah stretching his arms overhead, off to her right. She suppressed a shiver. Those muscles should come with a warning label.

"Not much to tell. I mean, when I was little, we'd just spend most of our time here, outside, in the yard, on the water. Sometimes we'd go to town for ice cream or a festival, or to Alex Bay for a drive-in movie, or when it was raining and we were driving our parents batty we'd go to Watertown, shopping at the mall or whatever."

"But you must have spent a lot of time in Willow Cove."

"Oh, sure." He cut his eyes her way, coupled with a wicked grin. "Why are you so interested?"

Gillian fidgeted. "I'm not."

"Okay."

"Who were your cousins, again?"

She had to keep him talking. She wasn't sure why, except it felt . . . safe. If she was listening to him talk about his family, she wouldn't have the time to ruminate on that thing he'd said, about her crushing on him. She reminded herself she was seeing *Sebastian*, today's dating fail notwithstanding. It disturbed her to realize she could so easily succumb to the siren song of Noah's pheromones, which seemed to thicken the air even worse than the summer humidity. Or maybe it was just her own perception, because he wasn't doing anything special—just sitting there, talking about his relatives, not making any attempt to make her fall for him. She redoubled her effort to focus on what Noah was saying, paying close attention as he detailed his family tree: his parents, Jamie and Iris, both still alive and still married, and good for them. One brother, Eric. Manny had never married, of course, and never had any children. Manny and Jamie were brothers and they had two sisters, and . . . and . . . around that time Gillian lost track of what he was saying. The only impression she was left with was he had what appeared to be approximately fifty cousins.

"Why don't you still have family vacations here?" she asked.

He shrugged and scratched the back of his head, that habitual gesture of his that she could have seen as annoying if it didn't show off his shoulders in such a wonderful way.

"Ah, you know," he answered, "people go their separate ways. All my cousins have their own lives . . . it's too hard to coordinate everybody's schedules."

"So it's just you and Manny for the summer, then?"

"Except he's spending all his time with Alyce."

"And where does that leave you? Who do you spend all your time with?"

"My garden."

"Liar. I've never seen so much neglect."

Still staring out at the river, Noah grinned broadly, his smile lighting up his whole face, and Gillian felt her stomach do a little flip.

"Seriously, have you taken a good look at it lately? Your garden is looking mighty sad. You'll want to spruce it up a bit before the competition."

"You should pay attention to your own garden."

"What are you talking about? My garden is fine."

"There's an unsightly pile of bricks in your driveway," he reminded her. "It's not exactly a good look. Unless you're going to insist it's a sculpture that's meant to be part of your garden design, and I'm not sure Louise is going to buy it."

"Why not? She's supposed to believe the travesty you constructed—excuse me, had constructed *for* you—is an actual garden."

"Touché."

"I'll get to the bricks," she grumbled. "I've got time."

"I hear Kennedy's free," Noah murmured.

"Shut up."

"This is a good truce."

Noah chuckled softly, and Gillian gave up trying to keep the smile off her own face.

After a few moments spent in peaceful silence, Noah asked, "Hungry?"

Gillian's first impulse was to say no, which horrified her. Had she been so affected by Sebastian's behavior at brunch that she was back to pretending she had no interest in food, even if she was developing a low-blood-sugar headache? Could she so easily fall back into those bad habits she'd worked so hard to eradicate after she removed Tucker from her life? Apparently so. Disgusted with herself and how impressionable she still was, she forced herself to be honest.

"I could eat."

Noah led her into Manny's house and rooted around in the refrigerator. Gillian forced herself not to stare at his ass. Failed.

She jumped when he said over his shoulder, "Yeahhh, not

looking good in here. Manny never was much of a cook, and it looks like he's only gotten worse. How far can baby gherkins and . . . I *think* that's cheese . . . take us?" He straightened up and checked the freezer. "Not even a frozen pizza," he muttered. Slamming the freezer door, he turned to face Gillian. "I'm sorry I got your hopes up."

"Don't worry about it."

"No, no, I feel responsible." Noah thought a moment, then said, "Interested in another boat trip?"

"Back across the river?"

"Nah, Willow Cove is going to be choked with people from the regatta. Let's shake things up, go a little farther than that."

"In the motorboat?"

Noah grinned. "We'll steal Manny's party barge. It could do with a bit more use."

Five minutes later they were heaving out into river traffic once again, the pontoon boat rolling on the waves as they made their way toward Alex Bay and a restaurant Noah promised would be worth the trip.

Gillian smiled to herself as the wind flipped her ponytail this way and that. Noah looked good at the helm of the bigger craft, despite it being large and clunky. It was definitely a step up from the boat they'd taken to get to Manny's. She was especially enjoying lounging on the cushioned bench seat. Who needed a yacht, anyway?

They pulled into one of the public docks and made their way through the crowds in the touristy area of town. Alex Bay had a very different vibe from Willow Cove, with far more summer people and day-trippers milling around more touristy gift shops, bars, and restaurants.

Noah led her down a cross street in a relatively quieter area to a restaurant half built from a house, with a glass-enclosed addition and tables on the wraparound porch.

"It's new. Very chic. I don't think it's been discovered yet," Noah said, ushering her inside.

"How do you know these things?"

"I make it my business." He winked as he held the door open for her, then came up close behind because she stopped abruptly in the foyer with nowhere to go. "Oh. Crap."

Apparently the new place had indeed been discovered, because it was crowded and noisy. But as Noah had said, it was indeed very chic. What Gillian could see of it, anyway.

"Imagine if this were the busy dinner hour," she said.

She had to almost shout to be heard over the din. Since it was between lunch and dinner, most of the activity seemed to be centered around the bar, but a lot of people were spilling out into the dining area. As Gillian wove her way through the crowd, she turned her head to make a comment to Noah about the modern decor, when she stumbled and nearly fell.

Noah caught her. "You okay?"

She wasn't sure how to answer that. Her insides had gone cold, and she wasn't sure where to focus. She did know she didn't want to get a glimpse of the bar area again. She looked up and into Noah's handsome face, now set with concern.

"What's wrong?" he asked, his eyes scanning her for illness or injury.

Almost against her will, Gillian's gaze drifted over to her right, and Noah looked that way as well. At first it was clear he couldn't tell what had upset her, but soon enough his expression cleared and he muttered, "Oh. I see."

There at the bar was Sebastian, nose burrowed in the highlighted blowout hairdo of a tiny young thing in an even tinier minidress.

"Come on," Noah muttered. He kept hold of her arm and put his other hand on her back, and Gillian appreciated the support.

Nodding to the hostess who was standing a few steps away, he said, "Table outside, please, if you can manage it."

The hostess led them through the restaurant toward a pair of wide-open French doors that led to the blessedly breezy and mostly empty deck.

Gillian's mind had gone blank when she'd first spotted Sebastian, but once she sat down at a table and had a moment to breathe, only one thought surfaced.

"I'm . . . really embarrassed you saw that."

"Saw what?" Noah scoffed, turning and tilting the table's umbrella so Gillian was completely in its shade. "The idiot at the bar with the wrong woman?"

She groaned. "I sure can pick 'em, can't I?"

"What's going on in there has nothing to do with you."

"Oh, I think it does."

"You know what I mean. If Sebastian is going to make that big of a mistake, it's all on him." Noah shrugged. "Hey, if you want to give him the benefit of the doubt, you can believe it's all a big misunderstanding." When Gillian laughed ruefully, he said, "No, really. There has to be a logical explanation. Wait, I've got it. She's his aromatherapist. His nose is buried in her hair because he doesn't feel well and the cure for his illness is in the fragrance of her shampoo."

"Her perfume too, apparently," Gillian managed to add in a hoarse voice, as from what she could see from where she sat, Sebastian had moved on from nuzzling the girl's temple to burying his face in her neck.

The girl giggled.

"She's quite the healer," Noah said.

"A selfless act, I'm sure." Gillian nodded. "She's a saint."

Then Gillian winced when Sebastian firmly locked lips with the girl, kissing her in a way he had never, ever come close to kissing Gillian, even in private. So much for Delia's theory that he was shy.

Noah leaned in front of her, intentionally blocking her view of the PDA. "Gillian, I'm so sorry. Look, let's go somewhere else."

She blinked, refocusing on the man in front of her. "What?"

"I shouldn't have picked this place. There are plenty of other ones. We can just—"

"Oh no, absolutely not."

"You shouldn't have to see this."

"You're right. But it's important I do, all the same."

Gillian meant to sound confident and cavalier about it all, but somewhere along the way she failed. To her utter humiliation, her voice broke, and she felt tears prick the corners of her eyes.

Noah put his hand over hers, as if to transfer some of his strength to her, and said firmly, "You definitely deserve better than Sebastian."

"I couldn't agree more. And yet he's what I got."

"Gillian, come on, now—"

"No, I blame myself. I got way too invested for no reason. I know better than that. But what's worse is I chose him, do you understand? I chose him, and I . . . I didn't even notice the pattern."

"Pattern? What pattern?"

Noah was giving her his full attention, which startled her and gratified her at the same time. It had been quite a long time since a man was so attentive—Sebastian didn't count, since he was attentive about all the wrong things—and it made her want to confess her darkest secrets to him. Which was kind of disturbing, considering their history. But she couldn't deny that Noah was obviously sincerely concerned about her, and that made her willing to trust him.

"Sebastian," she said slowly, "has turned out to be almost exactly like my ex-husband."

"Your ex-husband cheated on you?"

"Probably," she sighed. "I had my suspicions. But that's not what I'm talking about right now." The server arrived, and Gillian decided she needed to regroup before talking more. "You know what, let me take a minute. I'll explain in a bit, I promise. First I need a drink."

After they placed their order for drinks and food, Noah asked, "So what are you going to do about it?"

"Do about what? That unseemly display at the bar? Leave them to it. What else?"

"Okay, if that's the way you want to play it."

"I do."

"But as your *frenemy* . . ." he started with a grin.

"Oh, here we go—"

". . . I'd advise you to light him up."

For some reason this tickled Gillian, and she started laughing until she snorted. She froze, eyes wide. "Oh God," she said, mortified. "That was attractive."

"It was charming."

"Now I know you're lying."

When the server came back with their giant neon-colored fruity drinks, Noah lifted his glass, and she clinked it with hers.

Putting the glass down, Noah turned thoughtful. He was dead serious when he said, "Gillian, everything about you is magnificent. If Sebastian can't see it, that's his problem."

She felt a flush creep up her neck, suffusing her cheeks, and she looked away. "Big words from you, frenemy."

"Why? It's the truth. I'm not trying to embarrass you; I just want you to realize you're great and Sebastian is an idiot."

Gillian wasn't sure how to respond, so she didn't. Instead,

they sat in companionable silence, sipping their drinks, until their food arrived.

Then she ventured, "So, what I started to say, about how Sebastian is the same as my ex?"

Noah nodded, once again giving her his full attention.

Gillian poked at her food with her fork. "This here. This was a problem."

Noah frowned, confused. "Why? Is there something wrong with it?"

"All kinds of things."

"Want me to get the server?"

"No, not that kind of wrong. If I had ordered this in front of Tucker, my ex, he'd have pointed out I shouldn't be eating pasta. And tomato cream sauce, no less—how awful. And I definitely shouldn't put cheese on it. And was I really going to eat a piece of bread?"

"Oh."

"If I ordered anything other than a salad—and it had better not be a taco salad—I'd get a lecture. All under the guise of his being concerned for my health, of course."

Noah paled. "Really?"

"Really."

"But you don't . . . you're not . . . I mean . . . you . . . you're healthy."

"I'm very healthy, but Tucker didn't see it that way. Did I want to keep gaining? I *didn't* 'keep gaining,' but he didn't notice that. Did I want to get diabetes and heart disease? Where was my self control? Unless I got to the point where I was a size two, I just wasn't trying hard enough. I didn't *want* it enough. And apparently it was a reflection on him. Or something. Who even knows, really?"

"Gillian, there's absolutely nothing wrong with you. You're so strong you can lift heavier pails of compost than I can. You can outlast me digging and weeding and planting in the garden. You walk all the time. None of that makes sense."

"It does when your parameters for 'healthy' are to look like Sebastian's new friend over there."

"And Sebastian did the same thing to you?"

"Remember that day at brunch? He was watching what I ate. He didn't say anything, so he gets one more point than Tucker. Then again, he didn't have to say anything to communicate what he was thinking." Almost as an act of defiance, Gillian ate some of her food before continuing. "Then another time, after that, when we went antiquing, he openly admired my stamina. Can you believe it? Just shopping. I think he really thought I was going to sit on a bench, all out of breath, and say I couldn't walk another step. Not to mention a couple of nights ago when we went for a walk and I suggested getting some ice cream."

"Don't tell me that was a problem. It's *summer*."

"Exactly. I didn't say I wanted a gallon tub and a giant spoon. I just wanted to enjoy a soft serve because it's freakin' *summer*."

"And he said?"

"'How about an ice water instead?'"

"Ouch."

"And of course, out it came: 'I'm just concerned for your health.'"

"There's something I don't understand, though. If Sebastian had issues with, well, any facet of you, why did he go out with you?"

"Repeatedly," she said.

"Including today."

"Let's not include today. Anyway, it's been my experience that some men . . . you know, I'm not sure how to put this."

"Just say it."

"Some men . . . well, they used to be called 'chubby chasers.'"

"Eugh."

"I know, right?"

"What do we call them nowadays?"

"Assholes," she said without missing a beat. "I don't mean men who like larger women are assholes. The assholes are the men who are attracted to . . . a certain type of woman"—and here she gestured at her body like a game show spokesmodel showing off a new car—"but fight against what they like and pretend to prefer a woman with a more socially acceptable body type." Gillian gestured at Barstool Barbie. "Meanwhile, deep down they like women who look like me. If they're insecure and afraid of being judged themselves, they keep it a secret, and . . . oh," she breathed, realizing. "I am an idiot."

"What?"

Everything finally clicked into place. Sebastian *did* have a cottage in Alex Bay, just as he said. He *did* have a boat, and it could very well have been a yacht. The thing was, she'd never have found out, because there was no way Sebastian had ever intended to bring her back to Alex Bay, let her visit his house, let her see his boat, or—God forbid—introduce her to his friends, the crowd he was laughing with at the bar right now. He'd planned on keeping their relationship, such as it was, locked away in Willow Cove.

She was his dirty little secret.

Gillian shook her head. "I just became older and wiser, I guess."

"Don't beat yourself up. You're not the first woman to be suckered by a charming guy who looks like—"

"Superman."

"Ironic?"

"Now it is."

"And you won't be the last."

Gillian looked at Noah. Really looked at him. Past the good looks and the muscles and all the superficial nonsense to what she now knew of him. This guy she hated, whom she'd damned as egotistical, obstinate, rude, and obnoxious, had been nothing but kind to her all day. While charming and courteous Sebastian had done nothing but judge her, plus he obviously was ashamed of her, or he was ashamed of himself for liking her. Likely both. Wow, had she always been this bad a judge of character?

Noah snapped her out of her reverie by asking, "So what's next, boss? You going to light him up?"

Gillian considered. "You know, I don't think I am. Sebastian has his problems, but I'm choosing not to be one of them."

However, when she and Noah left the restaurant and passed Sebastian and his group of friends, she couldn't resist giving Sebastian a quick pinch on the ass. When he jumped, startled, she just winked at him and moved on.

“Corinne?” Noah nearly dropped the stack of tea towels he was about to stuff into a cardboard box as he answered his phone. “How, uh, how are you? Is anything wrong?”

“Why are you assuming something’s wrong?”

“Well, it’s just . . . you don’t normally call.”

There was a pause on the other end of the line. Noah tensed, worried his ex was irritated with him—her most common reaction to him during the last few months of their relationship and subsequent breakup—but instead she sounded contrite.

“Yeah. Sorry. Time sort of gets away from me. I’ve been busy.”

Another pause. Maybe she was waiting for Noah to ask what was keeping her busy and distracted, but he didn’t feel like it. He’d always been Corinne’s biggest supporter as she worked on getting her sculpture recognized in the art world—in his darker moments he wondered if she’d only hooked up with him because he’d had a gallery to show her work in—but that wasn’t his job anymore.

“How . . . how are you doing? The marina?”

Noah also didn't feel like going into all those details with her. Maybe he was afraid she'd judge him for not finding out about the financial issues before he leapt, or maybe he simply didn't feel like explaining the whole saga to her. Because she wasn't a part of his life anymore. He noted his reaction, filed it away as interesting, and gave her the simple answer.

"Yeah, fine. It's going fine. All coming back to me."

"Good. I'm glad."

"Corinne?" Noah prompted. "What's up?"

"You said you wanted to talk to Aidan."

He had said that. Repeatedly. Ever since she asked him to move out. He'd just never expected Corinne would make it happen. "Of course I do."

His mild irritation with his former girlfriend dissipated at the thought of finally getting to talk to her son. His de facto stepson, if everything had gone a little differently.

When Noah heard a rustling on the other end of the line and Corinne's muted voice encouraging Aidan to say hello, Noah exclaimed enthusiastically, "Hey, kiddo!"

"Noah?"

"Yeah, it's me, buddy! How are you? What's going on?"

Noah refrained from asking Aidan if the boy missed him—it would not have been cool on his part, even though he desperately wanted to know.

After a short pause, where Noah heard more encouraging words from Corinne, Aidan said, "I started karate."

"Karate? That's great—"

"I go with Ed. He's a green belt."

"Is he one of your new friends?"

"He's Mommy's new friend. She comes too and watches us."

Ah.

"Well, that's great. Proud of you, buddy, trying new things. Are you excited for T-ball too?"

"Uh-huh. I have to put on my gi now. That's my karate uniform. Ed's coming. Bye."

More rustling, and then Corinne was back on the line. "Sorry about that."

"No, no, I'm . . . glad he's doing well. Does he like . . ." *Ed?* ". . . karate?"

"Yeah, he's really into it. All that kicking and shouting."

Noah smiled as he imagined Aidan in a little white uniform, bellowing his lungs out. Next to Corinne's new boyfriend. Ah well.

"We really should get going," Corinne prompted, but it was gentle.

"Right. Right. Yeah, of course. Thanks for letting me talk to him."

"I'm sorry he wandered off. He really does miss you, you know."

"Tell him I miss him too."

After the call ended, Noah realized he'd kind of been hoping Aidan would ask him where he was and when he was coming home. But it was better this way. He didn't want Aidan to be sad, and now Noah knew he wasn't. Noah could still talk to him occasionally, and maybe Aidan could visit Willow Cove someday, and Noah could take him boating. But the little boy had moved on, and so had Corinne. And, really, so had Noah. There was no point in clinging to the past when there was no place for him there.

Noah sighed and looked around his house with its new, more minimalist look that he'd only managed to achieve after spending days and days packing up extraneous Retha miscellany. (Really, how many tea towels did one person need, anyway?) He'd enjoyed Marie Kondo-ing the shit out of the place to make it more his own, instead of feeling like he was a squatter in some strange woman's house. And the stuff that didn't spark joy in him? It was about to be history.

~

Noah pulled up to the thrift store in the main shopping district, hopped out of the truck, and rounded the back to fold down the gate, reminding himself to note how pleasant his surroundings were. This town was his home now. He was staying. Imagine that. He'd had his doubts a couple of months ago, but now . . . something had shifted. Besides getting acclimated to the weather and taming his allergies and letting Corinne and Aidan go. For the first time in a long time he felt a little glow of . . . hope. Which may or may not have been thanks to a certain blonde he suddenly felt . . . fond of. Almost more than fond of. Despite the fact that, after they'd spent the day of the regatta getting on better terms, and after she'd emotionally kicked Sebastian to the curb where he belonged, she'd declared she was getting back on the dating app horse.

That was fine. Noah could wait.

What he was waiting for was another matter. The specter of the garden competition still loomed. Gillian would find out what he'd been up to, and once he'd stolen her trophy, their tentative friendship and any possibility of anything more would end abruptly. But he'd cross that bridge when he came to it.

Right now he was enjoying chatting with her every now and again without arguing. He couldn't deny the little lift he felt whenever he saw her . . . like right now, in fact. Even though she was coming down the street beside a man he'd never seen before. Which meant it hadn't taken her very long to start talking to new guys online. Ignoring the completely irrational feeling of jealousy suffusing him, Noah turned around quickly and climbed into the bed of the truck to start unloading the boxes and furniture.

It wasn't like he could ignore the couple completely, however, as Gillian's date had a voice that carried a good distance. "You don't really *fill* the prescriptions, though, do you?" he was asking.

Noah caught only a few words of Gillian's reply, but it amounted to a reassurance that she, as a pharmacist, did indeed do just that.

"You mean you do stuff *for* the pharmacist, right? I mean, he doesn't really let you do prescriptions all by yourself."

He could practically feel Gillian bristle from several yards away. Or maybe it was Noah getting riled up. Was this guy for real? He allowed himself a quick peek over his shoulder. A short, paunchy man sporting questionable facial hair and wearing a baseball cap, cargo shorts, and three-quarter-length crew socks, with highly suspect manners and a severe lack of awareness as he challenged Gillian's professional credentials? Please.

The restraint Gillian was exerting revealed itself in her clipped tone. Her voice was strained when she answered, "I *am* the pharmacist. There is no 'he.'"

"Come on," her date scoffed.

"Come on" indeed. Noah was very much wishing this guy would come on, just a little bit closer, so he could drop a heavy seventies-era brass table lamp on his noggin. He was more than ready, but Gillian stopped walking, forcing her date to stop as well. Noah cast a furtive glance her way: feet planted shoulder-width apart, fists on her hips, fully facing her date. Noah had seen this power stance of hers before and knew the weenie was about to get a beatdown. He snickered a little as he refocused on the piles of stuff in his truck.

"Quint, do we have a problem here? Are you implying I'm incapable . . ."

Gillian drifted off. Now Noah was dying to look over again

to see what she was up to. Did she get tired of using her words and just squashed this Quint guy like a bug? Noah certainly would have. Did she walk away instead, realizing he wasn't worth the effort? Noah tried to resist peeking. Failed. He straightened up, hoisting an artificial ficus tree in his arms, and found himself staring right into her eyes. She looked away quickly. Was she . . . embarrassed? Couldn't be. This was Gillian Pritchard, after all.

"Let's just go," she muttered.

"Back to your place?"

Gillian's restraint finally deserted her. "Absolutely not! We met half an hour ago!"

"Yeah, but I figured . . . you know."

"No, I *don't* know, *Quint*. Why don't you enlighten me?"

"Well," he said, "not every guy would be, you know, interested."

"Oh *really*."

It definitely wasn't a question. It was more of a dare for him to continue. Noah winced as Quint took the dare.

"You should be grateful. You're lucky you matched with me. A woman like you isn't, you know, many guys' taste, but I'd be willing to—"

"How *dare*—"

"Gillian Pritchard!" Noah bellowed, dropping the ficus onto the sidewalk.

Before it even registered in his cranium what his body was doing, he leapt out of the truck bed and jogged over. He wondered if Gillian would let him touch her, even in a friendly way, especially when her defenses were in the red zone because of Quint. He decided to risk it. He could take a punch.

Dropping an arm over her shoulders and daring to kiss her on the cheek, he said, with as much enthusiasm in his voice as he could muster, "I haven't seen you in days. Tell me you're free Friday night. I still owe you drinks and that expensive dinner I promised you."

Gillian's eyes were wide and her mouth fell open a bit, but she didn't answer. Good grief, he'd rendered her speechless. He squeezed her shoulder with his left hand and stuck out his right toward her date.

"Hi. Noah West. Good to meet you."

Quint didn't shake his hand, oblivious to the fact that he should have been grateful it wasn't in the shape of a fist. To Gillian, he said, "Are . . . are you dating this . . . ?"

"Oh hey, no jealousy, dude, though I totally get it. You've gotta know Gillian's a free agent. She's got men lined up around the block for a chance to take her out. I'm lucky she even gives me the time of day. A woman like her shouldn't have to be exclusive."

Quint squinted at her. "Just how many men *are* you seeing right now?"

"Oh, Noah's exaggerating," Gillian said, putting her arm around Noah's waist.

He barely had time to enjoy her soft warmth pressed up against his side before she pinched him—hard—through his T-shirt. He smiled tightly to keep from crying out but emitted a little squeak he was sure Gillian heard. She pinched him again.

"I never said I was interested in exclusivity, though, Quint," Gillian continued. "If you've got a problem with that, well, I'm afraid it's just not going to work out. Why don't we part ways right now, so we don't waste each other's time?" When Quint hesitated, confused, Gillian waggled her fingers to move him along. "Buh-bye, now."

Soon enough, Quint went, with only one or two disbelieving backward glances. Noah made sure his arm stayed around Gillian until the other man turned a corner and was gone for good. Before he could remove his arm, Gillian gave him a mighty shove.

"And what the hell was that all about?"

"I was helping you."

"I don't need any help, thank you very much."

"Really? Because that douche didn't look like he was ready to take no for an answer."

"Noah, I can take care of myself."

"Don't you talk to these guys online first? I mean, couldn't you tell—?"

"Hold on. Are you blaming me?"

"No, no—"

"You'd better not be."

He held up his hands in surrender. "Sorry. I didn't mean it that way."

"Look," she sighed, "everyone's on their best behavior in chats and texts and emails. The ugly truth comes out when you meet them in person. Like our charming man Quint, there."

"Can I ask you something?" Noah blurted out.

"What?"

"Is . . . is this online stuff worth it, if that's the best you can do?"

"The best I can do? *What?*"

"I mean, Quint is even a comedown from Sebastian, and that's saying something."

She started to retort but stopped and took a steadying breath. Instead of whatever she was going to blast him with, she said, "I'll find someone worthy of my time. Sooner or later."

Noah studied her before turning away. "I'm sure you will," he tossed over his shoulder.

"Are you *patronizing* me?"

Gillian's voice was still close. She was following him. Noah fought back a smile at that.

"I'm just going back to my truck. If you'll excuse me. I'm terribly busy."

Gillian took in the piles of boxes. "Leaving? Don't forget to write."

"Very funny. I'm finally cleaning out some of Retha's stuff."

Gillian watched him unload the last of the items from the truck, and Noah fought off the urge to flex. "There are a lot of nice things here," she said.

"Oh, believe, me, the neighbors pointed that out, tried to convince me to keep all of it. If you want something, speak now. A silk ficus, maybe?"

"You're offering me a fake plant? *Me?*"

"There's always a first time."

"Not on my property, there isn't." Then she pulled something out of a wicker laundry basket and looked at Noah. "You're getting rid of the gnome?" She actually sounded hurt.

"You didn't want it. You made yourself perfectly clear."

"Well, yeah, but . . ." She trailed off, staring at the figurine.

Noah prompted, "But what?"

"Nothing. It's just . . . it's brand-new. You could return it to the garden center."

"Lost the receipt."

"Or, you know, keep it. Put it in *your* garden."

"You mean leave it hanging upside down from the pergola in effigy?"

"I don't know what you're talking about."

Openly grinning now, he hoisted a couple of boxes in his arms and headed for the thrift store. Gillian, still holding the gnome, got there first and opened the door for him.

"Wait a minute," she said as he passed her in the doorway. "The proprietor can be a really tough nut. If you don't want to end up having to take a bunch of rejected stuff home, you'd better let me help you."

"What? Why? What can you—"

But Gillian didn't let him finish; instead, she strode up to the donations counter and slapped the bell with her palm. "Dennis!" she called loudly.

There was nobody behind the counter; Noah saw that quite clearly. But in the fraction of a second it took him to blink once, a pasty man appeared in the exact spot that was empty only a nanosecond before. Noah jumped. Gillian didn't.

"What do you want?" the man—Dennis, apparently—asked Gillian with a bit of a wheeze. "Or are you just here to visit me?"

Dennis put on what he must have thought was a charming smile, but which really came off as a creepy leer. Noah shuddered. Gillian was unfazed.

"This is my . . . uh . . ."

For the infinitesimal amount of time Gillian hesitated, Noah wondered what she was going to call him.

"This is Noah," she said simply. "He's new in town. He bought Retha's house, and he's donating some of the stuff she left behind. Just accept it, all right? Don't keep him here all day while you hem and haw over an old edition of a *Reader's Digest* condensed book or each and every crocheted pot holder."

Dennis was ready to argue, it seemed. "I need to look at all the items. I can't trust this guy not to hide half a ham sandwich at the bottom of a box. I'll get roaches."

Noah spoke up. "I swear there are no ham sandwiches—"

Noah didn't seem to exist, however, because Dennis never spared him a glance. He continued to direct his comments only to Gillian, cutting Noah off. "I can't simply accept these items sight unseen. I have standards."

"It all belonged to Retha, Den'," Gillian repeated. "You know it's good. You also know it's clean." As Dennis ruminated on this, Gillian whispered to Noah, "He's about to give in. Quick, go get the rest of the stuff before he reconsiders."

"I thought thrift stores were *grateful* to get donations," Noah whispered back, close to her hair, which smelled amazing. Wait. No. Smelling her hair was too creepy.

"Most thrift stores aren't run by Dennis. So move it before he bans you for life."

Noah reluctantly tore himself away from the warmth of Gillian's body and her delicate scent and fetched the rest of the donations, not stopping till the truck and sidewalk were clear and everything was heaped on or in front of the counter.

While he brought in the last load, Dennis busied himself scrutinizing a lace curtain as though it were a classical painting he suspected was a forgery.

"Why is he donating all this?" Dennis asked Gillian, still ignoring Noah.

"Why are you donating all this?" Gillian asked.

Noah rolled his eyes, leaned closer to her again, and whispered, "Let's just say lace isn't exactly my thing."

Entirely unbidden, he found himself thinking about lace of a different kind. Perhaps worn by Gillian. That would be another matter entirely.

Noah took a step back and cleared his throat. "Don't need it. Got my own stuff," he said, grateful the hoarseness of his voice would come across as gruff.

"What about that?" Dennis pointed at the gnome Gillian was still holding.

She looked down at it as though surprised it was still in her arms. She stammered for a second before replying, "Not for donation. I'm keeping it."

"Oh no," Noah groaned. "Where's it going to turn up next? Headfirst down my chimney? In pieces on my front porch?

"I said I'm keeping him," Gillian said. "I like him."

And that made this odd experience worthwhile. "How about this, Dennis?" Noah ventured. "Take what you want, throw the rest out. I don't want any of it."

Dennis addressed Gillian. "I'll take all of it," he said, although he made it sound like a hardship. "But on two conditions. I get the gnome. And a date."

"With me?" Noah asked.

That finally got Dennis to look at him. It wasn't a pleasant look.

∽

"You could have said yes and then canceled later," Noah grumbled, swinging his truck wide around a corner, too irritated to take more care navigating through the town.

"What, sell myself for your convenience?" Gillian scoffed from the passenger seat as she cradled the gnome in her lap.

"I didn't say *sell.* What do you take me for?"

"That's what it would have amounted to. And to *Dennis.* You hate me that much?"

I don't hate you at all.

Noah was grateful he managed to keep that thought to himself and not blurt it out. After all, Gillian had already made him do stranger things than voice his feelings.

"What am I supposed to do with all this crap now?"

"There's always the town yard sale in September."

"A *yard sale*?"

"Well, you don't have to make it sound so repulsive. It's a big deal around here. Very respectable, good for the community, popular activity. And a great way to meet your neighbors."

"I've met enough neighbors, thanks."

Noah backed the truck into his driveway, keenly aware that the arm he'd stretched across the back of Gillian's seat as he looked over his shoulder was perilously close to her. If things were different, he could twine his fingers in her hair. But they weren't.

"Help me unload?"

Gillian laughed outright, flinging open the cab door. "I'll see you around."

She jostled the gnome at him to pretend it was waving, then headed for her own house without a backward glance. Noah wondered if she'd finally place the gnome in her garden, but he knew better by now. Of course she'd never let a tacky gnome sully her carefully tended, detailed design. He looked from Gillian's yard to the expensive layout he and Kennedy had cooked up. A study in opposites. His was professionally executed, with bed borders that practically looked laser cut and a smattering of plants—no flowers. He had no idea what the plants were. Couldn't name a one. He just knew they were chosen for their own sharp lines and austere, dramatic profiles. *Ugly . . . cold . . . unfeeling,* Gillian had said of his garden, and she was right. Meanwhile, Gillian's flower beds were as luxurious, rich, and abundant as the gardener herself—a riot of color and form, yet all of the potential chaos under strict control. Most important, it was beautiful. Truly beautiful. *Where's the heart?* she'd asked. Well, there it was. Right there. In her yard. One that definitely was primed to win all the awards.

Gillian should get the trophy, he knew. Not just because she had the best garden, but because she was a good person, someone who definitely didn't deserve to lose a competition that meant so much to her solely because of some underhanded plot Louise had cooked up. With him.

Noah knew Louise would never let him out of their deal. But he wouldn't be able to sleep at night if he took first place over Gillian. He couldn't do that to her. Something had to give.

CHAPTER 21

"Hey, whoa!" Gillian cried.

She stopped her careful pruning and ran over to Noah's yard. He had marched out of his house, yanked what looked like a brand-new sledgehammer out of the bed of his truck, and stomped into the middle of his new garden. Now the madman was swinging the tool in a wide arc like a golf club. At her shout, he stopped the momentum of the swing, stumbling a little.

"What are you doing?" she exclaimed as she reached him.

"Taking care of my garden."

"Uh, gardeners usually use things like this." Gillian waved her pruning shears.

"You do it your way, I'll do it mine." And he hoisted the sledgehammer again.

"Hold on!" she shouted, and he lowered the tool once more.

"You know, you're really cramping my style, here," Noah said, scrubbing his scalp with his free hand.

Gillian came a little closer and took a good, long look at him. Which was a pretty painless thing to do, she had to admit. Today's T-shirt was a light gray heathered one with a faded business name and logo on it, evidently from someplace in California, and it was just as tight-fitting as his others. Gillian realized she'd be perfectly content to watch a steady parade of Noah's T-shirts every day until he ran out. Then he could lose them altogether. That wouldn't be a terrible thing.

"If your style is Wreck-It Ralph, then I've got to wonder why you've chosen gardening as your artistic medium."

"I didn't choose the gardening life. The gardening life chose me."

"Looks like you're trying to end it, though."

"That's the idea," he said, his voice terse, and he started to swing again, aiming for one of the concrete planters flanking his new poured walkway.

"You're not . . ." she said, loudly enough to startle him out of his renewed assault, "you're not going to win a trophy with a pile of rubble."

To Gillian's relief, Noah settled the head of the sledgehammer on the walkway and leaned on it like a cane. She felt better when he wasn't swinging away.

"Why not, though? Couldn't be any uglier than what I've got right now."

Oh. He'd taken her words to heart. And now she felt bad.

"Look, I'm . . . I'm sorry . . ."

"No, don't be," he said quickly. "You were right. This"—he swept his arm in an arc to encompass everything in his yard—"is not what the competition is about. You don't have to talk to Louise. I accept that this breaks the rules, so *I'm* breaking *it*."

"You're not competing?"

Gillian felt an irrational lump of disappointment in her gut. In some twisted way, she'd sort of been looking forward to going head-to-head with Noah. Mostly because she knew she'd win, and then she'd be able to gloat about it—and she would—but it was also . . . something else. The competition bound them together, in a way. Silly, she knew, but she liked the connection it gave them.

"Oh, I'm stuck. Can't get out of it. But I can affect the outcome."

"Okay, I have no idea what you're talking about right now." Gillian dared to reach out and put her hand on his bicep—*holy hell, talk about concrete*—to keep him from renewing his assault on his unsuspecting garden. "So maybe you could fill me in?"

Noah studied her, his hazel eyes losing their fire, and he took a breath. "Sure. Care to sit?"

He gestured at a concrete bench, which looked like the most uncomfortable thing imaginable. Instead she gently eased the sledgehammer out of his grip and said, "Come on. I'll get you some lemonade."

Once they were seated at the tiny, white wrought-iron table at the back of her yard, lemonade and a plate of shortbread cookies in front of them, Gillian waved to him to start whenever he was ready. Noah heaved a sigh, and Gillian got the feeling he was assessing what, exactly, to tell her, and how much.

When he did speak, his first words startled her. "Why does Louise March hate you?"

"Wh . . . *Louise*?"

"Yeah. She really doesn't like you, and she's not afraid to show it."

"Well, I don't like her either. Nobody likes Louise."

"I can see that."

"Do you?" she ventured.

"Do I what? Like Louise? Not at all."

"Noah, what's this all abou—"

"What did you do to her?"

"Why do you assume I did anything to her?"

"Hatred like this doesn't come out of nowhere. Did you . . . I don't know . . . beat her in the garden competition one year?"

"No, she's never competed. How she named herself chair of the gardening club and the competition's head judge remains a mystery for the ages, but there you are."

"Did her husband hit on you or something?"

"Noah!"

He shrugged, taking a cookie off the plate. "Then explain it to me."

Gillian couldn't believe she was going to share this information with someone she barely knew, especially if the someone was Noah West, of all people. But there he was, sitting across from her, his knee almost touching hers under the little table, waiting. So she told him.

"I got boobs."

Noah nearly choked on a bite of shortbread. "What?"

Gillian sighed. "I grew boobs, and she didn't approve."

For a moment, Noah looked dumbfounded. Then he started snickering. "Well, what did she want you to do with them? Store them in your bedroom closet and only take them out for special occasions? More important, how is that any of her business?"

She wasn't sure how to explain this. She never had been successful before—not to people of average size, anyway, and most definitely not to men of *any* size. But hey, she was feeling adventurous today. Maybe it was the way Noah was looking at her, with a mix of fascination for her plight and anger at her tormentor. Gillian wondered what had transpired between him and Louise to make him detest her as much as she did. Because it looked like there was no love lost between her new neighbor and her old nemesis, the one she'd never asked for.

Gillian said carefully, "Some special people like Louise feel it's their God-given right to express their opinion about a young woman's body, especially if it's a negative one. No, it wasn't her business, and it's not anybody else's either . . ."

Oh God, there was a catch in her voice. This was even harder to talk about than explaining Sebastian to Noah. Was it because of the memory of the way Louise treated her when she was young and impressionable, new to town and unaware of the woman's penchant for trying to boss everyone around, even a fifteen-year-old? Or was it because of what she'd gone through yesterday with Quint? Gillian had sworn to herself she was unaffected by Quint's comments because she'd heard them a thousand times before and knew they were unfounded, but maybe they had gotten to her. Maybe on some level they always would. Regardless, she couldn't admit that to Noah, so she stuck with the Louise narrative.

"Go on." Noah's voice was soft. Not softly threatening in a sexy way, like it had been when she'd confronted him about his rule violation. That sound had unsettled her in an instant and made certain parts of her body hum in response. No, now he sounded caring and supportive. And this unsettled her in a completely different way.

"Louise," she continued, "has strong opinions about a lot of things—and people—even if she has no right to."

"I've noticed."

"So she thought that I, being a . . . *certain size,* should try to . . . minimize those renegade breasts. Minimize everything about myself, in fact." Gillian was gratified to see Noah gape in shock. Yeah, she'd felt the same way the first time Louise March had approached her and tried to tell her how to dress, how to walk, how to talk. *Cover up,* she'd urged. *Speak softly. Demurely. Don't call attention to yourself.* "Because apparently if a young woman is . . . you know . . . the 'wrong' kind of size or shape, she should hide herself in shame. According to Louise. Who informed me the rest of the world felt the same way. I used to work in the summer rec program. The proto–mean girls at camp, who were around eleven years old, used to call me Miss Piggy—how original—and Louise let them. Once I even caught Louise laughing when they said it."

"What happened? I really, *really* hope you told them to go fuck themselves."

"Of course not. They were eleven. I did melt all their plastic boondoggle lanyards in the bonfire, though. They never did find out it was me. As for Louise . . . I was only fifteen, and I'd been taught to respect my elders."

"You didn't do what she said, did you? Become less?"

"Of course not!" She smiled as Noah let out a relieved breath. He seemed invested in this. "If you haven't noticed, I'm a bit of a contrarian."

"No," he said sarcastically.

She nodded earnestly, pretending he was sincere. "It's true. So I went the other way. I became . . . more. Of everything. Just to spite her. And she *hated* it. Talked about me behind my back, tutted at me to my face, you name it. She's hated me ever since."

Noah, agitated again, but this time in sympathy for her, growled low in his throat and rubbed his hand over his mouth. "Well, I'll say it if you didn't—fuck her."

Gillian froze, astonished. He didn't say *Good for you.* That's what everyone always said when she talked about instances when she stood up to people, when she spoke up in defense of her size. But Noah didn't say those patronizing words. Didn't even think of saying it. She could have kissed him for that alone. And the thought made the heat rise in her cheeks. She desperately hoped it wasn't enough for Noah to notice, but apparently he did, because he was staring again.

"I mean," she stammered, trying to recover, "do you think I lost the garden competition four years in a row because my entry wasn't good enough?" She gestured around them, and Noah shook his head, amazed. "That was just Louise deciding I don't deserve nice things because of the way I look. I suppose I should thank her, really. The way she's been treating me all these years helped make me . . . me." She waited. Noah said nothing, just continued to gaze at her. "So," she rushed on, "why did you want to know? What did the harpy say about me this time?"

"Well, for one thing, she doesn't approve of your gardening style."

Gillian rolled her eyes. "Tell me something I don't know."

"And . . . then . . ."

Noah stopped and shook his head. She watched his face become reddish under his tan, and he looked down at his hands, which were now clenched between his knees. His sudden change in demeanor startled her.

"Noah?" she prompted in a hushed tone. "What is it?"

"I . . . I don't know how to say this. I thought I could . . . but . . ."

"Okay, you're scaring me now. Just tell me."

"Louise . . . basically, she . . . she encouraged me to enter the competition and promised if I did, she'd make sure I won, just so you didn't."

"She *what*?" Whatever Gillian had been expecting Noah to say, it wasn't that.

"I said no, if that's worth anything. But you know Louise."

"Wouldn't take no for an answer," Gillian supplied, and Noah nodded. "She certainly expects to get her own way all the time."

"But when I told her there was no way I was getting involved, she found a way to make sure I had to. Now I'm going to win, no matter what." Noah fidgeted, looking miserable. "That was why I said Louise approves of Kennedy's design. She doesn't care what it looks like, or who did it, as long as it's a 'worthy' entry. It shouldn't win, not over your hard work. I can't take the trophy from you."

"So don't."

"I have to. I'm sorry. I'm so sorry," he said, suddenly lurching to his feet. "You're going to hate me from now on, and I wouldn't blame you. There was a time I didn't care, but now I do. Now I wish you wouldn't hate me. I know that isn't possible; I just want you to know that if there was any way out of this, I'd take it. I like you, Gillian. I really do. You're a good person, and you don't deserve this. I hope you can forgive me someday, but I won't blame you if you don't. Being your friend for a while, though . . . it's been the best part of moving to Willow Cove. I'll miss it."

Gillian grabbed his forearm as he tried to extricate himself from the little grotto. He looked down at her hand as though it burned him. "Don't walk away, Noah, please. Nothing Louise engineers to hurt me is worth losing you as a friend. I like you too. And if she's using you to get to me, that's not your fault."

"But I agreed to it."

"You said you had to?"

Noah sighed. "Yeah, she's kind of got me by the balls on this one."

"Then explain it to me. Sit. Please."

He sat, and Gillian let out a small, relieved breath.

After a moment to regroup, Noah said, "Louise . . . she'll seize the marina for nonpayment of back taxes if I don't go along with being her ringer. You know, just your usual extortion."

"Wait. Wait." Gillian shook her head as if to get all this information to settle into a pattern that made sense. It didn't work. "*Extortion?* How . . . ? This is a rinky-dink small-town garden competition."

"Don't say that. It means a lot to you."

"Sometimes I wonder why."

"Because." Noah leaned forward, resting his elbows on his knees. "You put your heart and soul into it, that's why. And it shows." He looked at their surroundings. "This is incredible. Your garden . . . it's an art form. Unlike that ugly thing over there—"

"Noah—"

"No, you were right when you said it. It *is* ugly. It doesn't deserve to win any prizes, even if I had designed it and built it on my own. Which I didn't. It's nothing like yours. Your garden is perfect."

Tears pricked the corners of Gillian's eyes. Where had the curmudgeonly Noah West gone? If he kept this up, she wasn't sure how she was going to react. Crying or hugging or something just as humiliating would definitely play a part.

"The extortion," she muttered, feeling fury bubble up inside her. It was bad enough Louise had loomed like a specter over her life for more than fifteen years, but it was another thing altogether for Louise to use her power to harass an honest business owner solely to hurt Gillian. "It doesn't make sense. What's she going to do, drive you out of business? This town needs the marina."

"The town could seize it for nonpayment of back taxes."

Gillian fidgeted, frustrated. She wished she had enough money to be able to write a personal check for the full amount of the taxes and slap it down on Louise's desk just to see the expression on her face. But although Noah hadn't talked specific amounts, she couldn't imagine she had enough to cover whatever he owed. Noah looked serious, concerned, even frightened, and that had to mean the debt was substantial.

"Okay, then," she said, now all business, "here's what you're going to do. You're going to stay in the competition and make sure Louise doesn't get her hands on the marina."

"Gillian—"

"Nope. That's nonnegotiable. It's the most important thing. There's only one problem, though. It's pretty obvious you violated the rule about the gardeners having to do everything themselves. Someone else might insist—"

"That Louise disqualify me."

"Right."

"But Louise is all-powerful."

Gillian took a breath. "Allegedly. I've heard rumors to the contrary. Some of her minions aren't happy with how she rules with an iron fist."

"There could be a coup in the garden club?" Noah whispered, eyes wide, a smile playing on his lips.

"Just rumors, mind. But if someone does manage to stage that coup before the competition . . ."

"I could lose."

"But she's still town treasurer."

"And she'll demand the money."

"That's why you stay in. But you're going to have to make the garden your own."

Noah sighed heavily and squinted up at her in a ridiculously handsome way. "I wouldn't even know where to start."

"You don't have to. I do. I'll help you."

"Who are you, and what have you done with Gillian Pritchard?"

The exaggerated look of bafflement on Noah's face made her laugh out loud. "I mean it. I don't want you to be the next target of Louise March's terrorist agenda against all that's good in Willow Cove. We fix up your garden, make sure it adheres to the rules, and let the chips fall where they may."

"Those chips you're talking about are going to fall to me, like she promised. I'll win the competition, and that won't be fair to you."

"Don't worry," she assured him with a smile, standing and brushing down her shorts. "I know deep in my heart your abomination of a garden isn't really better than mine, no matter whose mantel the trophy ends up on. The marina is more important. So let's get started. But no sledgehammering. Construction, not destruction."

Noah stood and gestured for her to go ahead of him, and she felt herself flush a little at his manners. She strode confidently over to his property, ready to elevate his stark, depressing design into something prizeworthy. Something that could beat hers. But when she studied Noah's austere, depressing layout, all creative thought left her. It was like the garden was a black hole that sucked away any uplifting, positive feelings at all, let alone any creative ideas.

Gillian held out her hand. "Gimme the sledgehammer."

"I thought you said—"

"Let's just say on second thought, I've realized a little selective destruction is necessary. We have to make this thing breathe. What did you and Kennedy do, buy *all* the sacks of concrete at the home improvement store?"

"Almost."

"It shows. Sledgehammer, please."

"Take your pills."

"What?" Noah stopped wrestling with a chunk of rubble to look up at her, puzzled.

"You're outdoors, the tree pollen is high, you're going to start sneezing. Listen to your pharmacist."

He rocked back on his heels and rested an elbow on one knee. "I'll have you know I have my allergies pretty much under control these days, thank you very much."

"You're welcome."

"Yeah, yeah," he muttered, ducking his head to hide a grin.

"You're going to tell me it was The Witch on Warsaw Street who really fixed you up, right?"

Noah paused. He could continue to needle her, or he could tell her the truth. He decided on the latter. "Never went," he said. "Some pharmacist helped me out, so I didn't need to resort to black-market herbs."

"They're not . . ." Gillian trailed off, prompting Noah to look up at her. She was standing a few yards away, broom in mid-sweep, her mouth slightly open, eyes alight. It was obvious she'd just had some sort of epiphany. "Car keys?"

"Right here."

Gillian dropped the broom. "Come on."

~

Gillian's sudden energy from her brainstorm rocketed them from the yard to the truck to the garden center in record time. Noah watched in fascination as she ricocheted from table to table and scooped up pot after pot of plants. Gillian excitedly rambled about how this was the perfect time to buy them—in the middle of the season when they were sold at a discount, but not so late there was nothing left. The garden center looked picked over to Noah, but Gillian plucked buckets of greenery with a practiced hand, plopping them on their pushcart until he could barely move it over the grass.

"Mm, some of these look mangy," she said, examining one half-wilted plant with a critical eye, yet placing it on the cart anyway. "I'm not sure they'd revive and fill out in time, but I have a few tricks up my sleeve. Let's get these, and then we'll go to another place I know."

Herb garden, Gillian had said on the way to their first stop. That was her brainstorm. Instead of pulling up everything in his garden beds—as sparse as the green stuff might be—they would add to what was already there, with the theme of herbs: medicinal and culinary. Noah had jokingly asked if they could sneak another kind of herb into the garden, and to his surprise Gillian had actually seriously considered the idea, until she came to her senses and said Louise would not be amused by the inclusion of some cannabis. Even if, Gillian had said, it had a lovely broad spread to its leaves, and the buds were actually quite pretty in their own way. They compromised by picking up some catnip instead.

Their second stop was a roadside greenhouse. Gillian had him zigzagging down some narrow roads deep in the countryside, away from the river and the tourists and the vacation spots. Here there was nothing but fields of high grasses, leafed-out trees arching over the road, and scattered houses at the ends of long driveways. She told him to stop at a weathered farmhouse under the shade of tall, old elms. When he pulled into the driveway she was out of his truck in an instant, hurrying up to the woman who came out of the house to greet them. Noah hung back, but Gillian beckoned him over.

Noah stood quietly as the women chatted about the plants Gillian was looking for. Common names as well as Latin nomenclature flew from their lips, and Noah lost the thread of the conversation. But he didn't stop looking. Gillian was alight, in her element, laughing and talking, the breeze teasing a lock of her blond hair into the corner of her mouth. She absently tugged it out again with a manicured nail, and Noah wondered not for the first time how she managed to always look so chic. Weren't gardeners supposed to wear stained overalls and scuffed boots and have black dirt under their fingernails? Gillian looked . . . well, beautiful. Always. Even when she was wrist-deep in a flower bed. Even when she was scowling at him (which was more often than he wanted, he was starting to realize), like when she'd glowered at him under the glare of the fluorescent lights in the pharmacy, furious at having to help him with his allergies. Yes, she was beautiful even when she was straight-up pissed off.

As if cued by the memory, Noah sneezed. Gillian raised one sculpted eyebrow at him. He sighed and retrieved a blister pack of allergy meds from his glove compartment, knocking back a dose with a swallow of warm water from a half-empty bottle sitting between the seats. Someday he was going to acknowledge Gillian was always right. Maybe even to her face.

He followed her and the proprietor into the greenhouse. It was a tight squeeze between the swayback, water-dampened plywood tables that ran along the sides and down the middle, so again he stayed a few steps back and let Gillian work her magic. She selected more pots, and still more. Noah had no idea where they were going to put all these plants, but Gillian seemed unfazed.

Always right. Especially about gardening. So he kept his mouth shut, pulled out some cash, and worked on trusting her.

∽

"I still don't know why we couldn't get the Dr. Seuss plants. They were herbs, right?" Noah asked, adding the plants they'd just bought to the ones already crowding the truck bed.

"The allium?"

"Is that what they're called? The purple poofballs."

"I never thought I'd hear Noah West utter the words 'purple poofballs.'"

"You know what I mean."

"Yes, I do. They're ornamental flowering onions. Unfortunately, they'd die back well before the competition, so you wouldn't have any 'purple poofballs' blooming. I could try to force some blooms, but I wouldn't risk it. Besides, we've got plenty of other plants to work with. But if you want poofballs next year, the bulbs have to be planted in the fall."

"This is exhausting."

"Not if you know what you're doing."

"And you do. Obviously." Noah hid a smile at the color rising in her cheeks. "Now we plant?"

"Of course not," she said airily, waving her hand. "We've still got one more stop to make."

"It wouldn't happen to involve lunch, would it?"

"Are you on the verge of fainting from hunger?"

"Not exactly."

"Good. Then let's go."

"You're cruel."

"Drive."

The next place Gillian directed him to was closer to home but still outside the town limits. His truck kicked up a cloud of dust as he pulled onto a rambling lot filled with piles of detritus.

"Why are we at a junkyard?"

Gillian pretended to be scandalized. "Never call Mick's place a junkyard!"

"But it *is* a junkyard."

"Au contraire. This is a highly specialized, environmentally conscious architectural salvage establishment—"

"Junkyard."

"No."

"Then can you explain the architectural significance of that tangle of rusted barbed wire over there with the 'Make an Offer' sign?"

"I . . . cannot."

Noah gave her a smug look as he parked the truck and was gratified to see Gillian smiling.

She told him they were looking for some ornaments to liven up his garden, preferably well-used items made of wood or metal that would add character but wouldn't clash too much with its current austere look. *Humanize the thing,* she said. Noah bridled at the implication he had a Frankenstein's monster on his hands, but he had already admitted he kind of did. So they were going to go for a junkyard chic look, apparently.

"Think rusted metal, weathered wood, faded paint, chipped enamel," Gillian said, leading him toward a barn where, she said, the "good stuff" was.

Noah stepped in front of her and walked backward, fingertips in his jeans pockets. "Junk, then."

"No!" She laughed. "God, how many times—"

"Gillian!"

A tall, grizzled man scuffed toward them across the yard, and Gillian beamed at him. "Mick, just the man I wanted to see. Noah, this is Mick, the owner. Mick, this is Noah West. He's entered the garden competition. He's going for a rustic theme, so we're going to look around for your rustiest items, okay? We'll leave the bale of barbed wire for some more deserving customer, though."

"Aw, I thought you were here to get my nephew's phone number."

Gillian grimaced but, obviously not interested in offending her friend, said lightly, "It's still a no, Mick. Sorry."

Mick's eyes slid over to Noah. "Guess you're already taken, then?" he asked her, then he nodded in noble defeat to Noah. "Treat her right, understand?"

Noah didn't know how to answer that and, surprisingly, neither did Gillian. After a pause that went on a bit too long, she laughed off Mick's comment—but didn't deny it, Noah noted—and grabbed his hand. "Let's go, *babe*."

She pulled him into the dim and dusty barn, leaving a dejected Mick behind, staring at his phone, likely texting his nephew the bad news.

Once they were well inside the barn, out of the brilliant sunshine, Noah looked down at their clasped hands, then at Gillian's face. She gave away nothing, just gazed into the distance as she waited for her eyes to adjust to the dim light so she could start hunting for garden accents. The last thing Noah cared about at the moment, though, was finding random vintage objects to stick in the dirt or whatever she had in mind.

Because she still hadn't let go of his hand.

Come to think of it, he hadn't let go of hers either.

It was going to get awkward in a minute. Or really, really good. He wasn't sure yet.

Just as he opened his mouth to speak—and wondered at the same time what exactly he was going to say—Gillian took a couple of steps forward and let her fingers slip from his. It was natural, it was casual, and it caused him a startling amount of disappointment. When he didn't move, Gillian looked back at him, smiled, and tilted her head toward the cavernous space of the barn, forcing him to look past her.

He felt his brain stutter and seize up. The entire space was filled with junk. *No, not junk,* he corrected himself as Gillian would have if he'd spoken it aloud. *Jonque.* The genteel cousin of junk. The weather-beaten, chipped, faded flotsam and jetsam of past eras. Tin, wood, glass, ceramic, enamel. Everything jumbled together with no real rhyme or reason: windows with and without glass in the panes, milk bottles, Ionic columns, doors, school desks, lamps, empty picture frames, church pews, woodstoves. Chandeliers hanging from rafters. Upended raw-wood pallets covered with doorknobs, door knockers, switch plates. Heat vent covers leaned against the walls in stacks. Tables piled on top of one another, four or five high. Old tools, old kitchenware, old stained glass windows, old leaded glass, old appliances, old paintings and prints, old toys. Harnesses, wagon wheels, wooden boat wheels. A full staircase winding its way to nowhere. He was pretty sure he caught a glimpse of an entire bowling alley's worth of lanes in the distance.

"What, uh, now what?"

"Now," Gillian said, eyes alight, "we hunt."

~

"How?" was all Noah could manage to grunt as he waded through the items in the bed of his truck. It was completely

jammed with all the plants they'd bought, as well as rusty tools, enamel basins, and the rest of the loot they'd gotten from ransacking Mick's place.

"What?"

Gillian reached up and helped ease an old single-blade hand plow from the truck bed. Not for the first time, Noah was impressed by how Gillian leaned in to demanding physical labor without hesitation, and how it contrasted with her refined appearance. She never worried about breaking a nail, and she never seemed to do so either.

"How are we going to put all this together to create a decent garden? And in my wrecked yard, no less? And how does it all . . ." He drifted off and helplessly waved his hand to encompass everything still in the truck or deposited on the driveway.

"Fit together?" she supplied.

"Yeah."

"Magic," she whispered conspiratorially, complete with that *look* again. The one that turned his knees to Jell-O.

Not that he was admitting to it. But when she fixed him with her singular wicked expression, complete with one cocked eyebrow and mischievous grin, his nerve endings did funny things.

"Well, come on!" she prompted, moving the plow away and reaching up for more stuff, and he realized he was probably staring like a dope.

Noah recovered and worked twice as quickly to unload the truck. When it was empty, he asked, "So we're done for the day?"

It was nearly evening, still hot as blazes, without a cloud in the sky despite the region's track record of frequently rainy weather, and he desperately needed a break.

"Are you kidding?" Gillian scoffed. "We've got to get planting."

"No," he countered, jumping down from the empty truck bed and taking a gallon pot of something that smelled good out of her arms. "I refuse. I'm exhausted, I'm starving, and I will not do one more garden-related thing. I may just eat this plant. Why do I want to eat this plant?"

Gillian laughed. "Herbs, remember? It's dill. It's probably making you think of potatoes or bread—"

"Please stop," he said, putting the pot down. "I'm begging you. Aren't you tired? Thirsty? Hungry?"

"I guess. A little."

"Okay, then."

"But—"

"But we still have work to do, and plenty of daylight to do it in, I know. So we work." Noah hesitated. "I mean, unless you've got—"

"A date? No, not tonight."

"But you're still meeting people on those dating apps."

"Mm, some." Gillian hoisted a couple of plants and carried them to the patio, settling the pots in the shade. Noah followed her lead and carried over more plants.

"Any second dates?" he asked.

"Not really."

She sounded rueful, and Noah wondered if he'd been viewing her adventures in online dating all wrong. He'd thought she was happily bouncing from one date to another, sharing a meal or drinks or coffee with a series of interesting men, and then she got to choose which one was going to be graced with the pleasure of her company for the foreseeable future. But after observing her with misogynist Quint, he was starting to think spending time with strangers, desperately trying to see if they had anything in common, was more of a chore than anything else.

He wondered if he should say something reassuring along the lines of *Well, you'll find someone good if you just keep at it,* which he really didn't want to say at all, when Gillian asked, "How about you?"

"Me?" he nearly squeaked.

"Yeah." She looked over at him with a smile while she unwound the garden hose hanging on the back wall of his house. "Have you met anybody here?"

Oh. That wasn't what he'd thought—or hoped—she was going to say. He regrouped and answered, "Not looking," which was the truth.

"One of those loners, huh?"

"Something like that," he grunted as he heaved more plants into the shade. They were running out of shade.

The faucet squealed when she turned it on. "Brought on by a recent breakup?"

Noah straightened and plopped his dirt-laden hands on his hips in what he hoped was a casual gesture. "How can you tell? Do I have some kind of mark on me only women can see?"

"I would lie and say yes just to freak you out, but you'd figure out the truth eventually," she said as she dragged the hose over to the plants.

"The neighborhood gossips told you, didn't they?"

"'Fraid so. Don't worry, though. I won't say anything."

"They'll manage to tell the whole town sooner or later, if they haven't already, so don't worry about it."

"I know. I'm sorry. It's what they do. Does it bother you, people knowing?"

Did it? He shrugged. Living in a small town meant his past was going to be common knowledge. There was no stopping that. And what difference did it make if his new friends—and random strangers—knew his romantic history, anyway? People broke up all the time.

"Did you love her?"

Gillian's question was soft, tentative. Still, he was startled that that was what she asked first. Not how it happened, not whether it was an ugly breakup.

"Corinne," he supplied. "Yeah, I did."

She nodded and directed a light spray of water over the plants they'd bought, a thoughtful expression on her face. "I'm sorry," she said again.

"It was time. For it to be over."

"Why?"

"Well," he said slowly, "sometimes love can be real, but . . . misplaced. I don't think she loved me as much as I thought she did. As much as I loved her." He swallowed the lump in his throat and continued, "Like an idiot, I kept trying to make things right, but Corinne . . . she was already gone, emotionally. Looking for someone better."

"Or maybe just someone different."

"I certainly couldn't give her what she wanted."

"And what was that?"

It occurred to Noah this was the first time he'd told anyone the emotional underpinnings of his breakup with Corinne. His guy friends mainly said something along the lines of "Ouch, that sucks" and "Have another beer." His new neighbors had tried to set him up with someone else as soon as they found out he was single. This was the first time he was truly talking about his relationship and its demise.

He looked at Gillian, who was waiting patiently, still misting the plants. Nurturing them, nurturing him. And he appreciated her for all that she was. "I don't think I ever figured it out. Maybe she didn't even know what she wanted. She was an artist—a sculptor—and I owned a gallery. I helped her out, exhibited her work, but my gallery was small. I didn't have the influence she needed."

"You're making your relationship sound transactional. What about what drew you together?"

"I can't even remember anymore. Besides basic physical attraction."

"But you got attached."

"I did. To her and her son."

"That complicates things."

"It's taken a while, not gonna lie, but I . . . I've moved on. I found out recently Aidan has as well, and it makes it easier—knowing he's not missing me as much as he had been. I mean, it's not easy to let him go, but I have to. Things change, and you've got to roll with it. There's no point hanging on to something that's just dragging you down." Noah took a deep breath. "I'm rambling. The bottom line is it's okay. I'm okay now. Really."

Gillian frowned, serious, a dubious look in her eyes. He certainly didn't want that. So he made a face and dug deep to locate his inner douche. "And, well, you know. Women, they get clingy, want to lock down all this"—and he gestured at his body. "So sometimes you gotta cut 'em loose before they get too attached."

His words had the exact effect he'd hoped for. Gillian turned the hose on him.

CHAPTER 23

This was absolutely bananas. Not the part about finding out her nemesis Noah West was actually a decent human being, although that was shocking in its own way. Not the part about realizing she was willing to help him create a decent garden. Naturally she'd jump at the chance to make something decent of the travesty he'd paid Kennedy to vomit up. And it wasn't even finding out that she and Noah now had a common enemy in Louise.

No, what shocked Gillian was that she'd actually enjoyed herself today. All day. With Noah. It was getting to be a habit, she realized. He could make her laugh, which he did often; he could actually brighten her day, like he did when he ran off Birdman; he could even protect her (not that she needed it) and take care of her, like he did when Sebastian stood her up.

Gillian was also shocked to realize she didn't want the day to end. And it didn't have to—not yet. She'd promised him food, and she was going to make good on her promise. So while he was changing into dry clothes, Gillian made herself useful by firing up his ridiculously large gas grill, which definitely hadn't been on the back patio when Retha lived there, and then hurried over to her house.

She dug around in her fridge to find something grillable, making a point of hiding behind the open door of the appliance so she didn't have to witness the massive amounts of eye rolling Inner Bette was displaying from the corner.

And she most definitely didn't run upstairs to her room to try to catch a glimpse of Noah changing. Because that would have been bad.

Pork chops, veggies, seasoning, a cast-iron skillet, a cutting board, and utensils, because she had no idea how his kitchen was stocked. Even though Carol, Arnette, and Judy had told her all about how Retha had left everything behind, Gillian couldn't imagine Retha not taking her precious pots and pans, and she had no idea if Noah had replaced them. Who knew what lurked in the hearts of men when it came to cookware—some were into it, and some were more inclined to melt everything down to create a car part or something. She realized she didn't know which type of man Noah was, and the thought made her pause. She didn't know this man. At all. Not really. But lately she'd been getting the feeling he really was a decent person. Better than decent. A really good guy.

Imagine that.

Hands shaking just a little bit from the discovery that she might, just *might*, actually like a real, live, available, *nice* man, Gillian carefully set the food and cookware on his patio table and then went back to her house for just one more thing, which she tucked onto one of the chairs. She started vigorously slicing up some zucchini to focus on something besides puzzling over her growing feelings for Noah. Her text alert chimed as she was getting alarmingly close to her knuckles with the knife. It was Carol.

Is that you at Noah's house, dear?

Gillian looked up and around, confused. Carol's house was

directly across from Noah's. How was she able to see Gillian on the back patio?

As Gillian started to reply, Carol texted again.

We're all so glad you're together. We've always said you'd make a beautiful couple.

Ah, the Greek chorus's collective opinion. They were probably all together right now, watching and waiting to see something develop between her and Noah. Wait. *If* something developed between her and Noah. *If.* Sheesh.

Gillian texted back, *I'm just helping Noah with his garden. He admitted Kennedy did him dirty, and we're fixing it.*

She was about to ask if they had purchased a drone that was flying over their properties, getting video of everything going on in their backyards, when she realized the women were probably all at Judy's house, where they could get a glimpse of at least part of Noah's backyard. If they were in the front corner bedroom on the second floor. Standing on a ladder. And using binoculars.

Gillian wouldn't put it past them.

Sure enough, the next text from Carol was *That doesn't look like gardening. That looks like dinner. You really should cut the zucchini a little thinner, dear.*

Yep. Binoculars.

Gillian laughed softly to herself and texted, *Do you want to come over and show me how it's done?* Then she put her phone down on the table and went back to slicing vegetables. Within moments she heard a tussle in the distance. Knife still in hand, she rounded the back corner of Noah's house to find Carol heading straight for her, Arnette pushing Carol back with her hands on her shoulders, and Judy just going along for the ride, as Judy was wont to do.

They all froze when they saw Gillian glaring at them—the knife in her hand probably didn't help—and waggled their fingers hello instead. Gillian furiously shooed them away. Arnette smiled reassuringly and pushed hard at Carol again, saying something low and threatening. Gillian didn't care what Arnette threatened as long as it got them all back across the road before Noah came out of his house.

Once she was convinced they were in retreat, Gillian returned to the backyard and started cooking. In a little while, Noah joined her on the patio. Carrying a tray of sliced vegetables, chicken breasts, and cookware.

One point—no, five—in the plus column for this guy.

Before she could get all those mushy feels again, she put on her armor made of snark. "I helped myself to your ug-ug he-man grill. I hope you don't mind."

"Somebody cooking for me? Why would I mind?"

"Yeah, well, don't just stand there, bud. You can help. Throw those veggies in the pan. The meat's almost done." She hesitated, looking at his tray. "Do you want to take the chicken back inside, since we have these pork chops?"

Noah looked at her as if she had three heads. "What? Of course not. Let's cook it all. I can sure manage to eat it all."

Noah flashed her a bright grin as she made room for him at the grill. This was way better than fighting over landscaping. When the food was nearly ready, Noah ducked back inside to get a bottle of wine, earning her eternal gratitude.

"Sit," she said when he reappeared. "Not there," she added quickly, gesturing with her tongs. "That seat's taken."

Noah took a closer look at the chair. "Seriously?" He picked up the gnome by its pointed hat like he was handling a dead fish. "You're not planning on grilling him, are you?"

"Of course not. Why would you think that?"

"Your track record." Gillian reached for the statue, but Noah held it out of her reach. "Uh-uh," he said. "After the pergola incident, I don't trust you with him."

"That's fair, actually."

"I'll keep an eye on him from now on."

"If that thing shows up in my garden again . . ."

"Garden? Pfft. I'll sneak into your house and leave him in your bed, like the horse's head in *The Godfather*. A little warning not to get too full of yourself with this contest."

Gillian wasn't even mad. Because now her head was full of the image of Noah in her bedroom. When he handed her a glass of wine, she took a healthy swallow to steady her nerves while she filled their plates.

"Oh my God," he groaned after the first forkful.

"What?"

"This is fantastic." Noah closed his eyes, a rapturous look on his face. "What did you do to this food?"

"Ah, that's a secret."

He shook his head in wonder. "Damn."

"What?"

"Nothing."

"No, you've gotta say it now."

Noah drank some of his wine before answering. "I was going to say . . . you're a woman of many talents."

"I'm a brilliant pharmacist," she reminded him.

"First and foremost, of course. It's just . . . you know . . . everything."

"'Everything' means what, exactly?"

"Amazing. You're amazing. All the time."

Gillian didn't know what to say, where to look. She certainly couldn't look at him. She picked up her fork with the intention of digging into her food, but all she could manage to do was push it around her plate. "Thank you," she whispered. "And the point of all this sudden flattery?"

"Well," Noah huffed, "I . . . I just mean . . . you . . . it . . . okay, come on, Quint, little mister misogynist? Dennis, the weirdo from the thrift shop? These are the only guys you've got chasing after you? *Why?* It doesn't make sense."

That was comparatively safer ground than the shocking experience of Noah West paying her compliments. More comfortable now, Gillian laughed. "Maybe it's the profile photo you took of me."

"*Nah.* I think it's the men of Willow Cove. Somehow there's something lacking."

"I tried broadening the geographical radius. It didn't bring in any better options. Don't forget Sebastian," she muttered.

"You don't sound happy with your dating adventures so far, it's true."

"Does it show?" She looked up from her plate to find Noah watching her sympathetically. "I don't know," she sighed. "Maybe it's futile. I'm just so tired of going out on shitty dates. I'm getting close to giving up. It didn't turn out like I expected. At all."

"Is that why you rejected Mick's, what, nephew, was it?"

"Yes, and the fact that it'd be tantamount to cradle robbing."

"Why'd you hold my hand and let Mick think we were together?"

Gillian's stomach leapt at his frank question. Yes, why had she? Even the very moment she'd reached out and grasped Noah's hand, large, strong, and rough, she had berated herself for it. She didn't have an answer beyond the excuse that she was so, so tired of men judging her, discussing her like an object they could pick up or put down at will. And Mick, well-intentioned as he might have been, had been doing the same thing, trying to set her up with yet another inappropriate guy. She was tired. She was just looking for a little respite. A break in the madness. And there was Noah, solid and steady, beside her. It was more instinctive than anything. It turned out her instinct had been right. Grabbing hold of him had comforted and steadied her.

Then she'd kept hold of him because . . . because she'd liked the feel of her hand in his.

She could tell him. Right now. She could admit she enjoyed spending time with him, enjoyed their conversations, thought they worked well together. Liked him. More than liked him.

Gillian opened her mouth to say all of that, confess her feelings to Noah and let the chips fall where they may. But what actually came out, accompanied by a coy little wink, was, "I held your hand so I didn't lose you in the barn."

"Come on."

"Sorry. The truth is . . ." She took a breath and rushed on. "The truth is I needed a little bit of reassurance at that moment. I'm sorry if it upset you." She paused. "*Were* you upset?"

Noah's voice was soft when he said, "Only when you let go."

~

When they finished their dinners, Noah brought out a bowl of strawberries. When the sun set, they sat in the dark, the only illumination coming from the kitchen window. When the wine was gone, they didn't even notice, because they were deep in conversation about, well, just about everything.

Gillian entertained him with tales of her lousy dates; Noah told her about his drive across the country and his adventures at the marina. Gillian talked about what her childhood was like in Philadelphia and then moving to Willow Cove as a teenager, and they compared notes about the summers years ago when they may have passed each other on the street and never noticed. Noah talked about his family a bit more, especially Manny; Gillian told Noah about her parents, now living in New York City, because they always did the opposite of what was expected of them and so moved to a big city for the excitement just at the age when they should have moved to a quiet retirement community and tooled around in golf carts instead of riding the subway.

Before either of them knew it, it was close to midnight. Noah roused himself when Gillian shivered a little bit.

"We shouldn't have stayed out here this long. I'm sorry."

"No, no, don't apologize."

"Still—"

"No, really."

There was a pause. An awkward one. Gillian stood. Noah stood.

"Oh, the dishes—"

Gillian started stacking them on the tray Noah had brought out.

"Leave them. It's fine."

"I can't let you—"

"You cooked. I'll wash—"

"No, I—"

Gillian turned just as Noah moved to protest some more, and suddenly they were face-to-face with only inches of space between them. Alone. In the cool dark of a summer night. Gillian desperately, desperately wanted to close the gap, and by the look on Noah's face, so did he. But she couldn't assume . . .

"I should go," she whispered.

Noah took a step back. "Yeah. Yeah, of course. I don't mean to keep you."

"It's okay. You didn't. Thank you for dinner."

"It was all you."

"Are you sure you're okay with the—"

"Fine, yeah. It'll only take a few minutes. Our friend the gnome can help me load the dishwasher. Gotta make him earn his keep somehow."

Gillian smiled. "Okay. I'll find you tomorrow? We can start planting."

When Gillian ducked into her house, she shut the door and leaned against it, letting go a huge, trembling breath.

"Holy shit," she whispered.

You like this boy, darling?

Inner Bette took a drag on her cigarette and studied Gillian through the haze of smoke curling up toward the ceiling.

"Is that my vodka?"

Alcohol stunts your growth. I'm doing you a favor getting rid of it for you. Now answer the question.

Gillian's voice held a tinge of wonder when she said, "You know, Bette, I really do."

How deadly dull. I expected better of you, my dear. Well, Inner Bette said with a sigh, *don't say I didn't warn you.*

"I think I'm willing to take that chance."

Life is full of little surprises, darling, Inner Bette said in a patronizing tone. *Now, do you have any more vodka?*

"I'm going to bed, Bette. I advise you to do the same."

And Gillian walked slowly up the stairs to her bedroom, in a bit of a daze over the day's turn of events. Little surprises? Yeah, this qualified. She turned on the bedside lamp and turned down the duvet, still trying to make sense of things. She rounded the bed to open the window a bit and drop the shade. A blaze of yellow light from Noah's window streamed across their driveways.

She couldn't help but look.

And there he was. Undressing. Doing the guy thing, grabbing his T-shirt by the neck at the back and yanking it over his head.

Great googly moogly.

Muscles sliding under smooth, tanned skin. Planes and ripples and movement. Smattering of chest hair. Broad back. Some sort of tattoo near his shoulder blade; she couldn't make it out.

Oh crap, she was staring.

And as if Noah could feel her eyes on him, he turned around and stared right back at her.

A pulse started beating, fluttery and fast, at her throat. A steadier pulse, much lower, kicked in as well, and turned into a throb when a slow smile spread across Noah's handsome face. Noah held up his index finger. *Wait.*

She would wait. Of course she would. She couldn't move. She was frozen in place.

He disappeared for what felt like too long. She thought she heard swearing coming from him, which dragged a nervous giggle out of her. A man's voice started talking. Not Noah's, perhaps a recording. What was it, and was she supposed to be able to hear what the man was saying? But when the voice was replaced by electronic blips and then loud, crunching guitars, she caught on.

Noah reappeared in the frame of the window, grinning at her while the Smithereens' "A Girl Like You" rattled the glass in her window and probably woke up half the street. Gillian couldn't seem to bring herself to care. She was captivated by the sight of a shirtless Noah and the mystery of what he intended to do next. She didn't have to wonder for long; her breath caught when, still holding her gaze, he let his hands drift to the waistband of his jeans, his fingers toying with the button. Popping the button. Gillian squirmed. His hand moved to the zipper.

And then he shifted away from the window again.

The song was still playing, the raunchy growl of the music contrasting with sentimental words about winning a special girl.

Gillian craned her neck as if she could get a better angle to see into his room. Where did he go? Why did he do that? Should she—

And then he reappeared, facing away from the window. The jeans were gone. So was any hint of underwear.

Gillian was pretty certain she was going to faint. If the sight of Noah West's bare ass, rocking side to side to the beat of the music, didn't knock her over, what in the world would?

Noah turning around, that's what.

And then she nearly fell out of her own window laughing. He was holding the gnome in front of him, in a very strategic location, the gnome's cheery little face smiling away at her. Evidently she was laughing loud enough that Noah could hear her as well as see her, and his smile brightened.

She pushed up her window screen and leaned out. "I don't think the gnome signed up for that."

To her dismay, Noah crouched down and disappeared. The music cut off. When he came back up again, he was on his knees. He rested his forearms on the windowsill. "You rejected him. He has to get work any way he can now."

"Is this a pity ploy to get me to put him in my garden?"

"Yes."

"Give me the gnome."

Noah's calculated pause made her breath catch. Then he growled, "Come and get him."

Reservations? What reservations? Weirdness? There was no weirdness. The only thing that would be weird would be Gillian ignoring the invitation. She was down her stairs and out her side door in an instant. Inner Bette may or may not have been in her kitchen, pouring another glass of vodka and judging her. She didn't care. Noah was already outside, unfortunately wearing his jeans again, barefoot, carrying the gnome.

When she reached him, Gillian said, "You do realize I'm never going to look at that thing the same way again, right?"

"I'm counting on it."

Noah handed it over; Gillian set it down on the driveway. She didn't want anything between them at this moment, least of all a goofy garden ornament.

Noah leaned close to her, his nose brushing her temple, and she closed her eyes. Somehow, after their long, exhausting day, his scent was still fresh, all soap and the good kind of perspiration.

His uneven breathing feathered the outer whorl of her ear. Was he nervous? Noah? She didn't think it was possible.

His lips grazed her cheekbone and he whispered, "You're so beautiful."

Now her breathing matched his—uneven, shallow. She wanted to reach out and touch him, not only to feel his body, but to steady hers, which was beginning to sway.

"Noah," she breathed.

"Mm?"

"If you don't kiss me right now, I swear I'll spontaneously combust."

He laughed softly.

"I'm warning you."

"Okay, okay. Bossy." Finally his hands were at her waist, and he pulled her to him. Gillian could feel the warm hardness of his chest through her thin blouse, and it made her light-headed. Just as he was lowering his lips to hers, he stopped. She opened her eyes to see him glancing across the street. "Do you think the old ladies are watching again?"

"Oh my God, you saw them earlier?"

"Hard not to." The smile accompanying his words revealed he had as much of a soft spot for the trio as she did. "They're everywhere."

"Well then," Gillian said, "maybe we should go somewhere where they can't spy on us."

"In a minute. I mean, if they are watching, we really should give them a little something, right?"

"What have you got in mind?"

And then Noah finally kissed her, his strong arms tightening around her, bending her to him. And she went. His lips were softer than she expected, the scruff on his chin raspy and rough. Gillian was grateful he was holding her, because she wasn't sure she'd be able to stand on her own at the moment. His familiar growl sounded in his throat as she opened her lips to him, now a different kind of frustrated—hungry instead of angry—and she felt the same way. She ran trembling hands up his chest and wrapped her arms around his neck, pressing herself to him, reveling in how his hard angles found a place in her softness.

Pulling away from her mouth with a small groan, he buried his face in her neck. "Okay," he murmured against her skin, the vibration making her shiver, "that's enough for them. The rest of the night is for us."

Gillian smiled and drew back, taking his hand once again. And again, it was warm and safe. But this time it also held promise. She started walking backward, tugging him toward her house. "The gnome stays out here."

CHAPTER 24

"Killing me. You're killing me."

"Are we talking about the strenuousness of gardening, or something else?"

The wicked glint in Gillian's eye made Noah want to toss aside his shovel, throw her over his shoulder, and carry her off to whichever of their bedrooms was closest. As he pretty much had been doing all week. It was a miracle they'd managed to get any gardening done at all.

He couldn't get enough of this woman. Not in one day, not in five days, and, when he dared to let himself think any further than the end of his nose, not for a good long time. He couldn't say the rest of his life; that would be absurd, considering they'd only just stopped hating each other. But he desperately wanted to see how far they could take this exciting, intriguing, and downright joy-inducing whatever-it-was between them.

Gillian apparently felt the same way. She dropped her trowel and crossed the yard to him. Good lord, the woman even made clunky boots and gardening gloves sexy.

"Well? What's it going to be?" she asked. "Are we planting the rest of these herbs before it rains, or—"

Noah knew the other option, and he vastly preferred it. Never mind that the garden competition, and the marina's future that hung in the balance by association, was only weeks away. As Gillian had advised him, just plopping plants into the dirt didn't make a garden. They needed as much time as possible to root, to be fertilized and nurtured until each living thing was lush and full and in perfect harmony with everything else around it.

Well, fuck that.

Even if he was going to win no matter what, what had become most important to him was that his garden had to be on par with Gillian's. His would be a complement to hers, a background that would let hers shine, so it had to look as good as possible. And Gillian was enjoying herself so much creating it. He loved watching her glow with pride as she shaped something from nothing. *Magic,* she had said, about what made it all come together. Well, she was the magic. And he wanted more of that, more of Gillian. In the bedroom, in his truck, in the kitchen, on the roof, for all he cared. Anywhere and everywhere. Being with Gillian was all that mattered.

Of course, not out in the open in the yard.

Well, okay, absolutely in the yard, if he had a stockade fence and maybe one of those white sail-like things that stretched across the entire backyard to shield it from prying eyes.

And now the thought of divesting Gillian of her wellies and her gardening gloves and every other last stitch of clothing right there, out in the open no matter what, was starting to get to him.

As if to punctuate the thought, a rumble of thunder sounded in the distance.

"Better get inside," he murmured, running his fingers up the back of her thigh and just under the hem of her shorts. "It won't be safe out here."

"The storm's pretty far away. The rain isn't going to get here for ages yet." Her low voice matched his, the vibrations playing off each other as their bodies met in the space between.

"Who's talking about the rain?"

"You're obsessed," she chided, but she didn't pull away. Instead, she pressed against him and drew his head down for a kiss.

And even now, days after their first kiss, after hundreds more, the touch of her lips on his could still bring him to his knees. Magic indeed.

Noah had a vague recollection that he had viewed Gillian differently not too long ago. Intense dislike, he seemed to recall. But that couldn't be right, could it? And if it was, well, damned if he could remember why he hadn't liked her. Something about how passionate and headstrong she was. Why had he found those traits irritating? Now her passion and the sheer force of her personality thrilled him and fascinated him and inspired him. And made him very, very turned on.

He kissed her again, and again, deeper each time. She had the sweetest taste, the softest skin, and an openness he could drown in.

Or maybe it was the sudden deluge they found themselves in, as if someone had overturned a giant bucket directly over their heads. Gillian gasped and staggered back a step, pushing her hair out of her eyes as lightning flickered.

"Guess I was wrong," she shouted over the thunder as another crackle of lightning flashed, lighting up the gloom for a moment. "Well?"

"Well what?" Noah shouted back.

"Come on!" And she moved toward the house.

"Nope." He closed the distance between them and stopped her, wrapping his arms around her again.

"You are *not* going to *Notebook* me right now, are you?"

"I was thinking more *Lady Chatterly*-ing you, but—"

"You're not serious."

Noah shrugged.

"We're going to get hit by lightning."

"I won't notice."

The rain came down harder, if that was at all possible. Noah didn't care. Their clothes were clinging to them and sticking to the other's. He didn't care about that either. Because when Gillian rose up on her toes and kissed him, he knew his reality was better than anything he'd read in a book or seen in a movie.

~

"What does this mean?"

Gillian's voice was sleepy and relaxed. Her finger lightly traced the tattoo on his shoulder, a child's drawing of a person's head with black hair and dark eyes and a big smile.

"It's a replica of an original artwork. Self-portrait, twenty-first century, wax on parchment. I was good friends with the artist."

"Very talented."

"He is."

"And is the artist working now?" she asked, stretching lazily under his sheets.

"Summering in California. Well, it's his year-round retreat in Desert Hot Springs. He has a studio there. It has a rocking horse in the corner and a hot-air balloon hanging from the ceiling. Very inspiring." He wanted to keep it light, but Gillian was looking at him expectantly. And he couldn't shut her out. His smile faltered a bit as he rolled over onto his back, his hands behind his head. "That's the problem with breakups—sometimes they affect more than the two people involved."

"You miss Aidan." It was a statement of deduction more than a question.

No point in hedging about this either, Noah reasoned. "I do."

"I'm sorry."

"He's a good kid."

"Hey," Gillian said quietly, her hand warm on his chest. "I didn't mean to make you upset."

"You didn't. I swear."

"But . . . ?"

"I loved him a lot," Noah said, his voice creaking. "I really wanted to be his stepdad."

"I don't know what to say." Gillian's green eyes were soft with sympathy.

"Nothing to say. Look, there is something I wanted to ask you. I do stay in touch with Corinne and talk to Aidan when she lets me. I don't know if that's going to continue now that Aidan's used to my not being around anymore, but if it does, will it bother you?"

Noah tensed, although he fought to keep his expression neutral. He was sounding like he already considered Gillian his girlfriend, which was more than a little premature. There was plenty of time for definitions and declarations later. Not now. Now was all about enjoying each other's company and seeing where it led them.

He needn't have worried. Like everything else, Gillian took it in stride. "Of course not. I understand completely. You should stay in touch with Aidan. Of course."

Noah kissed her, grateful for her patience. "Late dinner?"

In their hurry to get horizontal after their workdays ended, they'd skipped some of the preliminaries, including food, and now Noah felt like his empty stomach was eating its way out of his body.

Gillian looked around for a clock. "Super late for a meal, isn't it? Almost, like, ten o'clock?"

"Not that bad, is it?" Noah leaned over the bed to pull his phone from his jeans that were on the floor where he'd kicked them off earlier. "Nine thirty."

"We'll have to go to one of the touristy places—they stay open late this time of year."

"I will endure the Edison bulbs for food."

∽

Noah and Gillian walked the dark residential streets hand in hand, toward the main street and all its brightly lit restaurants, bars, and shops. Gillian was right—nearly every establishment was still open, and they had their pick of restaurants. And somehow, with Gillian beside him, those damned strings of lights looked magical instead of cheesy. Noah smiled to himself. Was he losing his edge already?

"You do realize we're going public for the first time," Gillian murmured to him. "What if we run into someone we know?"

"If we run into Carol, Arnette, or Judy, they'll throw us a party."

They didn't meet up with Carol, Arnette, or Judy, but they did bump into Ben coming out of a dark storefront, locking the door behind him.

"Ben," Gillian started slowly. "What're you doing?"

Her friend lit up at the sight of her and gave her a warm hug. "Don't tell Jenna. Hey," he greeted Noah, who nodded back.

"Don't tell Jenna what?"

"Top secret, okay? Trust me?"

"First tell me whether you're breaking into the empty building or busting out of it."

The man grinned as he jingled the set of keys. "Neither. I've got a side hustle in between trucking runs. Some odd jobs, a little carpentry."

"Why would you take on more work? Trying to get out of the house, away from Jenna and the kids?"

"Of course not! I am, however, very interested in planning a vacation soon. And for that one needs a little extra green. Or, you know, a lot. I figure if I really dig in between now and spring, I can either take Jenna on a relaxing, romantic Alaskan cruise for two, or I can take the entire family on a chaotic trip to Disney. Whatever Jenna wants."

"That's sweet," Gillian said. "I promise I won't tell."

"You're the best." To Noah, he said, "Isn't she the best?"

Noah looked at her fondly. "She really is."

This finally caused Ben to look at them a little closer. "So I was going to say . . . Fourth of July cookout at Casa Masterson-Page? Excellent view of the fireworks over the river from our back deck. And bring a date?" He looked at the two of them pointedly until Gillian nodded, smiling, confirming she and Noah were a couple. "Right. Yes. Great. Fantastic! Congratulations! Is this something I should tell the wife, or should I let it be a surprise?"

Gillian and Noah looked at each other, and Noah felt himself go all gooey when he saw that Gillian looked nervous. This cookout would be the first time they'd spend time with her friends since he and Gillian had gotten together. He hadn't even asked, but it was evident she hadn't told them yet. Noah didn't mind. In fact, he completely understood. To go from mutual loathing to . . . this . . . took a lot of explaining. He wouldn't have had the energy if he were in her shoes. Whatever the case, the most important thing at the moment was easing Gillian's mind.

"Sure, we'll be there," he told Ben, squeezing Gillian's hand. "What can we bring?"

"Nothing. There is nothing you need to do other than make this lovely lady right here happy. Okay?"

"Okay. We'll bring beer."

"Excellent choice."

As Ben headed home, Noah put his arm around Gillian's shoulders and whispered close to her ear, "I hope you were ready to break the news to your friends."

She reached up and grasped his hand. "You make it sound like that's a scary thing. I'm not afraid of them."

"*I* am. Jenna in particular."

"Well, that's just wise. But I'm happy to bring you as my date. A real date. Not one of those sad, weird trials I've had too many of recently."

"I'll make you proud."

She beamed up at him. "You already do."

Noah didn't know what to say, or if anything would even come out if he tried to speak, since his entire chest was flooded with a warmth he hadn't felt in a long, long time. So when he dared to form words again, he said, "So what's Ben working on in here?"

"I don't know," Gillian said, climbing the two shallow concrete steps up to the door, cupping her hands around her eyes, and peering into the empty shop. "Looks like he was sanding the floor. This place has been empty since last fall. I wonder if there's something new going in, or if Ben's just doing some work while it's in between tenants."

"It's got a 'For Rent' sign in the window," Noah said.

"Guess there aren't any plans for it yet, then." Gillian stepped back and looked up at the small corner building. "It could turn into anything. Over the years, this has been a bistro, a candy store, a T-shirt shop, a clothing boutique . . ."

"Is it cursed? Is it built on some ancient burial ground?"

"No," she laughed, taking his hand again and leading him

toward the restaurant they'd chosen. "Turnover is high in town, but when the right business comes in, it can stay for decades."

"What was the last business that was in here?"

"Right up your alley. An art gallery. They usually do well, in season—we have a lot of local artists who need representation. The off-season is tough, so running a gallery has to be a labor of love or a side interest . . . What?"

Noah realized he'd stopped walking and was staring at the building. He shook himself. "Nothing. Let's eat."

CHAPTER 25

"Yay! You always hated dating apps; now you can delete them!"

"*Don't* delete the dating apps," Jenna deadpanned.

"Why not?" Delia countered. "God, you are so cynical. It's obvious Gillian doesn't need to keep up her dating profile now that she's in love—"

"Whoa, whoa, whoa, whoa," Gillian protested. "Slow your roll, there, sunshine. I did not use the L-word."

"You don't have to—I can see it on your face."

"That's just the bad pharmacy lighting."

Gillian knew it would be risky to announce to her friends during her dinner break at work—and by group video call, no less—that she was seeing Noah, but it would have been far more dangerous to surprise them by showing up as a couple at the cookout on Friday with no advance warning. No, she knew they needed time to acclimate before they descended on her and Noah en masse, derping all over the new couple, demanding to know how they got together and how they felt about each other and what their long-term plans were. It would send the poor guy running for the hills. Her too, come to think of it.

"We're just, you know, spending time together, that's all," Gillian hedged.

"Well, I think it's great," Gray said, appearing beside Delia on her screen. "It's about time you got a little sumpin'."

"Thank you?"

"Dammit, Powers, I've been looking all over for you," Eli exclaimed, dodging his cat, Blanche, who had decided now was the perfect time to strut between Eli and his computer and flick her tail in his face. "What are you doing at Delia's?" he asked, spitting white hairs. "You said you wanted to run the backhoe this afternoon."

"Delia and I are experimenting with her new soldering iron. Your construction can wait another day."

It was slow going, but Eli was finally making good on his dream of building a ropes course on his plot of land with an eye to having outdoor activities for groups of kids.

"You're not getting paid for today," Eli snapped.

"Wait—you were paying me?"

"Obviously not."

Now it was Leah's turn to squeeze into Eli's screen. "Gray, your loss was my gain—*I* drove the backhoe today. So thanks for that. Now, can you guys keep it down? I'm trying to choose my classes for the fall semester."

"Yeah." Eli changed tack. "Let's keep it down. Or I'm holding all of you responsible if Leah bails on college."

"Not a chance," she murmured to her boyfriend. "Social work is my calling and my destiny." She kissed Eli on the cheek. "And when I finish this, don't forget we're watching a movie." Turning back to the camera, she said, "Gillian, I'm thrilled for you. Don't listen to these knuckleheads."

"I'm with Leah," Ben called as he passed behind Jenna in their kitchen. "Goah all the way."

"Goah?" his wife repeated, leaning back to intercept him and take the can of soda he'd just gotten for himself.

"Well, Nillian just sounds dumb as hell."

"And Goah's better?"

Gillian stifled a groan. "Guys, we don't need a couple's name, okay? The only thing I'm asking is that you *be cool.* Can you manage that?"

Ben stole the phone from Jenna and gave Gillian an extreme closeup of his serious look. "Can I ask him what his intentions are?" he intoned.

"Absolutely not."

"Can we threaten to kill him if he breaks your heart?" Gray asked. "I'd *so* be up for that."

Gray held up a virtual high-five for Ben, who returned the gesture.

"Nobody threaten anybody. Just be welcoming, and for God's sake, act normal for once in your lives."

~

"This is not normal," Gillian muttered out of the corner of her mouth.

"What are they doing?" Noah muttered back.

"Trying to be welcoming?"

Seconds ticked by, and not one member of the group spoke. Gillian and Noah were frozen in the doorway to the back deck, crowded by eagerly smiling, but apparently all suddenly mute, friends. The only creature in motion was Fredo, Jenna and Ben's dog, who was taking the opportunity to dare to raise his snout close to the table and sniff out what food might be available for stealing.

"Say something," Noah urged Gillian.

"*You* say something!"

"Mom, will you get her away from me? She's bugging me."

Zoë, Jenna and Ben's older daughter, squeezed through the thicket of adult legs to complain about her sister.

"Hey now," Jenna said to her, "can't you see we have guests?"

The nine-year-old turned her somber brown eyes on the new arrivals. "Oh. Sorry. Hi. You're Aunt Gillian's new squeeze?" she asked Noah.

"Zoë!" Ben admonished her with a hollow, very fake laugh. "Where are you getting this?"

"I have ears. You guys aren't very quiet."

"What else have you heard . . . ? You know what? Never mind."

"Now, are you going to get Olivia away from me or do I have to do something drastic like send her off with a traveling circus?"

Jenna grabbed Zoë's shoulders in a death grip. "Honestly, I do not know where she comes up with this—"

"You use that threat all the time."

"MommyMommyMommy, Zoë's being mean—" Five-year-old Olivia came to a screeching halt when she spotted Noah. "You're really tall. Like Unca Eli."

Jenna bugged her eyes. "Manners! Have we taught you nothing?" She sighed. "All right, let's start over. Girls, say hello to Aunt Gillian's friend Noah. Noah, these are our girls, Zoë and Olivia."

"Hi," was all Noah managed to say before Olivia grabbed his hand.

"You have to come play with us. Unca Eli too."

"Olivia, he just got here!" Jenna tried to rescue Noah, but Olivia would not be deterred, nor would Zoë. She grabbed Noah's other hand, as well as nabbing Eli.

"I wanna play soccer," Olivia declared flatly, dragging Noah across the deck, away from the food and drink, and down the stairs.

"No! We have to play basketball," Zoë argued. "Look at them—they can actually, you know, make baskets!"

"What about me?" Ben asked plaintively. "Don't you want to play with your ol' dad?"

"No!" the girls scoffed.

"We play with you all the time," Olivia said.

Zoë added, "And you're terrible at basketball."

"I want soccer!" Olivia insisted.

Gillian fought back a laugh at Noah's befuddled look. "You going to play?"

"Do I have a choice?"

"Nope," Eli said. "Go with it and be grateful O doesn't want to play d-r-e-s-s-u-p," he spelled. "That lasts hours."

Olivia cocked her head, deciphering, but gave up and started tugging on Noah again.

"It's fine," he said to Gillian and went willingly, only casting one longing look at the cooler of beers.

Once the girls and their captives were far enough away, Delia grabbed Gillian by the arm and sat her down. "Everything. We want to hear *everything*. Especially about the sex."

"Not comfortable with this conversation," Ben declared.

"Neither am I, Ben," Gillian said. She most certainly wasn't going to tell her friends about sex with Noah.

"Maybe I should go referee the game," he offered uneasily.

"Aren't you manning the grill?" Jenna reminded him, retrieving her drink and sitting on Gillian's other side. "Oh, and Gillian needs a drink. Ben—"

"Come on!"

"But I can't miss any of the dirt."

Ben shook his head and headed for the kitchen, turning back in the doorway to say, "I'm fetching a drink for Gillian, because it's obvious she's going to need the fortifying effects of alcohol while the two of you interrogate her. And then I'm absenting myself, because I am not okay with this. Man your own grill."

"Less drama, more margarita," Jenna demanded. "Love you!" she threw in, then rounded on Gillian. "Well?"

"Guys . . ."

"This looks like a conversation I want in on." Gray assessed the tableau from the doorway, set his casserole dish on the table, and dragged over a chair. "What's going on?"

"Noah," Delia whispered, eyes wide.

"Well, *yeah*. Looks like this one's a keeper, right? Despite his first impression. *Impressions,*" Gray corrected.

"I thought *you* were bringing a date," Ben said to Gray, coming out of the house with a pitcher of margaritas and a glass already poured for Gillian.

Gray threw his arm around Delia. "I've got my date right here."

Delia swatted at him good-naturedly.

"Don't toy with her affections," Jenna scolded.

Ben held out the glass to Gillian, and Gray intercepted it. "Oh, thank God. Alcohol."

Ben sighed heavily and went back inside for another glass.

"So we're talking dirty details about the new man?" Gray asked. "Finally?"

"Shush," Jenna said in a low voice. "They're back."

She got up and bustled around the grill as Delia said to Noah and Eli, overly cheerfully, "Hey! Game over already?"

"There was a snail in the driveway," Eli explained. "Olivia didn't want to smush it."

"Did you suggest relocating it?"

"She said the snail was obviously going somewhere, and it wouldn't be fair to interrupt. She's watching it to see where it's headed. Could be a while."

"Oh. That's nice. Have some cheese and crackers."

Accepting a bottle of beer Eli handed him, Noah dropped into the spot vacated by Jenna and murmured to Gillian, "They were asking about the sex, weren't they?"

∽

The rest of the day passed in a blur of food, drink, chatter, and good-natured arguments, peppered with occasional demands for attention from Olivia, who got restless once her more introverted sister had retreated to their tree house with a hot dog and a book and pulled up the rope ladder after her. All the friends were on their best behavior and refrained from interrogating Noah; instead, they made an effort to have normal conversations with him. Every once in a while one of the group would pass by and give Gillian a little squeeze on her shoulder or her waist, or would give her a hidden thumbs-up, to communicate they all wholeheartedly approved of Noah and were more than willing to forgive him his earlier transgressions.

"It's like he's a different person," Delia murmured to Gillian late in the evening as they retrieved the desserts from the fridge.

Gillian set down a strawberry pie on the counter. "Yeah, he's great."

"Okay, *what* was that?"

"What was what?" Gillian asked absently. "Oh, we forgot the ice cream."

"That tone. You sounded way too iffy. Do you not like him or something? You look green."

"I tried Gray's kale and spinach casserole. Just to be polite. I noticed you, however, did not."

"I know better. Now, don't change the subject. What's going on?"

"Nothing's going on," Gillian insisted. "Noah is wonderful. We've been having a good time. Now can I please get these ice-cream tubs out of my hands before my fingers fall off? Get the scooper."

Noah *was* being wonderful; that wasn't a lie. And they had been having a good time, not just that day, but every day since they'd gotten together. Delia was right, though—it really was like Noah was a different person. Gillian got a weird feeling in the pit of her stomach as she wondered who the true Noah was: the egotistical, stubborn grump she'd hated so vehemently, or the kind, attentive gentleman with the wonderfully filthy carnal side she'd gotten acquainted with lately. Was it actually a dichotomy she should be worried about?

Apparently she was standing there ruminating for a few seconds too long, because Delia got up in Gillian's personal space.

"Okay, Jenna's busy outside, so I'm going to channel her for a minute," Delia said, and she poked Gillian's collarbone. "Snap out of it! Whatever is going on up there"—she tapped Gillian's temple a little too forcefully—"shake it off. Noah is officially a good guy, we were wrong about him, and the two of you are obviously getting along, so embrace it. Enjoy it. And get rid of your dating apps, for cryin' out loud."

Gillian knocked Delia's finger out of her face. "Come on, before the ice cream melts."

They loaded up the desserts onto trays and carried them outside. Noah was sitting in a chair by the outer railing of the deck. Olivia was on his lap, facing him, straddling his left knee, and talking nonstop. Noah was actively carrying on a conversation, not just tolerating her, and Gillian's heart skipped a beat. Definitely not the irritable grump from weeks ago. She thought of Aidan, and she realized Noah had plenty of practice connecting with little kids.

As Gillian dished up the pie, she watched Noah reach under his chair and pick up the paper bag he'd brought with him. When Gillian had asked him what was in it, he'd refused to tell her. Now he revealed a box of sparklers, and Gray passed him the lighter that had been sitting on the table since they'd lit the citronella candles.

Olivia, in raptures, ran around the deck with two blazing sparklers in each hand, then dashed into the gloom of the yard to show them off to a still reclusive Zoë. That got her sister out of the tree house and demanding two of the sparklers.

Despite her usual penchant for cynicism, especially when it came to men lately, Gillian felt her heart starting to melt. It was official: Noah really was a good guy. He'd been through so much lately, it was no wonder he'd been grouchy at first. She knew now that curmudgeon wasn't his default mode; this was. This generous, kind, funny, thoughtful, handsome, and sexy guy. The guy who brought sparklers for her friends' kids, whom he'd never met. The guy who fit right in with her group of friends and tolerated—and even enjoyed—their quirks. The guy who was looking at her warmly right now, his brilliant smile lighting up the darkening evening, framed by the golden light trails from the sparklers the girls were waving around in the yard behind him.

When the first fireworks lit up the night sky, Gillian sat on his lap and dared to hope, for the first time in a long time, she'd finally found a man who lit her up like those sparklers, a man she could trust enough to let herself fall.

CHAPTER 26

"Come on."

"Have you taken leave of your senses? Do you not realize the competition is this Sunday?"

Noah gently tugged on Gillian's arm. "Drop the shovel. Drop it. Drop. it."

Gillian let herself be pulled up and boomeranged into Noah's chest. "I am not a dog with a bone," she growled.

"Prove it," he growled back, kissing her for good measure.

What was meant to be a small peck turned into something deeper and more passionate, which Noah could have fallen into easily, but he refrained, pulling his head back to say, "That is not what I had in mind."

"For once?"

Noah hesitated, then admitted, "Okay, true. But no. *No.*" He pulled back again when Gillian reached for him. "We are getting away from all things even remotely related to gardening. We are getting away from dirt and fertilizer and deadheading and—"

"I told you," she said, giving his waist a squeeze and turning away again, "I have too much to do."

"Because you spent all your time helping me get *my* garden ready."

"Hey, I have no regrets. You need to win that first-place trophy and get Louise off your back. Now you have a fighting chance. But I'll be damned if I give up second prize to the half-assed pile of peonies Walter and Annabelle Fetzner always offer up."

Noah had no idea who Walter and Annabelle Fetzner were, but he had a pretty good idea they were her usual garden rivals. He buried the pang of guilt he felt for taking up all of Gillian's time for weeks. None of this was fair to her, and yet she unselfishly gave all of her time and effort to make sure his garden was respectable. And she wasn't going to win first prize. Again. She'd reassured him repeatedly she would regroup and enter the competition next year, but that made his heart hurt. He wanted all good things for Gillian right now. Not in a year.

"And," she continued, "yours could do with some sprucing up by now too, you know."

"Wha . . . it's fine!"

She cocked one eyebrow. "You said you could handle it on your own. 'Go ahead, work on your garden, Gillian. I've got this.' But you haven't pruned a thing in weeks, have you? Or thinned the mint? And I don't know how you managed to do this, but somehow you let the bee balm dry out. Look at those poor crispy edges on the leaves. Those are *herbs*, West. Basically weeds with a flavor. How did you let them get into such a state?"

"You're a mean taskmaster."

"Just don't get cocky—Louise could still ding you if she doesn't approve, and we can't have that. As for me, if I'm going to take second place, that pile of bricks *there*"—she indicated the load of pavers that had been languishing at the end of her driveway for weeks—"needs to be magically transformed into a short walkway *here*." And she indicated a spot at the edge of the driveway pavement that would lead into the magical landscape that was her garden. "I've got all day, and I intend to—"

"Later."

"There is no later!"

"Trust me, okay?" he pleaded. "Just come with me for today, clear your head, and we'll deal with the brick path in plenty of time. And I promise to thin my mint."

"This goes against every instinct I have," she protested, although Noah was heartened to note she had finally dropped her shovel and was grudgingly allowing him to drag her out of her backyard.

"Then maybe you need to reevaluate your instincts." Once Noah got her closer to her house, he said, "I've got the perfect idea for today."

"Driving around town and checking out the other entrants' gardens?" Gillian asked hopefully.

Noah glowered. Gillian rolled her eyes.

"Go get your hiking boots," he ordered, "and fill your biggest water bottle. Meet me back here in five minutes."

"Where are we going?"

"You said you liked hiking but you hadn't done it in a while. So we will go hiking. On that favorite trail of yours you told me about."

"Do, uh, do you even know how?"

"Do I know how to walk? Yeah, I think I figured that out more than thirty years ago. Now, go!" Noah waited till Gillian went into her house, then he quickly made a call, ducking through his own back door. "Ben. Five, ten minutes tops and we'll be clear."

"On it."

"You're not doing this by yourself, are you?"

"No, no, of course not. The guys are in, and Alyce is taking the kids so Jenna can help too. We got you."

"Thanks. I really appreciate it."

"You know we'd do anything for our girl."

~

Gillian let Noah drive and, after a quick pit stop at the café for take-out coffee and muffins for the road, she directed him to turn inland. More than an hour later, they traveled down a small town's brick-storefronted main street. At the edge of town, Gillian pointed out an unassuming gravel parking lot with a small sign and a couple of picnic tables.

"We're here."

"And here is . . . ?" Noah asked as Gillian hopped out of the truck and sat down on one of the benches to adjust her boot laces.

She smiled brightly at him. "Have you forgotten what an Adirondack trailhead looks like? Come on. Day's a-wasting."

"This is your favorite place to hike?" Noah peered into the tree cover. "Um, aren't there bears in there?"

"Don't worry, they aren't interested in you."

"Just promise me you aren't trying to lose me in the woods so you can rush back home and work on your garden."

Gillian pretended to consider for a moment. "You know, that's an excellent idea. But no. I haven't brought enough snacks, and I couldn't leave you to fight the bears over the berries you might find off the trail. Couldn't live with myself."

"Ah, so you do like me."

Reaching up to clasp her hands behind his neck, she murmured, "No question about that."

Noah was heartened by her words and the kiss that accompanied them. "Okay, lead on. Now . . . what is this, a mile? Two?"

"Oh, more like eight. Maybe ten."

"Ten?"

"I'm going easy on you. This trail is mostly flat. No mountain climbing today."

"Not today? What about tomorrow?"

"That remains to be seen. Let's see how you do with this first."

She led him into the woods, down a shaded trail that ran alongside a roiling river. Entirely unlike the massive, heaving St. Lawrence, this river was fast-moving, shallow, and rocky, with small waterfalls that threw up a refreshing spray. And even though the path was indeed mostly flat as promised, the scenery was beautiful, and his hiking companion was beautiful—at least, from what he could remember, as he spent several miles seeing nothing but her back as she outpaced him—Noah soon had serious regrets about suggesting they go to Gillian's favorite spot on their day out.

"Wait. Stop, stop."

Gillian turned back. "Something wrong? Pebble in your boot?"

Noah realized he could have used that as an excuse, but no. He decided to be honest. "I just need a break," he panted. "Don't you need a break?"

"A break from what?"

"Jesus," he muttered, dropping onto a flat rock close to the river. "Please, sit. I'm begging you."

Gillian was obviously fighting back a laugh as she joined him. "What's the matter?"

He guzzled about half the contents of his water bottle before he answered. "Nothing. I'm fine. Great. Fabulous. Entirely out of shape, apparently."

"No, you're not." Gillian ran a hand over his bicep admiringly, and he felt a little better. Until she said, "You just need a little more cardio in your life."

"Yeah, yeah. And you haven't even broken a sweat."

"I'm used to it. I like walking, you know that. Come with me sometime. On the nice, safe, level streets of Willow Cove."

"Ha ha."

"You've got to get out of that marina office more often, you know."

He sighed. "Might as well. It's not like my staff would miss me anyway."

"What are you talking about?"

"Ah, you know," he said. "Jerry was a good boss, always trained his folks well. The place runs like a well-oiled machine whether I'm there or not. The staff certainly doesn't need me to . . . to . . . stock the rack of sunglasses or gas up a boat. Honestly, most of the time I feel like I'm just in the way."

"I'm sure that's not true."

"Mm," he hummed noncommittally, "you'd be surprised."

"Does it bother you?" Gillian asked as she unlaced her boots, peeled off her socks, and dipped her toes into the river, her polished nails glinting as she wiggled them in the foam.

"What, that I came all the way here to take over a business I could have managed from California?"

"That's not true either."

"Yeah, you're right." Noah followed Gillian's lead and stripped off his boots and thick socks to cool his feet in the water. "And if I had, I'd have missed out on all this."

"My killing you by degrees on a death march in the Adirondack wilderness?"

"I'm pretty sure I can see the town buildings over there in the distance, so I doubt we're on a survival hike. No, I mean if I'd stayed where I was, I'd never have met you. And that would have been a terrible turn for my life to take."

"You hated me."

"Until I got to know you. Now I—"

Noah's words stuck in his throat as he realized what he was about to say. He loved her? Was that what was about to come out of his mouth? Did he mean it, or had he just had his head turned by a charming, gorgeous woman and he was feeling impulsive? Wasn't he supposed to be dating all sorts of women on the rebound to get over Corinne instead of having serious—really serious—feelings for someone?

"You what?" Gillian prompted.

Still the words wouldn't come out. Noah got the feeling this was a now-or-never moment and he'd just blown it. Even though Gillian didn't seem bothered, what he'd just done—or failed to do—bothered him. If he meant it, if he actually believed he loved Gillian, why couldn't he say it?

"Now," he said instead, "I let a beautiful, smart, clever woman talk me into things I never thought I'd do, like going on a thirty-mile uphill-the-entire-way hike. And create a garden. That could never, ever hold a candle to what she's capable of."

He held out his hand, and she took it. Noah desperately wished he could have said what he wanted to instead of these compliments that, while genuine, didn't come close to how he was really feeling. He hoped Gillian would be patient with him until he could say those three important words he felt in his heart, but which firmly lodged there and wouldn't budge yet.

"Do you miss California?" she asked, and not for the first time Noah noted how she was always willing to ask him questions about his life and his thoughts and his feelings. He'd never felt this seen by anyone, never felt like the person with him truly wanted to know everything about him. Because she was so up front about things, Noah always tried to answer Gillian honestly and completely.

"Sometimes."

"Because of Corinne and Aidan?"

"Not exactly. More like what they represented. At the time they meant home. And an identity. Like my art gallery. You know. 'Noah West, he's the guy who owns the Mesquite Gallery.' Now I'm 'Noah West, the poser who thinks he can fill Jerry

Spencer's shoes, even though he hasn't touched water in fifteen years that wasn't coming out of a lawn sprinkler.'"

"How did you manage to give up art just like that?"

"I think it was because it was attached to Corinne, to be honest. Her sculpture, the two of us circulating in the art world. So when I needed to stop thinking about Corinne, art went with it. I wanted to get away so badly I sold my gallery. Then I came out here and set up a new life. I mean, I do miss it. I really liked discovering artists that needed representation, connecting them with people who could appreciate their work."

Not for the first time, Noah's thoughts drifted to the storefront they'd seen on Willow Cove's Main Street. It was an intriguing space—huge windows, right on a corner in the middle of the commercial district, nice open floor plan. The place gave him ideas . . . but then he stopped himself. He wasn't sure he had the bandwidth to entertain those ideas without his brain short-circuiting. Surely he had enough to deal with already, didn't he? And he could satisfy his interest in art in more conservative ways.

"I haven't forgotten about art entirely," he told Gillian. "You're an artist, after all—just a different kind. You create living art, and it's pretty cool that I can help you make a composition with plants and flowers."

"It's not the same, though."

"It's enough for now."

"Is it?"

Noah pushed the image of the empty storefront out of his mind and flicked a little water from the river at her. "Yes," he said, kissing her for emphasis. "It is. I'm happy where I am."

He hoped it didn't imply he was happy the way they were now, without the stickler of an L-word coming up. Because, he realized as Gillian smiled and pressed her forehead to his, he wanted even more out of life, and he got the feeling Gillian played the biggest part in that.

Maybe, he thought, his gestures would fill in where words failed him.

Late in the afternoon, after they finished the hike—Gillian completely composed, Noah sweating and exhausted—they stopped at a rural pub so he could recover and eat nearly his body weight in lost calories. But when Noah got the all-clear text from Ben, he insisted it was time for them to get back to Willow Cove. Because he couldn't wait one extra minute to see Gillian's face when they got home.

The sun was setting, casting purple shadows over their yards, when Noah pulled his truck into the driveway. Gillian was distracted, collecting her things, and Noah nervously fidgeted next to her, waiting for her to notice.

She didn't notice.

"Today was fun," she said when they climbed out of the truck.

"It was."

"I'd better shower and get ready for tomorrow. Early shift at the pharmacy."

She was going to go into her house? Without looking?

Noah never said he was a good actor—in fact, he was pretty sure he was hot garbage, since the last time he'd been onstage was in second grade, when he'd played a tree, but he tried his best now. "Wait . . . what's that . . . is something wrong with your . . . what is it, again? Salvia?"

That got Gillian to turn her head, but she didn't seem worried about checking it out. "What about it?"

"It, uh, it looks . . ." He had nothing. What could possibly have gone wrong with one specific grouping of plants in her beds? He gave up. "Let's check it out."

Yep, a really bad actor. But it was enough to get Gillian down the driveway toward her backyard. Then again, she was so focused on the flower bed in question that she didn't notice any changes to her yard till her foot landed on a brick paver. Even then it took her another moment or two to realize she was standing on bricks instead of the dirt path she'd started to cut days ago.

"Noah," she breathed, awestruck, and his heart bloomed in his chest until he thought it would burst. "What . . . ?"

"Wasn't me. Obviously."

"You knew, though."

As she marveled at the newly inlaid brick path, which, judging by her expression, was exactly what she'd planned, Noah started a video call.

"Do you love it or do you love it?" Jenna demanded loudly.

Gillian spun around, beaming. "You guys!"

"All Noah's doing," Ben said.

Gillian turned to Noah, her eyes bright with unshed happy tears. "You stinker."

"Not the reaction I was hoping for, but I'll take it."

She launched herself into him, wrapping her arms around his waist and squeezing tightly. "I love it." She tipped her face up, smiling. "I love you."

Noah kissed her. It was the least he could do. Because the words still wouldn't come.

CHAPTER 27

"Ready for this?"

"Born ready."

But if Gillian was born ready for this garden competition, why was she sweating and fidgeting as if this were her first year competing, not her fifth? Because it would be her fifth year losing, thanks to Louise. Gillian stared out at her garden, which was perfect down to the last bloom and leaf, adjusted her wide-brimmed hat, and debated with herself, as she'd done all morning, whether she should have worn her hair up instead of down.

"You look beautiful," Noah murmured beside her.

"Stop."

"You do. I feel like the hired help next to you."

"Well, you didn't know, and I didn't think to tell you."

Most of the gardeners made a major occasion of the competition, dressing in their finest garden party attire. Gillian usually trotted out some frilly dress with flowered pastel fabric, a tight bodice, a full skirt, and lace touches here and there.

Noah was dressed in his usual outfit: a T-shirt, baggy jeans, and clunky construction boots. Even so, Gillian couldn't imagine him looking any better.

"What?" he asked, and she realized she'd been staring. "Should I go change?"

"No. You look wonderful—as always—just the way you are. I mean it. And Louise . . ."

"Doesn't care what I wear," he finished for her when she faltered.

"I was going to say Louise can stuff her expectations."

"Look, Gillian, about this contest—"

"Noah. Don't." She put a hand on his arm, and he gave up, looking helpless and distraught with guilt. "This year you're going to win, and for a good cause. I can wait one more year. Of course, next year I'll kick your ass," she added with a wicked grin.

"You think I'm going to keep up this gardening thing next year?" he asked, incredulous.

"I'm afraid I'm going to have to insist."

"As you wish," he murmured, his voice warm, and Gillian nearly melted into her new brick path.

To fight off the fluttering in her heart, she turned around and pretended to scrutinize Noah's garden as if she hadn't done it a dozen times that morning already. All the herbs were in place and flowering as best they could, given the time constraints. Gillian consoled herself by recalling how frequently she'd fertilized, and with her own magic compost, and tried to stop berating herself that she hadn't done more.

After all, his garden looked pretty amazing for not having existed a couple of months ago, and she was certain it would have been a real contender for second or third place even if he hadn't had an arrangement with Louise. Although she'd led the way on choice of plants and overall concept, Noah had offered up plenty of good ideas, and he had a great eye when it came to selecting rustic items at the salvage yard. They were sprinkled here and there in the beds—the plow that had been so much trouble to transport from Mick's, a chipped enamel colander, a flatiron, a rusted metal scale with a potted plant on each plate, a graniteware coffeepot, a metal stool, and something that she wasn't able to identify but that looked cool with its wooden base and cast-iron flywheel. There was even an anvil. Gillian also had insisted on hanging a rustic metal-and-crystal chandelier from the pergola where she'd once hung the gnome.

The gnome, however, did not play a part in either of their gardens.

"Nope," Gillian said suddenly. "It won't work."

"What are we talking about?" Noah asked as he checked his phone for the time. The judges would be coming by at any minute. Gillian's and Noah's gardens were the two last stops on their route.

"We're missing one last thing."

"Impossible," he said. "You have every plant imaginable in your garden. I have all the herbs. I have antiques. I have a freakin' chandelier. You have a brick path and a birdbath and a fountain and a damn astrolabe on a pedestal. What could we possibly . . . oh." His expression cleared as he realized. Gillian nodded at him. "I'll be right back."

Within seconds Noah reappeared with the gnome.

"Where do you want him?" he asked. "Your garden or mine?"

"I'm going to lose anyway, so I might as well take him."

Noah drew back as Gillian reached for the statue. "I'm going to win anyway, so *I* might as well take him."

"He fits best in my garden."

"I found him."

"But you gave him to me as an apology gift."

"Which you refused."

Gillian bit her lower lip but couldn't stop herself from smiling. "Are we actually fighting for custody of the damn gnome?"

Noah laughed as well. "We've lost our minds."

"Give it here."

"Hey."

"Hang on. What I mean is we'll put it at the edge of my brick path so it can greet the judges. When it's time for them to judge your garden, we'll put it there."

"That's fair."

He set the gnome down where Gillian indicated. It was almost the exact spot where the first shrub of the boxwood hedge had been, the one he'd ripped out and dragged down the driveway. Which had made Gillian hate him. For a while, at least.

But Noah was not the person who irately ripped out hedges and blithely made people hate him. He was a good person at heart, and what a huge heart.

"Noah . . ."

A strong breeze kicked up, and she grabbed at her hat as it tried to make a break for it. The sun had gone behind a cloud, and Gillian smelled rain. Just what they didn't need. Her garden looked its best in the shining sun. But then again, it didn't matter this year. The prize was going to Noah, and that was just fine. Fine enough that she was willing to feature a tacky gnome in her perfect garden.

Before she could get her words out—and she wasn't even sure what she wanted to say to him—two SUVs pulled up to the curb. Three women and two men, all well past retirement age, made their way up Gillian's driveway. Beside her, Noah took in a sharp breath. She knew how he felt. Her heart rate picked up, and her stomach clenched. *Showtime.*

The judges were all very congenial, shaking hands with her and Noah and reminding them of the rubric they would use as they assessed both gardens. After Gillian put on a welcoming smile and directed them up her new path, she and Noah hung back in the driveway and exchanged glances as they realized: Louise wasn't among the judges.

Noah went out to the curb and looked up and down the street, then looked back at Gillian with an exaggerated shrug. No Louise.

Meanwhile, the judges cooed and gasped and murmured at her flowers, her shrubs, her ornaments, her composition . . . all the things that made up a prizewinning garden. Some scribbled furiously on their clipboards and pointed out this and that, while others bent to examine buds and leaves or smell a flower. Gillian caught snippets of their comments on the breeze: *Lovely, just lovely . . . Have you seen this? . . . Nice use of . . .*

The rest of their words were lost under a rumble of thunder. Gillian desperately hoped they'd hurry up. Noah came back up the driveway with his hands in his pockets and a bewildered look on his face.

"I didn't do anything to her, I swear," he muttered when he was back by Gillian's side.

"Maybe we should ask the other judges where she is."

"I don't care where she is. The point is she's not *here*. And if she's not here, then this whole thing will be fair."

"We don't want fair. We want you to keep the marina."

"Why don't we worry about that later and just let you win like you deserve to?"

Gillian wanted to argue, but the judges were back, clustering around her and congratulating her on another marvelous entry for the fifth year running. Gillian gracefully accepted their compliments and answered their questions while Noah moved the gnome, and then she ushered them over to Noah's garden. A spatter of rain hit the pavement, and the judges eyed the sky with trepidation. Noah reached into his back pocket for a red mini umbrella about the size of his palm. In one smooth move he popped it open and held it over the frailest-looking woman, who brightened with gratitude.

Noah caught her eye and grinned as he held the umbrella aloft. *What a heart,* Gillian thought again. And she felt her own heart ache with affection. No. Love. She loved Noah. She'd said it, and she'd meant it. She loved her stubborn, crabby, supremely annoying neighbor? Yes. She did. Because he was also a kind, gentle, generous, compassionate man. And sexy to boot.

The judges oohed and aahed and praised Noah's garden as much as they had hers. One judge pointed at the relocated gnome in delight and a few minutes were spent trying to determine if there were twin gnomes. Once Gillian and Noah explained they shared the one gnome, the judges smiled and nodded and started scribbling their scores.

The heavy rain held off, fortunately, and Noah put away the umbrella as the judges excused themselves to confer. Gillian and Noah exchanged nervous looks, and each reached for the other's hand at the same time.

"This is ridiculous," Noah laugh-whispered. "When did I start caring about who's going to win a garden competition?"

"Welcome to my world," Gillian whispered back.

"Your world is weird. But I think I like it."

Gillian tugged on his hand, pulling him closer. She would have more than willingly kissed him right then and there, but suddenly there was a very short, stooped old woman between them, clutching a trophy.

"Ms. Pritchard, once again it is an honor to view your handiwork in the garden. And Mr. West, what a debut. We're so happy to have you as part of the Willow Cove gardening community."

Gillian's and Noah's grip on each other tightened.

"Now, we confess this was quite a difficult decision, but we feel we've scored the gardens as fairly as possible. And we recalculated our scores twice!" she exclaimed, her eyes twinkling. "Other gardens have won second and third place, and we'll make our way back to those to give them their prizes. But first place can be found right here."

"It had better not be a damn tie," Noah muttered, and Gillian giggled.

"Oh, we don't do ties, Mr. West," the judge said. "Mainly because we only have one trophy. No, first prize undoubtedly goes to—"

"Stop right there!"

Noah tipped his head back and groaned loudly. Louise was marching up the driveway. Oblivious to her dark mood, the judges greeted her congenially and asked where she'd been all afternoon. But Gillian looked past the furious woman to bug her eyes at the three people coming up in Louise's wake: Carol, Arnette, and Judy.

Best to confront the situation head-on, Gillian decided. "Ladies, did you kidnap Louise?"

"No!" Judy protested. "Not *exactly*."

"They might as well have," Louise sniffed. "Trapping me in my office for hours."

"We just had some questions," Carol said disingenuously. "Legitimate ones. About the tax code."

"Lots of questions," Arnette added, nodding vigorously. "We ran a little bit overtime."

"They made me miss the judging this afternoon! They did it on purpose. I tried to leave, and they locked the door!"

"Tax code?" Noah repeated. "You ladies are interested in town tax codes?"

"Oh, it's a fascinating subject," Carol said as Judy blurted out, "Absolutely hate it."

"Do you mind?" Louise interrupted. "There's a garden competition I need to judge."

"Actually, it's over, Louise," one of the men said. "Sorry you missed it."

"Not sorry," Judy muttered.

"It's over when I say it's over," Louise snapped. "Give me the score sheets."

Louise thrust out her hand, and all the judges dutifully turned over their papers, which she started rifling through immediately, grunting and muttering at the notes.

"As you can see," the other man said, pointing at the tallies, "the winners were quite clear. We were definitely unanimous on the decision."

"Mm, I've visited all these gardens frequently all summer to see how they were coming along. In fact, I made the rounds yesterday. I can't imagine they've all changed very much in twenty-four hours, so I'll be assessing these scores with that in mind."

"Would you like to sit down, Louise?" Noah offered, gesturing toward his patio.

The woman shot him a ball-shriveling glare. "No. *Thank* you."

Noah shrugged and looked at Gillian again, eyebrows raised, an amused smile twitching his lips.

Everyone waited in silence—even Judy—as Louise studied the scores. She squinted at Gillian's garden, then at Noah's. One of her patented withering looks landed on the gnome. Noah and Gillian let loose soft snickers.

"Taking this seriously, are we, Mr. West?"

"Nothing wrong with a little levity, Ms. March."

"Not if you want to win this contest. Gardening is a very serious business."

After another moment she sighed, straightened the papers, and looked at the people clustered around her. "Second- and third-place winners are clear," she said, echoing the words of the other judge. "Now, for first place." Louise held out her hand again, and the judge holding the trophy turned it over to her. "Ms. Pritchard." Gillian prided herself on not snapping to attention, despite the tone of Louise's voice that virtually commanded it. Louise took a breath, started to speak, stopped, looked her up and down. "You look very . . . festive today."

"Thank you."

"Brave choice of frocks."

Gillian wanted to say, *I wore my strongest pushup bra just to annoy you,* but she refrained.

"Although your outfit implies your next stop is a royal wedding, at least there's a sense of occasion about you. Mr. West . . ." And Louise let the comment trail off there, although the contrast was implied. "Impressive work, both of you. But the clear winner—"

"They've worked very hard," Carol cut in. "We've seen them out here night and day."

Noah nudged Gillian and mouthed, *Told you.* Of course they'd been watched by the old ladies all summer.

"I was unaware you had any interest in gardening, Carol," Louise said over her shoulder.

"Oh, yes. We love gardens. And competitions."

"As I was saying. The clear winner—"

"And gnomes," Judy said.

"Excuse me?"

"We like gnomes too."

"There's no accounting for taste. In any case, the winner—"

Arnette said, "Actually, there's something we like even more."

Louise heaved a weary sigh. "What, Arnette?" she asked dully.

"Investments."

"Investments?" Gillian repeated, wondering just where this was going.

"Mm, yes." Carol smiled warmly. "Especially investments in local businesses. Marinas and the like."

Gillian felt Noah tense up beside her.

"What did you do to my marina?"

"Back taxes have been paid in full," Arnette announced.

"I . . . wait . . . what?" Noah could barely get words out. "How?"

"Our dead husbands, who had pensions and life insurance," Carol said. "And our own wise—"

"Investments," Arnette finished for her. "We're whizzes at the stock market."

Once Noah's brain apparently successfully processed the information, he protested, "Ladies, I can't . . . I don't have the money to pay you back—"

"Oh sweetie, you don't have to," Carol said.

"I can't accept the money as a . . . a gift."

"You're not doing that either," Judy said. "You've just gotten yourself a board of directors. Now, I always thought the outside of the building needed painting—"

"Do you *mind*!" Louise snapped. "I would like to award this prize before the gardens die back for the winter."

As Gillian and Noah shared another look, Noah smiled broadly.

"Doesn't matter," he said congenially, holding Gillian's gaze.

Gillian grinned as well. He was right. With the taxes paid, Louise had nothing to hold over his head. The scores had already been tabulated; the other judges hadn't been influenced by Louise or anything else. It was as fair a tally as could possibly be. The only thing that would keep Louise from awarding Gillian first prize was lingering resentment.

Without another word, Louise thrust the trophy at the winner.

CHAPTER 28

"That monster."

Noah was still angry at Louise. She got her back taxes, and the marina now had a board of directors. Well, cheers to that. He could work with the ladies. Better than "working" with Louise. The point was the taxes were paid, and Louise's extortion of Noah had no teeth—the trophy was due to go to the rightful winner.

And yet Louise had still bestowed the first-place prize on Noah's garden.

Until the other judges got involved.

It was quite the melee, he had to admit, especially considering who was involved. Five previously fragile, feeble judges suddenly started wielding their clipboards like inmates brandishing trays in a cafeteria riot. The neighbor ladies joined in, arguing loudly. He was pretty sure at one point Judy had Louise on the ground and was biting her calf, but he might have imagined that part.

Everyone had cleared off about an hour ago, and now it was just him and Gillian lounging on his back patio, working hard on their goal of getting as tipsy as possible to celebrate that the garden competition had finally come to a conclusion.

"Louise is a peach, I told you," Gillian said, delicately sipping some champagne. "It's always been her firm belief the prize should go to anyone who isn't named Gillian Pritchard, so I wasn't surprised in the least." She raised her glass high. "To the winner."

Noah clinked her glass with his. "I can't believe it."

"You can't believe you won, or you can't believe the other judges wrestled the trophy away from Louise, kicked her out of the gardening club, and made me the actual winner? Or that Arnette chased Louise down the street and nearly all the way back to her house, throwing mulberries at her?"

Noah threw back his head and laughed heartily. He wasn't sure if the part about the mulberries was true, but he had seen Louise scoot off, Arnette hot on her heels, although she was bustling, not running. And in the confusion he did hear Arnette shout, "You leave Gillian alone from now on, or you'll answer to me!" So anything was possible. What mattered now was that he was sitting peacefully on his shaded patio, in his newly designed, prizewinning garden—even if the prize had been temporary—and, most important, he was here with Gillian.

Sighing, she stretched her legs and slipped off her pumps. Noah reached down, lifted her left leg up, and rested her foot on his thigh. He put his glass on the table and massaged her instep with both hands. Gillian's shoulders visibly relaxed, her eyes drifted closed, and she made a small, contented noise in the back of her throat that sent Noah into near-paroxysms of lust.

"You know," he ventured, pausing in his ministrations, and Gillian cracked one eye to look at him, "you designed and planted both gardens. So technically you won either way."

"Yes, but this is the correct outcome," she said serenely, "because that damned first-place trophy is now on my mantel, where it's always belonged." She closed her eyes again and waved her free hand. "You may proceed."

Noah lifted her other foot into his lap and continued the massage, smiling. "I want to throw you a party."

"You may."

"You won't mind if I conspire with your friends behind your back again?"

"If I'm going to be celebrated, I don't care how it happens. Make it so."

"Yes'm."

~

"So you snatched defeat from the jaws of victory, eh?"

"Something like that."

One week later, as promised, Noah threw Gillian a party in honor of taking first prize in the garden competition. Also to celebrate her in general, also as he promised. Noah had filled both their yards with lanterns and fairy lights, food and drink, and all their friends. He had friends in Willow Cove now. He liked that.

"Well, congratulations on your forty-five-second victory, anyway." Manny chuckled, tipping his beer bottle and draining the last drops as he watched Noah light his grill. "You know the trophy belonged to Gillian the whole time, right?"

"No doubt. She's amazing."

"Oh *really*?"

"Cut it out."

Noah glanced around nervously, even though everyone else was in Gillian's yard, admiring her plants and flowers.

"I've been hearing a lot of things about the two of you."

Noah groaned. "Oh no."

"I'd rather hear it from you, though."

With a huge sigh, Noah slumped into the nearest chair,

rubbed his face with both hands, and said, "I don't know, Manny. She really is incredible."

"Enough to love her?"

Noah was silent for a minute. "Doesn't matter," he finally said. "I had my chance to tell her, and I blew it. And the longer I let this go on . . . the less it matters. Because it's too late."

"Too late," Manny snorted.

"Seriously, I was too much of a coward to tell her how I felt when it counted, and I can't manage it now. Pretty soon she's going to get fed up with me, and I'm going to lose her, and it'll be all my fault."

"Ah, the West family cowardice."

"What?"

Manny sighed and scratched the back of his head. "Look . . . when I was your age, I missed out on a lot—missed out on the woman I loved—because I was straight-up chickenshit. Don't make the same mistakes I did."

This brought Noah up short. He'd always thought Manny never cared enough about any woman to devote himself to one. Not that his uncle had spent his life bragging about being single and dating a lot of women; he just hadn't talked about his personal life at all, and the vibe he gave off was it was best not to ask. He remained private, his personal life a mystery.

From what Noah could glean from his dad, which wasn't much, Manny had spent most of his youth "tomcatting," a word they'd laughingly picked up from an earlier generation—probably Noah's grandfather, who had lovingly teased Manny about his unmarried status while at the same time sounding proud that he had a playboy son.

It sounded, though, like Manny actually might be willing to divulge some details about his past now, so Noah asked. "What mistakes?"

"Thinking you'll live forever, that you've got all the time in the world. And then you wake up one morning, look in the mirror, and you see this." And he indicated his face—still handsome, but decidedly older, with freckles, age spots, bushier eyebrows, and a few wrinkles. "And who wants this?"

"Alyce, apparently."

"Meh," Manny grunted, waving his hand dismissively. He looked away, deep in thought, and Noah's heart squeezed.

Jenna and Eli's mother had come to the party with Manny, and Noah hadn't noticed any signs they were having difficulties, but he had been a little preoccupied and could have missed them. "What happened? Did the two of you have an argument?"

"We're not talking about this, son, because it's my business."

"You brought it up."

"We're talking about you and Gillian."

Cantankerous old coot, Noah thought, but with affection. He reached into the cooler at his feet and pulled out two more beers, handing one to his uncle. After popping the top and taking another couple of swallows, Manny appeared to have a change of heart. Out of the blue, he muttered, "When I was younger than you, I had my heart set on Alyce Thatcher. I was crazy about her."

"Who's Alyce Thatcher?"

Manny turned a baleful eye on Noah. "Use your brain, son."

"Oh. Alyce. Gotcha."

"But . . ." Manny sighed and didn't say anything more.

"What happened?"

"Maria happened. And Ellie. And Joanne. And—"

"Okay, I get it."

"And by the time I realized I was ready to settle down, Alyce Thatcher had become Alyce Masterson."

"So what did you do?"

"I found Rona. And Joanne again. And Frannie. And Joanne again. And—"

"But you never married Rona or Joanne or Frannie. Although Joanne sounds like she was a contender."

"No, I did not. And Joanne was not a contender. Because it was always Alyce. I buried it deep, of course. No need to be picking at a scab for decades. But when I saw her on that dating app, I . . . I couldn't believe my luck. And I went for it."

"And now you have Alyce."

"And look at all the years I wasted. I'm glad she had a good marriage, I'm glad she has Eli and Jenna and her granddaughters, but sometimes I wonder what life would have been like for us if I hadn't been stupid in my youth." Manny fell silent for a moment. "All I'm saying is talk to Gillian right now. Don't be a dope like your ol' uncle. Don't waste decades like me. Make a move before you're overwhelmed by shocking amounts of ear hair. Because pretty soon Gillian Pritchard is going to become Gillian Somebody-Else if you don't snap her up right now."

"She's not up for auction, old man."

"Old age is a cold and lonely place, take it from me. So don't let her get away. If you know you love her."

"I do. It's just . . . I can only manage to say it in my own head. I can't convince myself to tell her."

"Having a conversation with the dumbest person in the room doesn't get the girl."

"Can you not, please?"

Manny made a grumbling sound deep in his throat and pushed himself out of his chair. As he made his way over to the crowd in Gillian's yard, he said over his shoulder, "Needs more lighter fluid."

"It's a gas grill, Manny."

Noah sighed, watching the scene in Gillian's garden backlit by the glowing lights. All the people they cared about most swirled around Gillian, but she was the center of it all, the shining sun. As always, Noah focused on her; everything around her was a blur. Her glow commanded all his attention and—he might as well face it—always had, ever since he first laid eyes on her through the windows of their houses months ago.

Manny was right—Noah *was* a dope. And Manny was also right when he said Noah shouldn't let Gillian get away. When he was comfortable making excuses, he insisted to himself he was taking it slow, making sure, not scaring her off or going too fast or saying things he didn't mean. He convinced himself he was doing the right thing. The entire time, though, he wanted to be with her, professing his love every minute of every day.

She'd said she loved him. Freely, confidently, breezily, just like she approached everything in life. He, on the other hand, had choked. Twice. Well, she always was far stronger than he was, and she certainly knew her own mind, while Noah had been busy flailing around trying to figure out who he was and what he wanted. He knew now, though.

Gillian turned, smiling at him, and his heart swelled. He was going to tell her. Right now.

"It's my turn!"

"No, it's mine!"

"You already had a turn!"

"That one didn't count!"

Then again, maybe he needed to break up a sibling fight first. Zoë and Olivia were tussling in the driveway, both pulling on the gnome. They'd been amusing themselves playing hide and seek with it all evening, but apparently their unusual sisterly peace had shattered. Just as the gnome was about to be.

Noah rose out of his seat as the gnome came loose from their grips and flipped into the air like a pop fly ball, and everything suddenly was in slow motion. He'd never make it there in time, he realized, not even if he tried to lunge for it. He watched it turn over and over in midair. His stomach flipped, and the one irrational thought he had in his head was he had to protect the gnome at all costs. It represented everything he and Gillian had gone through to get to this point, and somehow, he felt, if it shattered on the asphalt, he and Gillian would fall to pieces as well. Ludicrous, but there it was all the same.

The figurine plummeted, and Noah winced. Here it came. The crash.

But there was no crash. He dared to open his eyes and found the gnome in the outstretched hands of Leah, who'd appeared out of nowhere and caught the statue. Noah let out a huge sigh of relief. She held it out to him, and he crossed to her and accepted it just as Eli scooped her up.

"Nice one," he said admiringly, kissing her.

"I've been practicing. How'd I do, coach?"

"I'm putting you in the infield when the fall softball league season starts."

Noah, ridiculously relieved, set the gnome down at the edge of Gillian's lawn, where it seemed to belong. He patted its head and straightened up to find Gillian beaming at him.

"You dope."

"I get that a lot." He took a breath. "Gillian, look, can we—"

"Are we eating this century, or what?" Manny demanded.

Noah sighed. Foiled again. "Yeah, yeah," he said to his uncle.

"I'll get the kebabs out of the fridge," Gillian offered.

Noah wanted to follow her into her house, but Carol grabbed his arm, eager to relive the events of the garden competition again, this time for Alyce's benefit. So he tamped down his urgency, told himself he didn't have a deadline, no matter what pressure he was putting on himself, and let Carol start telling the story for what had to be the thirtieth time that week.

~

After food, drink, more food, and more drink, Noah found he didn't mind putting off his confession to Gillian. The night was warm, the food was good, the drinks were exceptional. Noah was grateful for his new group of friends who had happily welcomed him into their group—even Jenna, which he had never thought would happen. Best of all, he had Gillian. She was by his side the entire night, and that made everything perfect.

Even better, when everyone was relaxing around Noah's table, Alyce wandered back into Gillian's garden, and Manny followed. No one else noticed, but Noah did. He watched every moment of his uncle's exchange with his girlfriend under the glowing string lights. Noah found himself pulling for Manny, feeling like their fates were tied. As though if Manny succeeded in telling Alyce how he felt, Noah would succeed in telling Gillian.

But then he saw Alyce roll her eyes, shake her head, and push at Manny, although not roughly. She followed that gesture with a gentle hand to the man's cheek, so it didn't look like a rejection, but it didn't look like a joyous acceptance either. Still, they rejoined the group together, and that was a good sign. As an excuse to intercept them, Noah tied off a bag of trash and crossed the driveway to throw it away in his garbage tote.

"Everything okay?" he ventured when Alyce and Manny walked by.

Manny grumbled.

Noah stepped in front of the pair. "Alyce. What did my uncle do?"

"Hey! Why are you assuming it was my fault?"

"Odds are it was, Manny."

". . . That's fair."

"What happened?"

Alyce heaved a sigh. "Your uncle *proposed*. Can you imagine? At our age? Honestly."

She walked back toward the group, shaking her head, and Manny let her go. Noah grabbed his arm. "Manny. Are you okay?"

"Ah, I'm fine," he said, waving his nephew off.

"I'm really sorry."

"Don't be. Who cares?"

"Okay, whoa. You said—"

"Marriage, yes, no, blah, blah—that part doesn't matter."

"Wait, wait. You said she was the one that got away. You said—"

"I know what I said, son. I was there."

"Manny!"

"Look," his uncle said in a gentler tone, "I'm fine with her not wanting to get married. It doesn't matter. What matters is I was able to tell her how I felt about her. After this many years. Do you understand? That's everything."

"And how does she feel?"

Manny actually smiled broadly. "The same. She feels the same. See why the other details don't matter? Besides, I'll win her over eventually," he said with a wink. "We ain't dead yet."

~

Maybe now, Noah thought. He could ask Gillian to help him fetch the desserts, get her alone in the house while everyone else was still outside. That could work.

But when it was time for dessert, it was Carol, Judy, and Arnette who cornered him in the kitchen.

"Why does this feel like an intervention?" he asked as the three women stared at him with concerned expressions.

Arnette began by saying quietly, "Noah, honey, you know we love you, right?"

Noah stiffened, wondering where this was going. ". . . Okay?"

"We're only doing this for your own good."

Oh no.

What was this all about? Was it something to do with Gillian? Were they going to tell him he wasn't worthy of her? Because that thought haunted him far more frequently than was probably healthy. Or were they going to tell him he'd destroyed Retha's house now that he'd redecorated it to his liking? Or had Retha's relationship with her boyfriend in Tampa ended, and they were about to tell him she was coming back to Willow Cove? And she wanted her house back?

He braced for impact. "Just say it, please."

"All right. Noah, as the newly formed board of directors of Spencer's Marina, we're hereby relieving you of your duties as general manager."

Noah blinked. "I'm sorry, what?"

"You're not happy there, dear," Carol interjected. "We can tell."

"And we've heard stories from the employees," Judy added. "Those stories are not good."

"Judy!" Carol and Arnette exclaimed.

"Hey, hang on, now. I'm a good business owner. My employees have always loved me."

"Never said you weren't," Judy said, shrugging and taking a swig of her beer. "And everybody likes you just fine, as a person. But they're complaining you're just in the way."

"But . . ." he protested, "I had ideas. About how to increase profits and liven the place up and—"

"And it's nothing the staff doesn't already know," Carol said gently. "They were just in a holding pattern between Jerry and you. They know exactly what needs to be done. Just leave them to it."

Arnette took over again. "Noah, the point is, you don't need to try to take an active role in the marina every day. Let the managers and the workers handle the day-to-day business like they've been doing right along."

"Be a man of leisure," Carol suggested. "Enjoy yourself. Spend all the time you want with Gillian. You're so cute together."

Noah started to protest—about the marina, not about spending time with Gillian, which he was all for—when he stopped and considered. Wasn't this what he had been telling himself right along? Why was he fighting it? Because of his pride—that he'd bought the marina and, dammit, he was going to single-handedly direct his new business, even if it was doing just fine as it was? Or had he been planning to immerse himself in the place because he needed a sense of belonging? He didn't need to find an identity in his work, not anymore. At least, not the one he'd bought in desperation as he'd flailed around, looking for a purpose after his life in California had imploded. He wasn't that guy anymore. Thank goodness.

"You know what, ladies? You're absolutely right."

They lit up, overjoyed Noah wasn't putting up a fight.

"We're so glad you see sense," Carol said, patting his arm. "Something else will come up, if you need something to occupy your time every day. We're sure of it."

"Maybe sooner than we think," he said, smiling mysteriously. When the ladies looked like they were going to press him for an explanation, he held out a baking dish. "Would you mind taking the peach cobbler outside?"

Noah followed them out the door, caught Ben's eye, and hitched his head for Ben to follow him. They sauntered over to a corner of his yard and Noah pretended to study the metal and wood contraption with the flywheel neither he nor Gillian had been able to identify.

"Know what that is?" Noah asked Ben.

"That's really why we're meeting back here like spies?"

"No." Noah took a breath. "I think I want to look into that gallery space you've been working on. Can you hook me up with the landlord?"

Ben nodded. "Absolutely."

"But, uh, would you mind not mentioning it to anyone? Just in case it falls through or I chicken out or something."

"Not even Gillian?"

"Especially not Gillian."

"You do realize she'd be more supportive about it than anyone else in Willow Cove, right?"

"I guess so," Noah sighed. "I just like keeping my plans quiet until they're more . . . certain. I've made enough missteps lately. I don't want this to be common knowledge in case it goes sideways."

"Understood. But I wouldn't worry. It sounds perfect for you. Gillian mentioned you had a gallery in . . ."

When he trailed off, Noah supplied, "A former life."

"Weird name for a city."

Noah rolled his eyes at Ben's goofy grin. Then he grew thoughtful again. "I did love the art world. Still do."

"Then you should go for it. I'll text the building owner right now. I think she'll be happy to keep that space the same. She was really disappointed when the last gallery closed."

"Thanks."

Ben gazed at the contraption in front of them. "So what is that thing, anyway?"

"No clue."

CHAPTER 29

It was close to midnight and the last round of the cornhole tournament had wrapped up when Gillian felt eyes on her. She sauntered over to Noah and slipped an arm around his waist. "You're staring at me. Why are you staring at me?"

Noah kissed her temple and answered, "How could I not? I—"

"Dude. I hear you and Eli are going kayaking on Wednesday. I want in," Gray said, high on life since he'd taken the cornhole trophy, even though it was just another bottle of beer with a daisy wrapped around the neck.

"Of course—anytime."

Noah sounded congenial, but Gillian picked up an underlying note of tension strong enough to make her do a double take. Noah's expression was placid, however, so she started to think she'd imagined it.

Until, after Gray walked away, tossed Delia over his shoulder, and marched off with her laughing and demanding to be put down even though she obviously didn't mind being manhandled one bit, Noah leaned over and muttered, "Isn't it time everyone went home?"

"Are you sick of them?"

"Yes. No. *No.* They're all great—"

"That girl," Gillian sighed, shaking her head at the sight of Delia reveling in Gray's attention. "When it comes to Gray, she's never going to learn."

Noah growled low in his throat.

"What's the matter?"

"Nothing. Not a thing. But—"

"Gilly, dear," Alyce said, taking her by the hand, "are you sure you're all right with giving me some of those daylilies you were talking about?"

"Yes, absolutely."

"Taking some won't hurt your garden?"

"Just the opposite," she reassured the woman. "Thinning them out is good for them. It's a little early in the season to divide them, but I think they'll be fine. I'll get my shovel and a bucket in just a second." Gillian turned to Noah. "You were saying?"

He sighed heavily. "Never mind."

Noah disengaged from her and walked away, clearly agitated, and Gillian found herself wondering why he was suddenly in a mood when he'd been congenial all day, even when the girls had nearly slaughtered the gnome, which, apparently, he'd become inordinately attached to. It had been a long day, she reminded herself, and Noah had planned and executed the entire party. Maybe he was just tired. Zoë and Olivia had already conked out on a pair of chaises by the patio, and the party was starting to wind down even for the adults.

Gillian dug around in her shed for an old five-gallon bucket and a spade, but when she walked over to the daylilies, Noah intercepted her.

"I'll do that."

"I don't mind."

"Give me the spade."

"I said I can do it."

"You're all dressed up. You'll get muddy."

"I have a washer and dryer."

"Gillian, give me the spade."

She blinked, then said, "No!"

She didn't know why she was feeling argumentative, only that Noah was being so stubborn and grumpy and she didn't know why, and that got her own hackles up.

Noah moved in close and, nearly nose to nose with her, rumbled, "Let. me. do. it."

Just as low and growly, Gillian countered, "I. said. no."

"Dammit—"

Dimly, Gillian was aware the party had quieted down. Was everyone else watching them? She didn't care. She was riled up now.

"You don't know how, and you'll make a mess," she pointed out.

"Like I haven't learned all this gardening stuff from you. Don't you trust me?"

"No."

"Yes, you do."

She did. It was just sometimes he got under her skin. "What's your problem all of a sudden, anyway?"

"I don't have a problem."

"A likely story. You've gone all crabby."

"Because I've been trying to—"

He stopped abruptly, making Gillian prompt, "What? What have you been trying to do?"

"I've been trying to talk to you! We need to talk."

Gillian drew back, alarmed. "Are you breaking up with me?"

"What? No! God, no! I just need to tell you—"

"That you're giving up the marina? I know. Carol told me."

"No, I—"

"You've decided to open a gallery in the empty storefront? I know. Ben—"

Noah whipped around. "Ben! You told her? That was in the vault!"

"Of course he didn't," Gillian cut him off before he could turn his full ire on their friend. "Ben tells Jenna everything, and *she* told me."

"Couldn't help it, man, sorry," Ben said sheepishly.

"I'm not sorry," Jenna said.

Noah turned back to Gillian. "Look, I have to say—"

"That you conned Eli into letting you run the backhoe, clearing the field for his ropes course? I know. Leah told me. And I also overheard Delia asking you to help her design some earrings for my birthday, so you should know I prefer gold—"

"For the love of God, woman, I'm trying to tell you that I love you!"

Utter silence in the garden.

In the glow of the string lights, Gillian could see a flush of red creeping up Noah's neck and suffusing his face. He looked away. She took his face in her hands to get his eyes back on her.

"I know that too," she whispered, a surge of joy putting a broad smile on her face and warming her down to her toes. "You show me every day."

"I wanted to tell you," he murmured, then glanced around, "in private."

"Oh, there isn't much of that to be had anymore, I'm afraid. You get me, you get this whole bunch here. So you'd better not wait till we're alone to kiss me either."

Noah smiled ruefully and pulled her close, kissing her deeply, and he wasn't even distracted by the rapturous sigh that came from somewhere in the vicinity of Delia.

"I love you so much," she whispered, her voice choked with tears, her forehead against his. "And I know you love me, even if you can't say it out loud."

"You caught onto that, huh?" he whispered back. "Well, I'm saying it now."

"Good."

"I'll say it every day, multiple times a day, from now on."

"Good."

"Now I think it's time your friends went home."

"Party's over!" she called. "Everybody out."

∽

Gillian opened the door and backed into her house, Noah matching her step for step like a predator. He kicked the door closed and moved in to kiss her, but then glanced past her into the darkened kitchen. "Hey," he said in a whisper, "is someone here?"

"No, everyone's gone." When Noah continued to look dubious, she added, "Maybe the gnome broke in."

"Are you sure Delia didn't ask to stay overnight or something?"

"No, of course not."

Noah didn't answer. He walked away from Gillian, frowning, and searched the kitchen, then walked through the dark living room. When he came back, he was shaking his head.

"Noah? What's going on?"

"I don't know. It was like . . . I saw some woman walk by. But all I saw was a peek of a . . . puffy skirt, like. With white stuff underneath."

"A crinoline?"

"I didn't drink that much, did I?"

"Not even close. But you've had a long day. Why don't you go upstairs and relax? I'll be up in a minute."

Noah nodded, gave her a small kiss, and climbed the stairs.

She turned to eyeball Inner Bette, who was lounging against her refrigerator. Gillian smiled placidly at her favorite phantom and opened the fridge door, which forced Bette out of the way.

So this is what happens, I suppose? Inner Bette asked, but not bitterly.

"It does, Bette."

He's all right, darling, Bette said as Gillian poured a glass of water and took a sip. *You've done well. I approve.*

Gillian nodded at her, and Inner Bette nodded back. For the first time since Bette had first started haunting her, Gillian thought she detected a hint of a genuine, kind smile on her face instead of her usual wry smirk.

"That'll do, Bette," Gillian whispered. "That'll do."

Inner Bette vanished in a puff of face powder, and Gillian suspected she wasn't going to see her again.

Gillian sighed, content. She and Noah were together. Finally, definitively. With nothing to fight over. Of course, something might come up that they'd argue over—correction, something *very likely* would come up—but Gillian knew they'd be able to work out any differences they might have from now on.

The future stretched out before them, bright and promising, and Gillian was going to be grateful for every moment, because they were going to be spent with Noah.

Tomorrow they'd clean up their yards. Water the plants. Take a boat out on the river and enjoy high summer in Willow Cove. Maybe they'd borrow Ben's key to the storefront and she'd watch Noah prowl the empty space, eyes alight, making plans. She smiled at the thought.

Right now, though, Noah was waiting for her, and he wasn't

waiting quietly. Powerful guitar music was blasting from her bedroom: the Muffs' punky onslaught of "Really Really Happy." Gillian's heart leapt. She wanted nothing more than to rush into Noah's arms and dance around in her underwear—with him. But first she paused on the stairs and pulled out her phone.

She had dating apps to delete.

ACKNOWLEDGMENTS

No author exists in a void (even though sometimes we feel like we do). There are always wonderful people holding us up. Here are mine:

My family members—especially Aunt Lil—who staunchly support me while not understanding anything about this strange profession and probably secretly ask one another, in covert whispers, where the heck I came from anyway? And has anyone looked into a DNA test?

My found family members—Carla Killian, Glynis Astie, Tracie Banister, and Kristina Braell—who never cease to amaze by also staunchly supporting me *without* the obligation of blood ties. Thank you for letting me message you incessantly whenever I'm avoiding my writing and editing deadlines. Also Anne Marie Weber, who helps me keep it together in general.

The wonderful people at St. Martin's who have helped make this second Willow Cove book a reality: Alex Sehulster, Cassidy Graham, Alexis Neuville, Alyssa Gammello, and everyone else at this fab publisher. Special shout-out to Christina Lopez, who went above and beyond to help shape *Hedging Your Bets* into a snappy, cohesive rom-com. Your patience is the stuff of legend.

Jordy Albert of the Booker-Albert Literary Agency, who believes in me more than I believe in myself, always patiently listens to me whinge, and is always there with a "You got this!" even when I do not, in fact, got this (until I do—because Jordy is always right).

And last but definitely not least, all the readers who have become fans of Willow Cove—hi! I see you and appreciate you!

ABOUT THE AUTHOR

Elizabeth Torgerson-Lamark

Jayne Denker is the author of romantic comedies, including *The Rom-Com Agenda* and the Welcome to Marsden series. When she's not hard at work on another novel (or, rather, when she should be hard at work on another novel), she can usually be found frittering away stupid amounts of time on social media.